Casper Potts and the Ladies' Casserole Club

Also by Ken Dalton

Fiction

The Bloody Birthright

The Big Show Stopper

Death is a Cabernet

The Tartan Shroud

Brother, can you spare a dime?

The Unsavory Critic

Non-fiction

Polio and Me

Casper Potts and the Ladies' Casserole Club

Ken Dalton

Different
Drummer
Press

For further information concerning *Casper Potts and the Ladies' Casserole Club*, email the author at ken@kendalton.com

Casper Potts and the Ladies' Casserole Club:
ISBN 978-0-578-71634-3

Humorous Fiction.—Casper Potts.—Luxury Senior Living.—Los Angeles Farmers Market.—Echo Park.—Boyle Heights.— I. Title.

ACKNOWLEDGEMENTS

A continued thank you to my artistic son, Hugh, who turns all my book covers into miniature works of art.

To Wendy Maxham, and the hardworking members of my editing staff.

To Dr. Ye, and the staff at Kaiser who saved me from a premature lymphoma death.

And to all the members of my writer's group, most who have passed on to that great computer in the sky where the printers never run out of ink.

Finally, to my wife Arlene, for remaining my lover and best friend. She took a big chance when she tossed the dice and married me. Sixty-two years later it looks like she rolled a seven.

This book is dedicated to my friends, Loraine, Bill, Jeanette, Merv, Eve, Nome, Lynette, Walt, and Charolette who live in an active senior complex similar to The Oaks, the posh fictitious facility in the hills above Hollywood that I created for this novel.

Without their input I would not have been able to write *Casper and the Ladies' Casserole Club*.

And those same friends requested that I inform the readers of this book that moving into their luxurious landlocked cruise ship was the smartest decision they ever made!

Prologue

One afternoon, Casper Potts was enjoying lunch in his apartment 1with one of the Ladies' Casserole Club members when he heard a scuffle at his front door.

Excusing himself from his current companion, he opened his door to find two women fighting over a marking pen attached to the Ladies' Casserole Club scheduling board.

What happened to change this introverted widower into the most sought-after male at The Oaks, a luxurious senior living facility located in the hills above Hollywood.

Chapter One

Casper, The Child

Casper was a cute, nine-pound, six-ounce baby, born to Mable and Harold Potts. The heir to the Potts family name entered the world in the town of Anaheim, California. Today everyone in the world is familiar with Anaheim as the home of Walt Disney's original Disneyland, but when Casper Potts wiggled his way into the world, Anaheim was a small town with many more orange trees than inhabitants.

While Casper grew from baby to toddler, his mother anointed him 'the perfect child' as he spent most of his days staring at the world around him and only cried when hungry or wet. But his mother's joy at her little boy's tranquil development was tempered by the fact that she was a consummate introvert with a disposition that befitted the only full-time librarian in the one library in Anaheim.

Her complete love, beyond her son, and Casper's father, and her career, was cooking. She enjoyed discovering new recipes and kept her larder packed with a vast variety of ingredients. Along with providing the best cooked meals in the neighborhood, she also preached the value of a good breakfast to provide the proper nutrition for the day ahead. Each morning, as she served her son, she would smile and say, "Casper, a healthy breakfast is the way to start your day," and that advice carried him through his wife's death and into the greatest adventure of his life.

Casper's father? He owned Anaheim's mortuary and spent most of his waking hours speaking with deceased individuals who were incapable of talking back.

Shortly after Casper's birth, his parents purchased their first home right in the center of a large development of four hundred houses. They chose their dream home from one of five exciting floor plans and Casper's father would point out to anyone who would listen, "Elevation changes and external architectural modifications made each house on our block look as if it had been individually custom built."

But Casper's father knew little about architectural design. As a mortician, his artistic vision was limited to applying the correct amount of powder and rouge required to make a dead face seem almost alive.

Casper's mother filled their new home with expensive, contemporary furniture, but going with the times, and considering her own conservative streak, she protected all of their upholstered furniture with clear, custom-made plastic covers. Sitting on a couch shielded with plastic tended to be uncomfortable, but Casper's mother felt that the assurance there would be no spills or tears to her pricey furnishings was more than worth the cost of her family's comfort.

So in Casper's case, his DNA combined with his upbringing placed him solidly on the introverted side of the bell-shaped curve.

During Casper's second birthday party, after Casper blew out the two candles on his cake, his mother and father presented him with a large piggy bank. To help him understand how to properly use his new gift, they gave him ten dollars in quarters so he could drop his quarters into the bank and listen to each twenty-five cent piece as it hit the other coins. Then his father gave him a brief lecture on the virtues of saving his money for a rainy day. But Casper, a boy who was born and raised in Southern California, seldom saw a rainy day. Regardless, he followed his father's advice and never spent his savings on gum, candy, or other frivolities. From his second birthday on, Casper saved and saved. As he increased in stature, he outgrew his piggy bank and his coins became dollars. Before he started his first job, Casper's bank account had reached a low four figure balance.

As Casper matured, and because his mother was the town librarian, he spent most of his time after school alone in the children's section of the library. When he was seven, his mother handed him a book about a good knight in shining armor who rode a white horse. The story told how the white knight rescued a fair maiden from the clutches of an evil knight who wore black armor and rode a horse darker than his armor.

At a corner table in the children's section, Casper read and reread the exciting story, and soaked up the illustrations of the good knight locked in mortal combat against the evil knight.

Often, Casper would set the book down on the table, close his eyes and drift off into the medieval time of King Arthur's court.

The good knight was in a jousting match with the evil knight and the hand of a fair maiden awaited the victorious knight. The two combatants mounted their horses at opposite ends of the jousting arena. They lowered their lances and charged at full speed toward each other with a low wooden fence called a tilt separating them. In a few seconds, the two combatants came together and the arena was filled with a cacophony of sound as the good knight's lance caught the evil knight with a direct hit in the center of his breastplate. The fair maiden's eyes closed as the lance of the good knight reached its target. For a moment, she couldn't be sure who had won, but then she opened her eyes and saw the evil knight fall to the earth with a thunderous crash.

When the good knight dismounted and bowed in her direction, the fair maiden covered her smile behind her lace handkerchief and offered him a shy nod.

Casper woke with a start when his mother gripped the shoulder of her sleeping son. On the drive home, Casper considered his dream and determined that he would spend the rest of his life emulating the good knight. He would grow up to be a man with honor. A white knight willing to lay down his life to defend his moral and social code.

Strangely enough that seven-year-old's decision, made while his mother drove home from the library, established the ethical path upon which Casper would trod for the rest of his life.

In elementary school, Casper was a bit of a loner, but he did develop a few friendships. Casper's mother, however, did not take to his schoolmates addressing him by anything other than his given name. Each time she heard a school chum call her son Cap, or Cass, or the Ghost, she would raise her voice above its usual whisper, so his school chums knew she was upset. She would say, "My son's name is Casper!" The words she uttered were his mother's attempt to protect her son from the slings and arrows of life with her own custom-made "verbal" plastic covers.

After four or five spoken admonishments from Casper's mother, his school friends, boys with perfectly normal parents, never returned to Casper's home.

While his mother was protecting her son from nicknames, Casper's father would come home every night with a long face and a mood to match. As Casper grew older, he decided that his father's chosen profession had rendered him incapable of conversing with live people. Before he became a teenager, Casper determined he would not follow his father's line of work.

Another twist of fate, however, dramatically changed Casper's life. His father was approached one day by the wife of a man who had owned a large orange grove. The man had just died and his wife wanted a funeral so expensive that she did not have all the funds to pull off the gigantic send off. The wife offered Casper's father a ten percent ownership of the orange grove in lieu of payment for the funeral. After some consideration, Casper's father accepted the deal.

A year later, in another fluke that totally altered Casper's future, his father suddenly began to waste away. He was diagnosed with pancreatic cancer and died within a few months, leaving Casper fatherless.

Not long after his father's funeral, Casper's mother was offered an outlandish sum of money to sell her ten percent ownership of the orange grove on the outskirts of Anaheim. The money from the sale of the orange grove had hardly been deposited into Mable's bank account when the fruit trees were ripped out and the Potts ten percent section of the grove eventually became the entrance to the Disneyland Hotel.

Chapter Two

Casper, The Teen

With her newfound fortune from the orchard sale, and the life insurance from her deceased husband, Mable decided to sell their Anaheim house and move closer to her sister's home in Los Angeles. After a week of searching, she paid cash for a home about three blocks northwest of the Farmers Market, in the Fairfax district of Los Angeles.

Mable, now with more discretionary money than she had during her life with Casper's father, boosted her son's weekly allowance to five dollars. He immediately deposited most of it into his savings account.

As a teen, Casper had shot up to slightly more than the average male height of five feet, nine inches, replaced his expression of curiosity with a look of attentiveness, and had begun to feel the twists and turns of teenage testosterone. However, Casper was too reserved to have a girlfriend like many of the boys his age.

Casper liked his new Fairfax neighborhood and quickly fell in love with the Farmers Market. Every day after school he would wander up and down its aisles. He'd stop at the Nut Shop to stare at a large glass bowl with the shiny metal hook inside churning the fresh brown blob of ground peanut butter to keep the oil from separating. Or he'd talk back to the myna bird perched outside a shop that sold postcards with pictures of palm trees, orange blossoms, and the Hollywood sign stuck into the side of a hill. Casper particularly liked the white coffee mug that proclaimed "The Farmers Market" in bright red letters.

One day, he broke one of his personal rules and spent some of his allowance on a Farmers Market mug for his mother and was pleased to see that she used the mug to hold her morning coffee until the day she died.

But unknown to the young Casper, the beguiling collection of shops, fresh produce, restaurants, fresh fish, gifts, and meat markets that made up his favorite haunt had never been planned to be a marketplace. Like the majority of the urban sprawl called the City of Angels, the Farmers Market just sort of happened.

During one of his afternoon walks, Casper noticed a plaque mounted on the wall of the administration building that read, "In memory of A. F. Gilmore, founder of the Farmers Market."

That aroused his curiosity and the next day he headed to the library where he read the history of the Los Angeles Farmers Market.

In 1880, a man named Arthur Gilmore had bought the land under what is now the Farmers Market and established a large dairy. Some years later, while drilling a well for water, instead of H2O, Gilmore discovered a lake of oil. So the dairyman switched from milking cows to milking the earth. To this day, The Gilmore Oil company has produced more than 50 million barrels of black gold.

But Gilmore's chance oil discovery was only the first part of the story that created the Farmers Market.

During the depression, local farmers were desperate to sell their produce, and the newly minted oil tycoon had a small area devoid of pump jacks at the southwest corner of his oil fields, bordered by Fairfax and 3rd. An inveterate entrepreneur, Gilmore rented the farmers a space large enough to park their trucks for fifty cents a day. Over the ensuing years, the farmers trucks were eventually replaced with permanent stalls, and finally roofed. In 1934, the collection of permanent stalls became what is known today as one of the premiere tourist attractions in Los Angeles.

Nowadays, unbeknownst to the thousands of tourists that cruise the aisles, there are still eleven pump jacks hidden from their view, pulling oil from

11

the Los Angeles basin's underground lake of oil, shown on a 1930's City of Los Angeles street map as the Salt Lake Oil Field.

Casper, satisfied with his newfound knowledge of the Farmers Market, continued his daily treks, but now he searched for evidence of the bygone days when thousands of oil pump jacks covered the ground.

A few months after Casper and his mother moved into their new home, they met their next door neighbors, Mr. and Mrs. Salvatore Delgado, who owned an upscale butcher shop in the Farmers Market.

Salvatore Delgado entered this country in his mother's womb after she and Salvatore's father, Fredrico, decided to leave their Tuscan village of Caldana, Italy.

Fredrico was an apprentice meat cutter who was anxious to move up to journeyman, but advancement in Caldana, a village with a population of less than five hundred, was very limited. After years of waiting for his turn, and his patience worn to the nub, Fredrico, his wife immigrated to Los Angeles, the land of milk and honey on the coast of the golden state of California.

The Italian immigrants moved into a small, one bedroom apartment in the Fairfax District, and a week later Fredrico was hired as a journeyman meat cutter at the Select Meat Market, located inside the relativity new Farmers Market. A few months after Fredrico had found work, Amalia gave birth to a son who was named, Salvatore, meaning savior in Italian.

Due to Fredrico's daily interaction with his fellow butchers and the customers, he quickly picked up English, but Amalia's motivation to become bilingual, home alone raising her son, faded as her son grew.

Salvatore, who attended the local schools, spoke perfect English, his father spoke passable English with an Italian accent, while Amalia's English never got much beyond, thank you, good bye, and an enthusiastic happy birthday every year to her son.

Following the old world tradition of frugality, Fredrico and Amalia were thrifty and saved every dollar they could. Many years later, when the owner of Select Meat Market casually mentioned that he was considering selling his business, Fredrico found himself shouting, "I'll buy it!"

And with every dollar they had saved, and a hard-fought for bank loan, Fredrico took over the Select Meat Market.

When Salvatore reached the age of fourteen, he would work an occasional weekend at his father's meat market, but Fredrico wanted his son to become more than a meat cutter, something he never had the opportunity to do. Fredrico wanted his son to graduate from an American university.

Salvatore did as his father had asked and some years later he completed his undergraduate education at the The University of Southern

California with a business degree that included an emphasis on marketing. Salvatore, however, did one thing that earned his father's disapproval. During his senior year at USC, Salvatore fell in love with a bright, young woman named Trudy, short for Gertrude, who lived to be the life of the party, or so he thought. Not long after he graduated, they married, and he soon discovered that his wife turned out to be more of a dull Gertrude than a party-hearty-Trudy. Soon after they exchanged marriage vows, Salvatore began to cast his fishing line into some different waters.

After graduation, Salvatore went to work with his father full time. Though Salvatore's real interest was growing and improving the business, he put his nose to the grindstone and learned the meat cutting trade in record time

First, he proposed they change the name of the business to Delgado's Meat Market, a much classier name then Select Meat Market, and his father wholeheartedly agreed.

Then he suggested they raise the prices on their finest steaks and chops. At first, his father resisted the concept, but eventually he agreed to try his son's recommendation. After six weeks, to his father's surprise, the higher priced meat was selling faster than the lower priced cuts.

Finally, Salvatore was poised to pull off his marketing coup de gras when his father had a stroke and mercifully died within a few days.

His mother, still unable to string five words of English together, perished the following month from what Salvatore knew was a broken heart.

His mother's doctor told him, "Mr. Delgado, we did all we could, but she seemed to lack the will to live."

After two funerals inside of six weeks, Salvatore implemented his final marketing plan for what was now his meat market: he placed a weekly ad in The Beverly Hills Courier. The copy extolled the benefits of shopping for the finest meats at Delgado's Meat Market, an exceptional store located in the world famous Farmers Market. The Courier was a free weekly newspaper that served the posh communities of Beverly Hills, Bel Air, Holmby Hills, Century City, Trousdale, Brentwood and Westwood.

Salvatore knew what he was doing. The Courier reached many of the most expensive homes in the Los Angeles basin and the ads ended up on the kitchen counters of some of the richest and most famous people on the earth. Within a month, Salvatore needed to hire two additional butchers as his business jumped up thirty percent.

After he became better acquainted with Mabel and her son Casper, Mr. Delgado offered Casper the opportunity to work four hours each Saturday at his meat market to give him a leg up on the meat cutters' apprentice ladder for the magnificent sum of fifty cents an hour.

Mr. Delgado, however, had a more important reason to offer Casper the job, a reason that at no time crossed Casper's innocent mind. Casper never noticed that every Saturday, about the same time he left his house to walk to his job at the Farmers Market, Mr. Delgado's wife would leave her home for her weekend position behind the notions counter at a near-by Woolworth's, leaving Delgado and Casper's mother with just a single driveway separating them.

As he had frequently strayed from his vow of fidelity, Mr. Delgado was ready, willing, and able to cast his fishing line closer to home. It took Mr. Delgado, a very handsome and sophisticated gentleman, several weeks to convince Mable that as a widow with needs she deserved all the love and affection he was capable of providing, as long as it took place on a Saturday.

If by chance he had observed the assignation between Mr. Delgado and his mother, his mother would have likely convinced him that she and Mr. Delgado needed their Saturday time together so Mr. Delgado could teach her the intricacies of the meat business. She, on the other hand, as a former librarian, would use her Saturday to explain to Mr. Delgado the ten major classifications of the Dewey Decimal System, beginning with 000—Computer science, information and general works—and ending with 999—History & Geography. So until his mother passed away, she and Mr. Delgado

16

continued their clandestine Saturdays-only companionship.

Casper's first job assignment at the Delgado Meat Market was to sweep up all the previous day's exhausted sawdust, now laced with blood, fat, and God knows what, and replace it with a fresh supply of clean, sweet particles of pine sawdust before the market opened to customers.

After six months of diligent effort, one of Mr. Delgado's butchers, Mr. Jack Lasco, was assigned to teach Casper the ins and outs of how to become a journeyman meat cutter.

Mr. Jack Lasco taught Casper:

• How to grind beef, and just how much beef melt (beef pancreas) to slip into the grind of the expensive ground round mix to brighten the color without modifying the taste, and most importantly, without getting caught by the inspector.

• How to keep track of the day and month the briskets and rounds of beef had been dropped into a large corning brine barrel located in the walk-in refrigerator.

• How to scoop a little more than a pound of ground meat onto butcher paper so the customer would always buy a little more than what they had asked for.

• Just where to hang a beef crown rib roast to dry-age the meat to perfection in the walk-in refrigerator.

- How to sweet talk the female customers so they would ask for you by name.

According to Jack Lasco, that was nearly every skill Casper would need to become a successful butcher.

By the time Casper received his diploma from Fairfax High School he had a light crop of whiskers that had to be shaved every three days. His countenance could be called very close to handsome, and he began to appreciate being admired by some of the females who shopped for their meat at the Farmers Market.

Chapter Three

Casper, The Adult

It didn't take Mr. Delgado long to spot the positive way Casper dealt with his female customers and hire him as a full-time meat cutter.

So Casper Potts, unaware that Delgado had hired him for his ability to attract female customers, spent the rest of his working life as a quiet, unassuming meat cutter at one of the exclusive and most expensive meat markets in Southern California.

Casper loved the part of his job when he butchered a fresh side of beef or a whole lamb, or when he'd place a full tray of freshly ground beef on display, or adjusted the plastic green parsley between the glistening rows of pork chops in the glass case. But he did not immediately take to the other part of being a meat cutter—chatting and smiling with the friendly female customers who stood on the other side of the meat counter. However, being an intelligent young man, Casper realized that acting friendly and acknowledging the

19

person who purchased the meat was a big part of the meat cutter's job, so he worked at improving his people skills, while never totally understanding the need for them. He became skilled at the required banter. After he pulled a whole chicken from the display case, bony yellow feet still attached, if Mrs. Ruiz commented, "Your apron looks spiffy today, Casper."

Casper would nod shyly and answer while he wrapped the chicken, "Thank you, Mrs. Ruiz, but not anywhere as spiffy as your dress. Is that new?"

As introverted as Casper was, he still understood that his goal was to keep his female customers happy. Mr. Delgado quickly noted on the days that Casper worked sales were seven percent higher than those days when he was off.

So day after day, month after month, and year after year, Mr. Delgado's Meat Market was Casper's life—cutting, grinding, and wrapping meat and saving a large percentage of his salary. Then one momentous day, after he had properly weighed, and correctly priced a package of ground round for Mrs. Shultz, she said, "Thank you, Casper. Should I assume a good looking man like you has a girlfriend?"

Casper forced a smile, and stated, "Not yet, Mrs. Shultz. By the way, I love your new hat."

Then Mrs. Shultz delivered the line that would change Casper's future. "Thank you Casper. You know, a lot of pretty, young girls your age attend my church."

After a few weeks of constant reminders from Mrs. Shultz, Casper attended her church where, as promised, he met many pretty, young girls.

He was a naive twenty-five-year-old living with his mother when he met his future wife, Margaret, at the adult bible study group held each Thursday evening at the church. A few students of religion attended the Thursday evening sessions to study the bible, while Casper and most of the pretty, young girls were searching for a spouse, or at least a trustworthy date for the weekend.

One Thursday evening, before the Bible class began, Casper spotted an irresistible female standing across the room, and for some inexplicable reason, he knew that he was looking at his future wife.

The young woman was very attractive, stood a few inches below his six foot height, and wore an outfit that was incapable of hiding her female shape.

Casper's congenital introversion combined with an overwhelming fear of rejection nearly caused him to chickened out. But he discovered a previously unknown hidden resolve and he approached her, forced a smile, and tentatively thrust his right hand toward her. "Hi, my name is Casper."

With a feeling of anxiety, she forced herself to respond "Hello. My name is Margaret."

Her hand moved forward, to shake his, and the moment their palms touched, Casper felt as if the two had been transported to their own private island.

Casper said, "Margaret, there's a little coffee shop just around the corner. I'd love to buy you a cup of coffee so we can get to know each other better."

Margaret was a woman who seldom made impulsive decisions due to her general distrust of everyone, but mostly men. This time, however, after gazing into Casper's azure eyes, she found herself saying, "I guess that would be alright, but let's wait until after the class is over."

Casper, his only motivation for attending the weekly Bible class now exposed, was eager to talk with his future soulmate, but it had taken him twenty-five years to find her so an additional hour was no problem. "Sounds good to me."

Sixty long minutes later the two left the church and walked around the corner to the coffee shop.

Once they were seated in a booth, Casper said, "Margaret, they make an outstanding cherry pie here. Would you like some? My treat."

"No thank you." Based on what Margaret's mother had instilled in her, she had to say no. If she had accepted his offer, what else might he expect from her?

The two finished their first cup of coffee with some light talk about the Bible class, and had started on their refills when Casper said, "I'd bet most people would call me an introvert. To tell the truth, I attend the Bible class just to meet girls, but you're the first one I've worked up the courage to ask to coffee after the class. You don't know how glad I am that you accepted my offer."

Again, Margaret stared into Casper's eyes, as if she hoped to find a sign that he was telling the truth. Not finding anything but his blue orbs, she responded, "You're welcome."

Relieved that he had successfully cleared a major hurdle, Casper relaxed, and said, "You sure you don't want some of that cherry pie?"

Margaret smiled, "No thank you, but I really appreciate you asking me again."

Responding to Margaret's smile and realizing he had a shot at finding his first girlfriend, Casper said, "Maybe I should tell you something about myself. I have a full time job as a journeyman meat cutter at Delgado's Meat Market in the Farmer's Market. I was born twenty-five years ago in Anaheim. I am an only child, with a mother who was a librarian and a mortician for a father. Looking back, I think that's why I'm so introverted. When my father died unexpectedly, my mother and I moved to this neighborhood, and I've already told you that I joined the Bible class to meet nice girls. What about you, Margaret? I'm all ears."

As Casper completed his abbreviated life history, a single tear slipped from her right eye.

A shocked Casper stammered, "Margaret, don't cry. I'm sorry if I said anything that —"

"No, no, it's not you. I was just thinking how lucky you were to have known your father."

As she dabbed her right eye with her handkerchief, Margaret realized that for some inexplicable reason, she wanted to tell this perfect stranger the secret that she had worked to keep suppressed for more than a decade.

"My mother is a checker at Safeway and works 9 to 6 each day. Her schedule gave me time after school each afternoon to do my homework. One day, when I was thirteen, I came home from school, completed my assignments, and sat down to go through our family photo albums. As an only child, that was something I did a lot, but on that day I noticed for the first time, there were no pictures of my father. Casper, I had looked at those old photos hundreds of times, but this time, as I was beginning adolescence, the absence of any pictures of my father caused an alarm to go off inside my head. Then my anxiety rose after I turned the pages further back and saw there were no wedding pictures of my parents. When my mother came home from work I confronted her. All of the color drained from her face and she sat down on the couch. She told me that to protect me she had made up the story about how my father worked in the far east oil fields, and died in an oil rig accident in Saudi Arabia. Then she sat me down next to her and told me the truth, that I had been conceived during a 'one-night-stand' in Las Vegas. When I was born, she made up a father's name for the birth certificate. Casper, my father wasn't a mortician.

24

He's just a nameless man who got my mother pregnant.

After an uncomfortable moment of silence, Casper leaned forward and whispered, "My God, that was a terrible thing for your mother to tell you."

With that comment, Margaret felt a tiny spark of hope that Casper could be trusted. "I agree. I don't think she set out to hurt me, but what she told me that day changed my life. Prior to that, I was a friendly, happy-go-lucky teen, but since that day I've been suspicious of everyone's motives, not just my mother's, but friends at school, the minister at our church, even you, Casper!"

Casper was truly shocked that Margaret's apprehensions included him, an individual who had never hurt a fly. Suddenly, he envisioned himself donning his shiny suit of armor and climbing onto his trusty white horse to rescue this damsel in distress.

He placed his hand palm up on the table. "Margaret, please put your hand in mine."

She hesitated. Then, as if a single rock tumbled off Margaret's dark mountain of mistrust, she placed her palm onto his.

Casper gave her hand a gentle squeeze."Margaret, you need to know that I will never lie to you. I will always protect you, and I will devote the rest of my life to earning your trust."

Margaret, comforted by the warmth of Casper's words and his hand, responded with a little smile and a hesitant nod of her head.

Now that he had rescued his lady from her angst, Casper said, "I'm fully aware that the next words out of my mouth will sound a bit crazy, but the moment I set eyes on you, I knew that we were destined to become soulmates. Margaret, will you do me the honor of becoming my wife?"

To say that Margaret was stunned at Casper's offer of marriage would be a gross understatement. Faithful to her inherent and general lack of trust in humanity, she quickly responded with a resounding, "No."

Later that night, Margaret interrupted her mother as she watched a show on TV. "Mother, after the Bible class I joined a nice young man named Casper for a cup of coffee.

Her mother jumped up from her easy chair and said in a voice laced with anger, "You allowed a man to seduce you for a cup of coffee?"

"Mother, he didn't seduce—"

"But I thought my example would warn you away from that sort of man?"

"Mother, I—"

"Promise me that you'll never talk to that man again."

"Mother, I am an adult, and if I choose to see Casper every week after the Bible class for coffee that is my decision to make."

"Be warned, I'll not be a part of anything that happens in the future between you two."

Her mother stormed from the living room. From that moment, their model mother/daughter relationship began a downward spiral.

Regardless of Margaret's deteriorating connection with her mother, her knight in shining armor persevered. After many trips to the coffee shop, and multiple marriage proposals, Margaret's belief in Casper's promise to love and protect her, grew to the point that she joyfully accepted his promise of matrimonial bliss.

The only fly in the ointment was that Margaret's mother refused to attend both their wedding. After missing the Christening ceremony of her granddaughter, Margaret never spoke to her mother again.

Once the the happy couple returned from their brief honeymoon in San Diego, and in anticipation of finding their own apartment, the two moved Margaret's belongings into Casper's mother's house.

Her first week home, Margaret dropped out of UCLA and concentrated all her efforts on becoming a wife.

During the second week, Casper's mother offered to teach Margaret how to prepare her new husband's favorite meals.

By the end of the third week, Margaret was comfortable cooking Casper his breakfast and dinner and Casper was delighted with the results.

Then, at the end of the fourth week, Casper's mother was struck down in a crosswalk by a hit-and-run driver.

After the funeral Casper realized there was no reason to continue searching for an apartment as he was his mother's sole heir, and now the owner of the family home.

During their second year of marriage, Casper and Margaret were blessed with the birth of a child, a girl they named Judith. She turned out to be the complete opposite of her mother and father, the textbook definition of an extrovert.

All through school, their daughter, Judith, was sociable with gaggles of giggling friends passing regularly through the Potts home. While matriculating at USC, where she majored in theater arts, Judith met her future husband, Albert Pann.

Once Judith's formal education was completed, she and Albert married and then worked together in the world of television where they developed a pilot that became an instant TV sitcom hit. Every week the program's credits would close the show with their now distinctive logo of Potts and Panns Productions.

One day, after Judith was old enough to leave with a sitter, Casper decided to surprise his wife and he asked Margaret out for a date.

Margaret frowned as she said, "A date? We're married. Married people don't date."

"Margaret, Judith is a beautiful daughter, and I love her more and more everyday, but she's the reason why we need to go on a date."

Margaret frowned. "I don't understand."

"Before she was born, we'd go out almost every week, to a movie or dinner. You need a break from the household chores, cleaning, changing diapers, and cooking. That's why we need to go out on a date."

Margaret smiled as she recalled the carefree days before Judith. "But can we afford a baby sitter and dinner?"

"I just received a raise from Mr. Delgado. We can afford it. And besides, I love you."

So the following Wednesday, after he received his weekly paycheck, Casper took Margaret to Du-par's Restaurant, located in the Farmers Market.

Casper, tired of looking at display cases filled with red meat ordered the Crab Cakes while Margaret opted for the Chicken Pot Pie, one of Du-pars signature dishes. Once they finished their main dishes, the two topped off their first date night with one of Du-par's famous Hot Fudge Brownie Sundae served with two spoons.

Casper was quick to note how much Margaret enjoyed that Wednesday night out, so a Wednesday dinner date at Du-pars became a regular weekly event.

A few months later, Mr. Delgado invited Casper and Margaret to join the Delgado's for dinner at El Cholo's, a well known Mexican restaurant close to downtown Los Angeles. Margaret and Casper beguiled by El Cholo's food, and the old world atmosphere at the venerable restaurant. Saturday dinners at El Cholo's with the Delgado's became their second weekly date.

Over time, Casper and Margaret sampled every item on the El Cholo's menu and eventually Casper settled on their amazing Spanish Omelet, while Margaret would select the Chile Rellenos combination plate, except during the months of May through October when she would switch to their Green Corn Tamale special.

While the two eagerly looked forward to their evenings out, Casper and Margaret, like all new parents scrambled to keep up their growing daughter, so the other five days of the week could not be considered dull. Baby Judith would not allow that to happen.

As a baby, she was curious about anything and everything. Judith seldom cried, and instinctively giggled when handed into the arms of a neighbor.

From age five to eleven, Judith easily worked her way through elementary school while her reclusive mom fought off her timidity and bravely put in her hours with the school PTA.

Casper's contribution to Judith's formative years was to take her to the library each Saturday. The two would select a stack of books to check out, then before her bedtime each evening, Casper would read the illustrated stories to his daughter. As she grew older, the books went from *The Cat In*

The Hat, to *Tom Sawyer*, to *The World According To Garp*.

One Saturday, while searching the library shelves, Casper discovered the same book that he had read as a child: the story where the white knight vanquished the dark knight. That night he read that story to Judith and she was so enraptured by the tale of honor that Casper purchased the book.

By the time his daughter reached high school Casper was confident that Judith was well read and would become a successful adult.

Although an honor student in high school, her top academic status did not put off her classmates. During her senior year she was elected Homecoming Queen. Judith received multiple invitations to the prom and eventually accepting the invite from the handsome, all-league quarterback. Margaret, who never quite understood her daughter's popularity, did something that she and her own mother had never done, shop for a prom dress. One Saturday, Margaret and Judith spent the whole day going from store to store until Judith found the perfect gown, conservative enough to get her mother's approval and sexy enough to arouse the ardor of her prom date.

Alas, the week after Judith moved into a sorority house at USC, Margaret and Casper reverted back into the same, mundane existence they had lived before their daughter was born.

Just how uneventful were their lives? Each morning the alarm clock woke them at six fifty am.

Margaret threw on a robe and fixed Casper's hearty breakfast. Then she packed him a lunch, and after he left for work, showered, dressed and did laundry, or cleaned the house, or shopped for groceries as needed.

While Margaret fixed his breakfast, Casper showered and shaved. Seated at the kitchen table, he consumed his sizable morning meal and read the *Los Angeles Times*. After he brushed his teeth, Casper gave Margaret a hug and a kiss, picked up his lunch box, walked to work and arrived at eight fifty each morning ready face his world of customers. Once he secured his clean, white apron with a tie around his trim waist, he checked the beef rounds that hung inside a brine barrel in the walk-in refrigerator, wrap a package filled with ground lamb, or just schmooze with one of his female customers.

Once his workday was done, Casper arrived home for dinner at precisely six-thirty-five each evening and Margaret served the evening meal at seven sharp. Once they washed, and put away the dishes, the two retired to the living room where they read, listened to music, and hopped into bed by ten,

For more than three decades of marriage, Casper, unlike many of his fellow workers at Delgado's, was aware that he lived a happy, quiet life, but he was content.

And Margaret? She still felt a tingle of happiness each time she recalled the day Casper first proposed.

But sooner or later, in all life, some sorrow will strike.

The week before the happy couple were to celebrate their thirty-third wedding anniversary, Casper returned home from work. When he opened the door, he noticed the lack enticing aroma from Margaret's latest culinary creation, an event he had looked forward to for more than three decades. As he walked into the living room, he found the love of his life lying facedown on the couch. He grabbed her wrist and her skin was cold. He gently turned her over and she wasn't breathing. Sobbing, he called 911. The ambulance arrived in five minutes, but there was nothing they could do.

Before he followed the ambulance to the hospital, Casper called his daughter. "Judith . . . I . . ."

"What is it dad? Is something wrong? Did something happen to mom?"

He hesitated, " . . .Yes, she died. They are taking her body to Cedars-Sinai Hospital on Beverly —"

"I know where that is. I'll be there as soon as I can."

When Judith arrived, the father and daughter hugged each other tightly, as if they were the last two people on earth. Moments later a doctor approached and told them that Margaret Potts had

33

likely died from a brain aneurysm sometime that morning.

Casper asked, "Doctor, did she feel any pain?"

Although the doctor didn't have a clue, the physician knew this was the proper time for a response that would help the family feel better. "Mr. Potts, Ms. Potts, I'm sure she never felt a thing."

"Thank you, doctor."

As the two walked to the parking lot Judith said, "Dad, I know how much you depended on mom. I can quit college for a year or two to help you out."

Casper shook his head. "No, your mother and I want you to stay in school and graduate."

With tears streaming down her face, Judith cried, "Do you need help with the arrangements?"

"Again no. You go back to school. I'll take care of everything."

"Dad, if it's okay with you, I want to pick out mom's final outfit for her to wear."

Choking back a sob, "Thank you. Now you get back to school. We don't want our daughter to flunk out of USC."

Back home in the empty dining room of his empty house, still stunned by the unexpected turn of events, Casper pondered what he was going to do with the rest of his formerly well organized life. He had a solid job that paid well plus a home without a mortgage in a good Los Angeles neighborhood, but he wasn't sure he knew how to live without

Margaret. To him, at that moment, his life was as empty as his home.

While he considered his future, his stomach rumbled signifying that it was time to eat. He rose, walked to the door of his kitchen, and as he stood outside the unoccupied room, he slowly realized that throughout his entire life he had never once prepared a meal. First there was his mother's cooking, then the various school cafeterias followed by Margaret's cuisine, combined with the date nights ar Du-par's and El Cholo. Every breakfast, lunch, and dinner had been miraculously assembled by someone else. That first night after his wife had trundled off her mortal coil, Casper decided to avoid his kitchen and walked to a neighborhood Italian restaurant where he satiated his hunger with a sausage and black olive pizza.

The following morning, Casper made his first and only attempt to fix his own breakfast. His plan was to assemble a simple meal of dry cereal, juice and coffee. But as Casper puzzled over how to make the coffee machine work, he became aware of the fact that he had never once used the device. Coffeeless, as he attempted to eat his wheat flakes with milk, he found they were as tasteless as cardboard, unaware that Margaret had always added a dozen golden raisins along with two heaping spoonfuls of sugar over the cereal. That was when he realized Judith was right. He did need help! After his disastrous attempt to make a simple breakfast, Casper ate his future morning meals at Denny's where they provided him with a plate full of eggs, bacon, toast, and a cup or two of hot, fresh coffee.

One Wednesday evening, a few months following his wife's funeral, Caspar sat, as usual, in Du-par's, where he perused his morning edition of the *Los Angeles Times* with his dinner.

As Casper took a bite of a delicious crab cake, the headline of a colorful, full-page, ad caught his eye.

SENIORS

LIVE AN ACTIVE

INDEPENDENT LIFE!

AT

THE OAKS

He scanned the pictures below the headline, intrigued by a perfectly decorated apartment with a balcony that overlooked a pool surrounded by beautifully landscaped grounds; a library lined with shelves full of books and comfortable overstuffed chairs; a dining room with smiling people sitting around a table and being served what looked to be a very tasty meal.

Had he owned a mobile phone, Casper would have called The Oaks at once. As one of the few people left in the planet who didn't understand the value of a smart phone, he had to wait until he returned home.

Once he arrived home, he keyed in the number from the newspaper ad and a female voice answered, "Good evening. You have reached The Oaks, where happy, active seniors live the good life. My name is Bridget. How may I help you?"

"Ah . . . I noticed your full page ad in the *Los Angeles Times* and . . . I guess I'm calling for more information."

Chapter Four

The Oaks

"You're in luck. The manager was just about to leave. I will transfer your call."

Casper didn't really want to talk to the manager and was about to hang up when a melodious male voice filled his ear. "Good evening. My name is Mr. Bradford. What can I do for you?"

"Uh, Mr. Bradford, I noticed your ad in the Times. I'm looking for more information."

"And your name is?"

For a second time, Casper contemplated hanging up. At this juncture, giving a stranger his name over the phone seemed like a very large commitment and all he wanted was some information that he could absorb at his leisure, in the privacy of his home. Reluctantly he relented and said, "Mr. Potts", feeling that providing only his last name would maintain a little distance between himself and the unknown man on the other end of the phone call.

"Mr. Potts, why don't we begin with the FAQ's?"

Casper's eyelids fluttered lightly as they often did when he was confused. "Excuse me?"

"I apologize, Mr. Potts. FAQ's are Frequently Asked Questions. Now, the number one question most people want to know is how much it will cost them to join the family here at The Oaks. We have an entrance fee for our one bedroom apartments is $550,000. That fee increases to $750,000 for a two bedroom apartment, and tops out at $1,250,000 for our brand new, three bedroom casitas that have a view of the Hollywood Bowl. That is the answer to our most asked question."

"I see. Then you're telling me that I would be purchasing a condo?"

Mr. Bradford sighed. Before he had been hired by The Phoenix Corporation, his knowledge of luxury retirement living would not come close to filling a thimble. But that all changed when one day, while eating lunch, he read the following Business Journal's article.

Jump on the Luxury, Active Senior, Retirement Bandwagon
A Lucrative and Booming Industry!

"To meet a future buyer's criteria as a luxury retirement facility, the establishment must offer the potential resident a standard of living far above the common, or average senior living facility by providing the following features:

- A living space large enough to accommodate a COMFORTABLE, standard-sized couch and at least one overstuffed chair.
- One, two, or more master sized bedrooms. All with square footage large enough to accommodate a KING-SIZED BED.
- One, two, or more bathrooms, each with bath and shower.
- A fully functional kitchen with, and this is very important, GRANITE COUNTER TOPS.
- Each bedroom, living room, and kitchen must be constructed with high ceilings to give THE ILLUSION OF SPACE.
- Added to the apartments, or living spaces, there must be opulent details that differentiate the luxury from the mundane independent retirement facility such as:
- Gourmet dining options offered off a menu and served by a uniformed waitstaff on tables covered with a white tablecloth.
- A minimum of one swimming pool.
- Secured aboveground, or underground facilities for parking.
- Immaculately landscaped grounds.
- At least one fitness center.

- Twenty-four hour security every day of the year.
- A fully stocked library.
- A twenty-four-hour coffee lounge with internet access.
- Card rooms.
- A movie theater.
- Luxury vehicles to transport the residents to doctor visits and shopping mall excursions.

Combine all the above items and you will have created a luxury senior facility where unreasonable fees will be disregarded by the residents because they will feel as if they had moved into the best suite of a five-star cruise ship."

From the moment Mr. Bradford finished reading the article, he had found his new career.

Without missing a beat, he launched into his sales pitch. "No, Mr. Potts, you will not be buying a condo. The entrance fee allows you to become a family member here at The Oaks. Your entrance fee will be returned, minus fifteen percent, to you or your heirs, for the following reasons:

If you move to another location; your own death; or because The Oaks is an independent, active senior living facility, you are required to vacate the premises because you contract a debilitating illness that requires full-time assistance. Under those circumstances, your

41

entrance fee would be returned, minus the aforementioned fifteen percent."

Casper was starting to feel some pressure, the same way he did when he last bought a new car. He attempted to slow Mr Bradford down by asking, "Mr. Bradford, I'm a bit confused about the difference between independent living and assisted living. Could you explain that difference to me?"

"Mr. Potts, it's really rather simple. The Oaks is for independent, active seniors, not for those seniors who, for what ever reason, require assistance."

Casper recalled his father's last few months on earth when he needed help getting in and out of bed, going to the bathroom, getting dressed. He even needed someone to push his wheelchair from room to room. He said, "Thank you. Now I see the difference, and I understand why you would return the entrance fee."

"Actually, since I've been the manager here at The Oaks, death has been the only reason a resident has left the The Oaks family."

Mr. Bradford's remarks about death sent a chill down Casper's spine, because until that moment, he had never considered the fact that someday, just like his parents and his wife, he would cease breathing.

Casper said, "Fine. Now I understand the entrance fee, but what happens if while living at The Oaks I fall and break a leg? All of the pictures in the ad show healthy people sitting by the pool. I didn't see a wheelchair, or a cane in any of those photos. What happens to people who live at The Oaks if they temporarily need a wheelchair or assistance?"

"Mr. Potts, as an independent living facility all who live at The Oaks must be ambulatory or capable of moving under their own power in a wheelchair. The Oaks family members, however, are allowed to remain for a short time while they recover from an illness, or a fall.They will however, be required to leave The Oaks once it has been determined that they will never be able to move about in a wheelchair under their own power."

Casper nodded. "Now, I have one more question. How much more does one have to pay to access the library pictured in your ad?"

"Mr. Potts, you've hit upon the best aspect of The Oaks. Once you pay your monthly rental fee for your apartment, all of The Oaks facilities are yours to use at your pleasure. An elegantly decorated apartment, the indoor and outdoor swimming pools, the gym, the card rooms, the library, the movie theater, and live entertainment on weekends are just a few of The Oaks' outstanding attributes. And don't forget, two full gourmet meals are included every day, seven days a week, served to you at your table by our impeccably trained staff."

"Mr. Bradford, how much is the monthly fee?"

"Mr. Potts, it varies, but let me say your monthly fee would fall between four and five thousand a month."

Casper glanced at the pictures in the ad and envisioned himself sitting at one of the dining tables, sipping a glass of wine, and discussing the pleasantries of the day with his new-found friends, and while the monthly fee seemed high, he could see that with a little belt tightening, it was doable."Mr. Bradford, I must admit that The Oaks sounds interesting."

"Mr. Potts, please stop by anytime you are free. Go to the front desk, ask for me, Mr. Bradford, and I will personally take you on a tour of our facilities, and after the tour, I will dine with you as we partake of one of our gourmet meals, complements of the management."

Casper was impressed by the calm, but authoritative tone of Mr. Bradford's voice. After a short moment of consideration, Casper said, "Mr. Bradford, I will meet you tomorrow at The Oaks. What would be a good time?"

"Let me check my calendar . . . Tomorrow around eleven-thirty would be perfect. Will that work for you?"

Casper said, "I recall you said I could partake in one of your gourmet meals."

"That's correct, Mr. Potts."

"I'm mostly curious about your breakfasts. Does breakfast qualify as one of your gourmet meals?"

Mr. Bradford paused. That was the first time a prospective buyer asked for breakfast. "Of course it does. Could you be here at eight?"

"I can."

44

"Excellent. I'll meet you at eight."

The Oaks was constructed some twenty years earlier by The Phoenix Corporation, a multi-billion dollar company that had built dozens of similar facilities throughout the country. The corporation's published mission was: "To provide an exciting lifestyle for seniors where they can discover a renewed youth to live out their golden years in a safe and peaceful environment."

What Casper didn't know at that time was that The Phoenix Corporation like many monolithic companies, had fallen into the trap of adhering to the Peter Principle—the theory that the majority of management personnel within a corporation rose to their level of incompetence. Mr Bradford's career with The Phoenix Corporation was a classic example of the Peter Principle in action.

Mr. Bradford's first assignment with The Phoenix Corporation was assistant manager at the The Cedars, an active senior facility located in Medford, Oregon, where he quickly became the apple of his boss's eye. Each day, Mr. Bradford would complete every task that had been assigned to him, allowing the manager to spend most of his time playing golf.

Week after week, Mr. Bradford trusted his future to the work ethic grindstone, and within a year his boss placed him on the list for promotion. But what the manager of The Cedars didn't comprehend, because he was playing golf, was that Mr. Bradford had only reacted to the daily tasks assigned him. Mr. Bradford lacked the X factor that separated the few true leaders in the business world from the multitude of followers.

In other words, if The Cedars were a railroad train packed with four hundred passengers racing across the tracks, and Mr Bradford realized that the train was approaching a potential derailment, he lacked the leadership qualities needed to make the right decision, at the right time, to avoid the disaster.

In spite of his lack of leadership ability, Mr. Bradford was promoted and shipped to Southern California where he became the manager of The Oaks in the Hollywood Hills, and into a position where he couldn't kick any unsolvable problems up-the-line. His desk was where the buck stopped, and he soon began to realize that he had reached his level of incompetence—his managerial career ceiling with The Phoenix Corporation.

The only true attribute that Mr. Bradford brought to his position at The Oaks was his ability to close the sale, a talent that held him in good stead with The Phoenix Corporation, but didn't do much to keep The Oaks functioning in a smooth and efficient manner.

The following day, after a quick shower and shave, Casper, with excusable ignorance as to what his life would be like living in an active senior facility surrounded by hundreds of other seniors, left his home. He drove north on Fairfax, made a right turn, then a left, then another left to The

Oaks, a series of aesthetically designed buildings, located in the Hollywood hills between Runyon Canyon Park and the Hollywood Bowl.

Far below The Oaks lay The Hollywood Bowl, the iconic performing arts landmark in Southern California. The Bowl had been presenting concerts and musical festivals since 1920 when the first audiences sat on wooden benches in what was called 'Daisy Dell' in Bolton Canyon. In 1922, after being renamed the Hollywood Bowl, audiences heard the Los Angeles Philharmonic, under conductor Alfred Hertz, for the initial season of Hollywood Bowl's 'Music Under The Stars' concerts. In 1927, Lloyd Wright, Frank Lloyd Wright's son, designed and constructed the first pyramidal band shell. Over time, the original band shell has been redesigned and/or replaced but the seasons of Music Under The Stars have continued to dazzle concert goers for more than eighty-five years.

As there were concerts performed at the Hollywood Bowl most every day during the summer months, The Oaks' buildings were conveniently tucked below a small ridge so the musical concerts did not disturb the seniors' tranquility.

At 7:55 am, Casper parked his car in a visitor's slot, got out of his vehicle and felt a bit dwarfed by the three-storied, beige-colored building that he faced. He noted the main building was freshly painted, but much less cozy than his three bedroom home in the Fairfax neighborhood.

He walked toward the front door that automatically opened as he approached, and Casper noted how handy that door would be if he had to walk into the building carrying bags filled with groceries.

He entered the building and stepped onto a floor made of highly polished marble. To his right was a desk and behind that desk sat a woman who'd shape was nearly as round as her face. She asked, "May I help you?"

"Good morning. My name is Casper Potts and I have an appointment for breakfast with Mr. Bradford."

She picked up her phone, pushed a button and mouthed a few words into the transmitter. She smiled as she set the phone down and said,"Mr. Potts, Mr. Bradford will be right with you."

After a few moments Mr. Bradford walked into the lobby and thrust his right hand in the direction of Casper. "Mr Potts. How good of you to drop in, and right on time."

Casper observed the man behind the voice he had heard on the other end of his phone conversation. Mr. Bradford looked to be in his mid-forties, plus or minus a few years. His height was a touch shorter than Casper's, six foot, one inch. Mr. Bradford had broad shoulders, and a pale complexion, as if he seldom ventured into the sun, and a pleasant face.

Casper reached for Mr. Bradford's hand and said, "I'm looking forward to the tour."

48

Mr. Bradford clasped Casper's hand. "Mr. Potts, that's what most people tell me, but I have a feeling that it's my promise of a gourmet breakfast, served by our impeccably trained wait-staff, that brought you here this morning. Let's go to the dining room. We can tour the apartments and the amenities after we dine."

Mr. Bradford had been correct. At this point, Casper was more interested in the gourmet breakfast than wandering through a few boring apartments."I agree. Breakfast first, and then the tour."

With a sweep of his hand, Mr. Bradford gestured to his left. "To our beautiful dining room. After you, Mr. Potts."

An hour later, Casper's belt was nearly bursting after breakfast that began with a glass of fresh squeezed orange juice, followed by a ham and cheese omelet, hash-browned potatoes, two slices of fresh tomato, two buttermilk biscuits hot out of the oven, four small jars of cherry jam imported from France, and the best coffee Casper had ever tasted.

Casper, dazzled by the quantity and quality of the food served, joined Mr. Bradford as they toured the apartments and amenities at The Oaks.

After the tour of the one bedroom and two bedroom apartments, and the three bedroom casitas, Mr. Bradford escorted Casper to his office where he began his sales pitch.

"Mr. Potts, what was your favorite of the living facilities we offer at The Oaks?"

Casper responded, "I felt more comfortable with the space and the views offered by the two bedroom apartments that overlooked the pool and gardens as compared to one of the smaller, one bedroom apartments."

Mr. Bradford said, "Mr. Potts, if you liked the two bedroom apartments, then you must have fallen in love with the three bedroom casitas."

"Mr. Bradford, the casitas were lovely, but I felt they were a little flamboyant for my taste."

While Mr. Bradford was a man completely out of his depth as the manager of a large, active senior facility, he was a born salesman. As one of the most successful life insurance salesmen west of the Rockies, he had the innate sense of when to push harder or to back off. In this case, he correctly translated Casper's statement, 'flamboyant for my taste', as the three bedroom casitas had exceeded his monitory limit. So all Mr. Bradford had to do was discover Casper's money limit, and The Oaks occupancy rate would increase by one.

Mr. Bradford said, "Mr. Potts, for you to move into a two bedroom apartment with a view of the swimming pool and the posh, landscaped gardens, you would be required to pay a $750,000 entrance fee."

Knowing that he would be spending more money than any other time in his life, Casper started to do some monetary calculations in his head while Mr. Bradford spread out some 8 x 10 photos of apartments in front of him. "Look! I have some pictures to remind you of the one bedroom apartments that you felt were cramped, and the two bedroom apartment we walked through today. I'm sure you recall that apartment with the extra bedroom and the outstanding views?"

Casper, fearing that things were moving faster than he liked, stood up. "Thank you, Mr. Bradford, for all your input. I appreciate the outstanding breakfast and the tour of The Oaks, but you are talking about me spending more than three quarters of a million dollars. I need to go home and figure out if I can afford to live at The Oaks."

Masking his growing concern that he could lose this sale, Mr. Bradford jumped up. "I can understand your anxiety, Mr. Potts, but I have another appointment scheduled in thirty minutes and the lady specifically told me that she was considering the very apartment in which you had shown such interest."

Casper smiled. "I will call you later today, or tomorrow morning with my decision."

Alarm bells sounded in his head as Mr. Bradford returned Casper's smile. Every successful salesman in the United States, and that included Mr. Bradford, knew that once a potential sale left the office without signing a commitment sheet and leaving a deposit check, the odds were very high that the anticipated sale would vanish and never be seen again.

With a warmth that belied his mounting angst, Mr. Bradford glanced at his watch and exclaimed,

51

"Mr. Potts, there's no need for you to go home to mull over your decision. I'm due for my monthly meeting with the kitchen staff, so you are welcome to stay in my office and look over the pictures and floor plans of the available apartments and casitas. Take all the time you need. Just let my secretary know if you have any questions and I'll return shortly."

The moment Mr. Bradford had closed his office door, Casper felt less pressured. He relaxed, sat back, and considered his visit to The Oaks. There was no doubt that The Oaks would offer him much more than living alone in his house. But could he afford it? And even if he could, did he want to place all his eggs into one basket, so to speak. After a second, and third look at the pictures and floor plans, he mentally added up his assets:

Margaret's insurance money and his savings account came to a little more than $265,000. That left what he would receive from the sale of his home. According to an article he had just read in the newspaper, he could receive around $500,000.

Casper then shifted mental gears and considered that if he did move to The Oaks, what were his living options: the million dollar plus casita, the one bedroom apartment without the view, or the two bedroom apartment with the view.

Without a doubt, the million dollar plus casita was out of his price range and frankly, he felt cost more money than anyone should spend for a place to rest his head.

Then he inwardly wrestled over the one bedroom apartment without the view. Financially, the one bedroom apartment would leave him more of a cushion, but after much consideration, he decided that remaining in his three bedroom home in the Fairfax district where he presently lived was the better choice than moving into the confined, one bedroom apartment at The Oaks.

That left the $750,000 two bedroom apartment. He admitted to himself that since his wife had died, his daily life had been very lonely. He considered the view from the two bedroom apartment, the gourmet food served by a professional staff, and the camaraderie he had seen during his tour of The Oaks.

If he did move to The Oaks, he knew that the entrance fee would take most of the money he would receive from the sale of his home, and most of his savings.

But on the other hand, having a trained chef prepare two gourmet meals a day, everyday, along with a trained waitstaff pushed his decision. With a touch of trepidation, Casper pulled out his check book and wrote the largest check he had ever written, $150,000, as a deposit on a freshly redecorated two bedroom apartment at The Oaks.

When he opened the door to ask Mr. Bradford's secretary to let her boss know that he had made his decision, Casper was a bit surprised to find Mr. Bradford standing next to her desk.

Mr. Bradford said, "Ah! Mr. Potts, it turned out that my meeting with the kitchen staff was shorter than I had planned. Have you come to a decision?"

"I have," and Casper handed the check to Mr. Bradford.

Mr. Bradford's face lit up. "Mr. Potts, let us return to my office."

They enter the office and as Casper sat down, Mr. Bradford pulled out a sheet of paper and placed it on his desk. "Mr. Potts, let me be the first to welcome you to our family here at The Oaks. Because we understand that many of our new family members still have to complete the sale their homes, your $150,000 deposit will hold the apartment of your choice for sixty days. But you need to understand that I will require the remaining $600,000 balance within that two month period."

"Mr. Bradford, I understand. I do have one problem with the check. Most of that money is in my savings account, so please hold that check until tomorrow afternoon to allow me time to transfer the funds from my savings into my checking account. "

"I fully understand," Bradford chuckled. "Not many people leave that amount of cash in a non-interest bearing checking account. Now, once you sign this commitment sheet, our business is done." He held his breath while Casper signed, and then exclaimed, "Congratulations, Mr. Potts, you are officially the newest member of The Oaks family."

As he shook hands to seal the deal, Mr. Bradford allowed himself an inward sigh of relief as he realized that the expensive ad he had placed in the *Los Angeles Times* had lifted The Oaks occupancy to three hundred and fifty-eight, a fill rate of exactly 89.5%, a bare fraction over the corporate standard of 89%, but just above the measurement that he knew must be met if he expected to retain his position as manager.

The following morning, Casper, still a little stunned at the rapid pace of change, called Mr. Delgado and informed him that, as of this phone call, he was retiring from the meat business.

Next, he called his daughter and left a message on her answering machine concerning his move to The Oaks.

Then he made a call to his bank to transfer funds from his savings to his checking account.

His fourth call was to The Meat Cutter's Union headquarters to inform them that he was now retired and to please start his pension as soon as possible.

Finally, he reached for his phone book. Pictured on the cover was a real estate broker with a phone number. Inside an hour, that same pictured real estate broker was sitting in Casper's living room.

Moments later, the broker left with a signed listing contract that included the stipulation that the escrow must close in forty-five days. Somewhat excited from his flurry of activity, a satisfied Casper walked to Du-pars for a celebratory early dinner.

After his early dinner, Casper contacted a company to move his worldly possessions to The Oaks as soon as the escrow closed on his house sale.

The following day, the broker called to inform Casper that his house had sold for his asking price of $550,000. After the broker's 6% commission, and a couple of miscellaneous fees, at the close of escrow, he would receive a check for $510,000. He added up his assets and he had enough to cover the rest of the required entrance fee of $750,000 and leave some toward rebuilding his savings account.

Satisfied that his life was now moving in the right direction, Casper was convinced that he would live out his remaining years in complete comfort in his apartment with a view, a well stocked library, and gourmet food served daily in the luxurious dining room by an impeccably trained staff.

But a few weeks later, after Casper moved into The Oaks, and following his morning repast of apple juice, Huevos Rancheros, four strips of crisp bacon, sourdough toast, imported dark cherry jam, and two cups of their excellent coffee, a loud rapid rapping on his front door interrupted his ritualistic, after-breakfast, leisurely perusal of the *Los Angeles Times*.

As a slightly curious Casper shambled to his front door, he had no concept that when Mr. Bradford had discussed the FAQ's concerning The Oaks, he had neglected to bring up one of the most important queries, the one that concerned what a handsome, viral, newbie male of the The Oaks' family should do and say when confronted by the formidable, unelected leader of the unofficial, and unsanctioned, Ladies' Casserole Club!

Chapter Five

Chicken Paprikash With Dumplings

Standing in the hallway outside of Casper's front door was Izabella Sandor, better known to some members of the The Ladies' Casserole Club as "Pain-in-the-ass Izzy" or just plain Izzy to her card-playing friends.

Clutched in Izzy's hands, protected with colorful potholder, was a warm earthenware container filled with authentic Hungarian Chicken Paprikash with Dumplings. She shifted the heated pot to her left hand and knocked a little louder the second time.

Not long after her parents had immigrated from Hungary, Izzy was born in St. Louis. She grew up in a neighborhood of mostly Hungarian immigrants, where she met, dated, and married Timur Sandor.

As a wedding present, Izzy's mother had given her the family Chicken Paprikash with Dumplings recipe. The detailed instructions were tucked in the center of a brightly decorated wooden box and surrounding the recipe were twenty-eight metal boxes, each filled with 100 grams of genuine Hungarian paprikas that ranged from sweet to fiery hot, a combination her mother was sure would cover all her daughter's spice requirements for the first year of her marriage.

While Timur worked to complete his law degree, Izzy was the breadwinner of the family with a full time job as a teller at a local St. Louis bank along with being the chief cook and bottle washer at home.

After Timur graduated in the top five percent of his class, he was recruited by a prestigious west coast law firm, and in spite of Izzy's misgivings at leaving her parents, the two made the move to Los Angeles.

Soon after their transfer to Los Angeles, Izzy emptied the last of the twenty-eight 100 gram metal paprika containers. She made a quick search in the phone book and discovered a small shop in The Farmers Market that carried all ranges of authentic Hungarian paprika. Izzy was relieved she could replenish her beloved spice supply whenever needed.

With her husband now a successful breadwinner, Izzy responded to her biological demands, became pregnant, and gave birth to a girl they named Zoe.

While Izzy stayed home and raised their daughter who also married a lawyer, Timur rose through the ranks and eventually became an equity partner in his law firm.

Year after year, Timur and Izzy moved up the financial, and social ranks of the Los Angeles legal community until they ended up in an opulent home that had been constructed on a view site in the Hollywood Hills overlooking the Los Angeles basin. But regardless of Izzy's wealth and standing, she was a true peasant at heart. Once or twice each week, she would give their live-in housekeeper the night off so she could whip up some authentic Hungarian food for her husband.

Life was good.

But a happy existence can turn to tragedy in an instant. Timur's contemplated retirement was cut short by an unexpected heart attack. Soon after his initial coronary thrombosis, he died—perhaps the result of too much paprika along with too many dumplings from Izzy's famous Chicken Paprikash— bringing an abrupt end to their marital bliss.

Not long after Timur's demise, while sitting on the deck of her massive home, Izzy stared across the LA basin at the high-rise buildings that made up the Civic Center of Los Angeles. Although she loved the view, Izzy decided to sell her home and move in with her daughter and son-in-law.

After a stressful six months of trying to live with her daughter's family in the smog-choked town of Downey, Izzy became one of the charter members of The Oaks' family.

Today, far removed from the ethnic neighborhood of St. Louis, or her mansion in the Hollywood Hills, or her daughter's three bedroom tract house in Downey, Izzy occupied a two bedroom apartment on the first floor of the west wing in The Oaks. She played Bridge and Pedro each week in the card room, art classes in the common room every Thursday afternoon, participated in the water aerobics class in the half-Olympic sized swimming pool, and never missed a movie in the media center as long as the film was made before 1990.

But since Izzy's move to The Oaks, one of her most important clandestine activities was the bribe of a bottle of California chardonnay she gave to the front desk night clerk, Alice, each week to ensure that she was the first of the Ladies' Casserole Club membership to receive detailed information concerning the latest male members of The Oaks' family!

Prior to the day that Izzy planned to dazzle Casper Potts with her now famous Chicken Paprikash with Dumplings, Alice, had presented Izzy with the following dossier as she went off her shift:

- Name—Casper Potts.
- Recently widowed.
- Age—sixty-years old. Birthday is June 26th.
- Full head of silver-gray hair.
- During his tour he indicated that gourmet food is very important.

- All females at The Oaks will consider Casper Potts a catch.
- Handed over $750,000 entrance fee as if money was no object.

Some of the Ladies' Casserole Club members didn't abide with Izzy's 'full head of hair' fetish, but she remembered the simple pleasure she received when she ran her fingers through Timur's hair.

With her inside information, and very likely a day's jump on the other women, Izzy was sure that once Casper Potts inhaled the aromas of her Chicken Paprikash with Dumplings, she would hold the upper hand with The Oaks's latest male arrival.

Although the small shop that carried her favorite Hungarian spices was located in The Farmers Market, it was a distance from Delgado's Meat Market, so until this moment in time, waiting in front of Casper's unopened apartment door, Izzy had never seen Casper Potts.

Casper opened his door and Izzy's heart skipped a beat as she noted that, as promised in the dossier, he did have a full head of hair. He was more than good looking, this man was as handsome as Robert Redford in his prime! Casper, totally unaware of what was about to happen, asked, "May I help you?"

Izzy flashed her most brilliant smile. "Hello! My name is Izabella Sandor, but as you are now part of the family at The Oaks, please call me Izzy."

Casper's initial impression of his unexpected visitor was her hair. It was a bright, straw color and he quickly determined by the wrinkles on her face that her tresses had been bleached of all natural color, something his now deceased wife, Margaret, had never done. Then he noticed the lady standing before him was very short, not much more than five feet tall, much shorter than Margaret's five feet, seven and a half inches. Finally, for a woman to knock on his door unannounced told Casper that this female was more brazen than . . . but at that moment he inhaled the bouquet of spice that radiated up from the pot she held between her hands, and he said, "My goodness, that smells delicious."

Izzy lifted the pot to Casper's nose. "It's just my Chicken Paprikash with Dumplings. I skipped breakfast this morning so I'd have the time to make this for you as my house warming gift." She carefully handed the pot to Casper, making sure he grasp the potholders first, hesitated for a moment as if she were waiting for a trumpet fanfare to fade away, then continued, "To Casper Potts, the newest member of our family at The Oaks."

Casper was both taken aback and intrigued. Somehow this woman knew his name, an item that bothered him a touch, but his concerns were quickly overcome by the fact that she had gone to great effort to make him something with such a powerful, but interesting aroma. In his sixty-years, no one had ever surprised him with food in this manner. Not his mother. Not his wife. No one!

But before Casper could open his door wider, as if to invite this intense female into his apartment,

Izzy pushed her way past him. As she entered the apartment, she glanced around and noted the newspaper sitting on the arm of what was very likely Casper's chair. She snatched the pot back from Casper. "I'll take the casserole into your kitchen."

Casper was more than anxious that a total stranger had entered his apartment without an invitation! In an attempt to regain control over the situation, he stammered, "Please don't go into my kitchen. I have some dirty cups in the sink."

"That's no problem. It's not as if I haven't seen a few unwashed dishes in my day. I also have a bag in my apron pocket with a little lettuce, celery, a tomato, and balsamic vinaigrette. All I have to do is whip up a little salad. That, and the Chicken Paprikash, will make a perfect lunch for the two of us. Casper, sit down. I'll put the teapot on and bring you a cup of tea to enjoy while you read the rest of your morning paper."

Casper, still a bit stunned, slowly accepted the reality that his abode had been successfully invaded. He eased into his recliner and marveled at his good fortune finding such a thoughtful neighbor. But as he opened his paper to the editorial section, there was a sharp knock on his front door. He started to set the paper down when Izzy burst through the kitchen door. "Casper, you sit back, relax and read your newspaper. I'll answer the door."

64

Izzy was ninety-nine percent sure who stood on the other side of Casper's door. She marched across the living room, opened the door, slipped into the hallway, and closed the front door behind her.

Chapter Six

Shrimp and Grits

Izzy was not at all surprised to find her rival, Delilah Madison, standing at Casper's front door with her own casserole in hand.

She said, "Del! I see you have arrived with your tired old Shrimp and Grits. My dear, I hate to bring this up, but according to my nose your shrimp seem to be a little off. Did you purchase those crustaceans last week? Next time that happens, I recommend you soak the little buggers in milk for twenty minutes. I've been told the casein in the milk will bind to the fishy odor. Then when you throw away the liquid, you throw away the smell."

"Izzy, I bought those shrimp just this morning and they are as fresh as the morning dew! Now, are you going to stand there and tell me that you made something different than your overly spicy chicken thing you throw into a pan with those soggy dumplings?"

Izzy hoisted herself up to her maximum height of five feet, three inches, and declared, "It's Chicken

Paprikash with Dumplings, and my dumplings are not soggy. Del, as usual, I beat you to the punch so move along. You might offer your casserole to the maintenance crew in the basement working on the sewage backup. Their nasal passages are used to the funky stench down there so I'm pretty sure they won't notice the reek of rotten shrimp."

Del glared at her casserole opponent and leaned forward so their noses were but a few inches apart. "Izzy, level with me. We're both paying off the night desk clerk with a bottle of chardonnay. What I don't understand is how you always get to the newbie's apartment before I do?"

"Just lucky, I guess."

But Izzy knew exactly why she always beat Del. The night desk clerk would gladly take a bottle of any chardonnay from anyone, but she went absolutely bonkers for a bottle of the Dry Creek, 2014 Russian River Valley Chardonnay. The wine cost Izzy a couple of dollars more, but the advantage she gained was well worth the extra money.

Izzy turned her back on her competitor, and said, "Goodbye, Del. Better luck next time." She reentered Casper's apartment, closing the door in Del's reddened face.

Standing in the hallway, warm casserole dish in hand, Delilah Lee Madison nearly threw the serving dish of Shrimp and Grits against the wall. But then she remembered her anger was aimed at Izzy, not the crew that would have to clean up the mess she had created. She put her head down and stormed away to lick her wounds in her three bedroom casita in the east section of The Oaks complex.

Delilah, Del to her friends, was a widow. In that way she was similar to Izzy, and ninety-seven percent of females living at The Oaks.

Her first and only husband, Jayden Madison, could proudly trace his lineage all the way back to the venerable James Madison, the American statesman and Founding Father of our country who helped write the Federalist Papers, the Constitution, and the Bill of Rights. But James Madison, in a total reversal of his original political position of supporting a powerful central government, later argued that the states should wield more authority than a central federal administration.

Jayden, just like the long deceased donor of his DNA, found it very difficult to make up his mind, not only concerning major political leanings, but also the simple day-to-day decisions of life.

On Jayden's final fateful day of life on this earth, while he was cruising at seventy miles per hour on the Hollywood Freeway, he noticed some red brake lights ahead. His indecisive heritage contributed to his last fatal moment.

He lifted his foot off the gas pedal and as his vehicle slowed, he tried to make a decision. Should he stay in his lane of slowing vehicles?

Or should Jayden switch into the lane on his left?

Or should he dart right and take the off-ramp to avoid the backup altogether?

Jayden's driving dilemma was a microcosm of his life. With his eyes and mind desperately seeking an opening to his left or right, he didn't realize his lane had come to a complete stop and by then it was too late.

The front end of Jayden's Jaguar plowed directly into the rear end of a stalled pick-up truck that had three small exchangeable tanks of LP gas, the size that people use to fire up their backyard grills, firmly secured to the tailgate.

Thus Del's husband's lifetime of indecision came to a spectacular conclusion inside a giant ball of fire. Jayden also became another highway statistic, the sixth fatality of the year along that particular four mile section of the Hollywood Freeway.

At first, Del was devastated by Jayden's sudden death.

As the memory of his funeral faded, her lawyers attempted to explain to her, time and time again, that her husband had been a very poor investor. They informed her that his indecisiveness consistently caused Jayden to buy stock and bonds at their highs and then sell them at their lows.

His catastrophic losses in the stock market were followed by an investment in six can't-miss movies but all six missed and Jaden's total investment in he world of entertainment was gone. His failed speculation in the movie industry, however, did provide Del with one reward, two seats, in the second balcony, but two seats none the less, at the annual Academy Awards gala in Hollywood.

Finally, in excruciating detail, the lawyers described how Jayden, in an ill advised attempt to reverse his disastrous stock market and movie blunders, decided to change his investment strategy. He invested his remaining liquid assets in four limited partnerships that constructed strip malls. Everyone of those turned out to be losers because they were always built in the wrong sections of the city at the wrong time.

No matter how hard her lawyers attempted to explain that her husband had somehow turned a one hundred million dollar inheritance into a single mansion in the Hollywood Hills worth about six million dollars, Del tuned out the truth.

When she allowed herself to think about her deceased husband, all she wanted to recall was that Jayden, her true Southern gentleman, was the man who had rescued her from the backwater of Savannah, Georgia.

Once Del's home was sold, and all the lawyer's fees had been paid, she still had more than enough to live on. In fact, she had enough to live four or five lives.

As the escrow on her Beverly Hills mansion dwindled down to less than thirty days, Del suddenly realized that she would soon be homeless. Rich, yes, but nevertheless on the street without a roof over her head.

One of her lawyers suggested The Oaks as the perfect place for her to live out her sunset years. He told her, "Del, give it a try. I'm not talking about a retirement home where people sit around in wheelchairs. The Oaks is like living on a cruise ship that never leaves the dock. In fact, that's where I plan to live once I retire."

Del, however, didn't feel like she was in her sunset years, so she first checked out a beach house at Malibu. But at a cool twenty-four million dollar asking price, the beach house turned out to be way too expensive, even for her! Then she checked out a brand new high rise condo in downtown Los Angeles, but the building was located next door to a large homeless encampment. It was not the neighborhood for a genteel woman from Savannah, Georgia!

As her escrow close date approached, she decided that The Oaks would be her emergency destination. If she liked it she could stay. If not, despite the fifteen percent she would lose of her more than million dollar entrance fee, she still would have more than enough money to find a suitable place.

The day after she moved into The Oaks, while eating lunch, Del, met a pleasant enough woman with a crazy nickname, Izzy.

And even though Del lived in one of the expensive casitas and Izzy in one of the lowly, first floor two-bedroom apartments, they became close friends. The two remained that way until one day

71

when they were playing bridge Del innocently mentioned an interest in the newest male member of The Oaks family.

"Izzy, did you see that new, handsome gentleman at lunch today? Sitting all by himself? A little bird told me his name is Henry."

Izzy, obviously agitated at Del's interest, threw her cards onto the table and exclaimed, "Del, his name is Harrison, not Henry. I guess my little bird is a little quicker than your little bird. I have the first dibs on Harrison. That is the prime rule of the Ladies' Casserole Club."

Del drawled softly, "Prime rule? The Ladies' Casserole Club? Just what are are you talking about, my dear?"

Izzy said, "Del, at this point, the only rule you need to understand is, as the club President, my casserole gets first crack at each new male member of The Oaks."

Now Del had grown up in the south where women were taught to respect their elders, but at the moment she wasn't sure who was the elder, she or Izzy.

The other bridge players, all members of the Ladies' Casserole Club, were aghast when Del stood and her tone shed all of her southern softness. "Izzy, I was unaware that there was a Ladies' Casserole Club, or that any rules existed, but as far as I am concerned, all's fair in love and war. My dear, if you want to make this a war, so be it. And don't forget, the south will rise again!"

She pushed her chair away from the bridge table and stormed out of the card room. From that day on, the battle lines of the Ladies' Casserole Club were drawn between Chicken Paprikash with Dumplings and Shrimp with Grits.

Chapter Seven

Mister Bradford Sort Of Saves Casper

After Izzy had spent her morning assembling the ingredients and cooking her casserole, and coughing up $32.00 for a bottle of expensive chardonnay, and vanquishing the barbarian, Del Madison, from Casper's gate, she was expecting somewhat more from her contrived luncheon date than what she received.

But the lack of a romantic spark in her lunch partner wasn't due to a failure on her part. She was completely unaware that Casper and Margaret, had spent three years in a slow courting dance, so Izzy's assumption that Casper had arrived at The Oaks in a pent-up state of sexual tension was completely and totally incorrect.

However, Izzy's imprecise forecast of her afternoon activities paled when compared to Casper's stomach problems after he had consumed more than his share of Izzy's highly seasoned casserole.

A little more than an hour earlier, Casper had eaten a gargantuan breakfast and now Izzy's peppery chicken and dumplings were searching for space in his already filled stomach. As gigantic gas bubbles were seeking an escape route, Casper, on the verge of pain, was pondering how he could graciously run to the bathroom for a handful of antacid tablets. Luckily, for both Casper and Izzy, at that very moment, there was a loud rap on Casper's door. The pregnant silence between them was interrupted before it swallowed both of them whole.

As Casper popped out of his chair, a loud belch burst past his lips. "Pardon me for that . . . I have to see who's at the door."

Izzy grabbed the empty dishes covered with the bright red residue of hot Hungarian paprikas and scurried into the kitchen.

After a second thunderous belch, Casper opened the door and stared into the smiling face of Mr. Bradford, the genial manager of The Oaks.

"Mr. Potts, I apologize for not joining you at breakfast this morning. I had a corporate conference call and, as I am sure you know from your vast experience in the business world, one must not miss an important conference call from the head office."

As a journeyman meat cutter, not the harried middle-manager of the billion dollar corporation that owned The Oaks, Casper did not have a clue why Mr. Bradford assumed that a meat cutter would know why anyone should not miss a corporate conference call, but as a polite gentleman, he nodded as if he understood.

"Mr. Potts, may I come in?"

Before Casper could answer, Izzy pushed her way past them into the hallway.

She turned, and gave the two gentlemen a warm smile. "Casper, thank you for the enjoyable lunch. I'm sure we'll do this again. Soon I hope." Then she spun and walked down the hall, empty casserole dish in hand.

Completely befuddled by much of the past hour of his life, Casper blurted, "You're welcome, Izzy."

Both Casper and Mr. Bradford watched the tiny woman turn right at the end of the hallway and disappear round the corner.

Mr. Bradford said, "I see you've already had the pleasure of meeting Mrs. Sandor. Lovely woman." The manager hesitated for a moment. "Although some of The Oaks family consider her to be more than a little forward. May I come in?"

Casper wanted to ask Mr. Bradford what he meant by, 'more than a little forward', but he decided the hallway would not be the most appropriate venue for his question. He gestured through the open door. Mr. Bradford entered, glanced around the living room and said, "Mr. Potts, I love the way you've arranged your furniture. And I love your little Christmas tree."

What Casper didn't know was that Mr. Bradford's complimentary statement about his furniture arrangement contained the exact phrase that he used with each and every new member of The Oaks family during the manager's initial visit to their apartments.

Casper, his roiling stomach his only concern, said, "Please excuse me for a moment." He moved quickly down the hall to his bathroom where he found the antacid tablets and rapidly chewed four of them into soothing powder.

As his stomach started to settle, Casper returned to his living room.Before he had the opportunity to offer Mr. Bradford a seat, the manager took the liberty and sat down on the couch. "Mr. Potts, as I told you earlier, I had planned on meeting with you at breakfast. I trust you enjoyed your breakfast of apple juice, Huevos Rancheros, four strips of crisp bacon, sourdough toast, four dollops of our finest dark cherry preserves imported from France, and two cups of our proprietary Wake-Up blend of coffee?"

Casper's normally stoic eyebrows jumped as Mr. Bradford listed each and every morsel of food and drink he had been served for his breakfast, right down to the number of spoonfuls of dark cherry preserves and the two cups of coffee he had consumed. Casper's pique intensified as he realized that without an invitation, or an appointment, Mr. Bradford had unceremoniously interrupted his tete-ta-tete with Izzy. His sense of annoyance grew as Casper attempted to comprehend why Mr. Bradford would be interested in a detailed list of the food he had consumed at breakfast.

Before Casper could organize his thoughts into a lucid question, Mr. Bradford said, "Mr. Potts, again I welcome you to The Oaks. As you settle in, I want you to know that my office door is always open to each and every family member at The Oaks. If you have any questions, or comments, both positive or negative, I look forward to your observations." Casper started to open his mouth to ask why what he had eaten for breakfast was so important that the manager had memorized it, but Mr. Bradford's eyes were closed and lost in the recital of his welcoming address. "Mr. Potts, that brings me to the reason I felt the need to meet with you today. My presence here is more than a simple welcome to The Oaks. Mr. Potts, as you sat in our dining room enjoying your first breakfast with us, I am sure you noticed that those living here at The Oaks represent a large and diverse community of a few males and many females. Granted, there are a couple of our family who are wheel chair bound, but the vast majority, like yourself, remain in the prime of their lives." Mr. Bradford paused, as if to give Casper a moment to process the importance of what he just stated, then continued. "And those males and females, of varying physical capabilities, partake in the many activities and clubs we offer at The Oaks. For example, we have an interesting stamp club that meets every Tuesday morning. We have our book club that meets each Wednesday just before lunch. A tap dance class meets every other Monday in the gym. Frankly, the activities and clubs are so numerous I don't have enough time to mention them all today. That takes me back to my personal observation that you seem to be in the prime of your life. Do you understand where I am going here, Mr. Potts?"

Casper arched his right eyebrow, as if he did, but he really didn't have a clue as to the thrust of Mr. Bradford's question.

"I see that you do, Mr. Potts, and as the man who sees himself in the mirror each morning as you shave, I am sure that you have noticed that you have been blessed with a handsome countenance." Mr Bradford paused to emphasize the following statement. "In a few words, Mr. Potts, you are a man who would be considered a catch by any woman who lives at The Oaks."

Casper felt a long forgotten tingle move through his groin as he realized that no female, not his mother, nor his wife, had ever informed him he was handsome.

Mr. Bradford continued, "And that brings me to my main point, a statement that I will call a cautionary tale. I am dismayed to report that with all the sanctioned activities, clubs, classes and opportunities for advancement offered here at The Oaks, we have a few unsanctioned groups, such as the secret Texas Hold'em poker game held each Thursday night in Mr. Sullivan's apartment.

Gambling in all forms is a violation of The Oaks's rules and regulations."

Casper was about to ask Mr. Bradford, if the poker game was such a secret, then how did he know games were being held each week? And if the poker game was in total violation of The Oaks' regulations and rules, then why did he allow the poker game to go on? In fact, Casper Potts was on the verge of becoming confrontational with the man sitting on his couch, something he had avoided much of his life.

He had grown up in a household of introverted parents. Married a wonderful, but extremely quiet woman. Worked his whole life as a butcher where the most controversial part of his day was deciding if he should give Mrs. Shultz or Mrs. Gonzales a package of bones for their dogs. He defused all potential confrontations by keeping a tray full of bones in the back of the meat display case so anyone who shopped there would be able to take a treasure home for their dog.

After sixty years of peaceful, non-confrontational existence, Casper was suddenly faced with a problem, but before he could open his mouth to respond, The Oaks manager continued. "Mr. Potts, trust me when I say that the illegal Texas Hold'em game pales when compared to the large band of females who have formed an amoral alliance is known as The Ladies' Casserole Club."

Mr. Bradford hesitated for a moment, as if waiting for acknowledgement from Casper that he agreed there was a licentious purpose to The Ladies' Casserole Club.

When Casper did not immediately respond, Mr. Bradford continued, "Mr. Potts, I'm not really worried about the dissolute actions of a few wanton women. I am concerned with the potential unsanitary food prepared by the Ladies' Casserole Club members. Each year the kitchen at The Oaks is inspected by the Los Angeles County Department of Health and they have the legal authority to shut down our kitchen if we do not meet all health standards. Consider the fact that any future casserole you might consume would be prepared in the kitchen of a Ladies' Casserole Club member which are not inspected by the Los Angeles County Health Department."

Casper mentally acknowledged there was some logic behind Mr. Bradford's rant, but he also knew that the kitchen his wife used to prepared their meals each day during their happy years of marriage had never once been inspected by the Los Angeles County Department of Health and neither of them nor their child had ever become ill from Margaret's home cooking.

Mr. Bradford, ignoring Casper's lack of attentiveness, rambled on, "A few moments ago, when you answered my knock, the lovely Mrs. Sandor left your apartment with an empty casserole dish under her arm. The woman you supped with today is the founding mother, so to speak, of the unsanctioned Ladies' Casserole Club."

An awareness slowly spread across Casper's features as he finally tumbled to the reason behind Mr. Bradford's visit.

Mr. Bradford smiled. "Ah, your expression informs me that you understand my concern. Mr. Potts, as the newest, and very likely the most virile male living in The Oaks today, I fear Mrs. Sandor will be the first of many Ladies' Casserole Club members who will try to capture your heart through your stomach."

Casper hesitated for a moment to be sure Mr. Bradford had completed his mission, but mainly to make a momentous decision that would change the course of the remaining years of his life.

Up to this point, Casper had led an extremely sheltered life. His existence had never once required him to defend himself against another human being. Not at home. Never at school. Not once during his happy marriage. Now he was facing a man who for some unknown reason had delved into various aspects of Casper's personal life, and had told him what he should and shouldn't do, and who he should and shouldn't associate with while living at The Oaks!

He determined that Mr. Bradford was attempting to bully him and that was the moment Casper decided to engage in a verbal battle with Mr. Bradford. In that way, he would maintain his masculine pride against this schoolyard bully!

For the first time in his life, a rush of 'fight or flight' adrenaline coursed through his body. His heart pounded and breathing increased. More blood flowed to his brain. Beads of sweat popped out on his forehead and goose bumps covered his arms.

While Casper's mind raced through untested and untried strategies on how to handle Mr. Bradford, he decided to stall for a moment in an attempt to come up with a successful plan of attack.

Casper offered his right hand to his enemy, "I thank you for your concern, Mr. Bradford."

"You are most welcome." Mr. Bradford jumped up and thrust out his hand to clasp Casper's hand.

With a vision that he was now a knight in shining armor about to vanquish his enemy, Casper metaphorically threw down his gauntlet.

"Sit down, Mr. Bradford! I have a few questions for you."

"Of course. I am at your service." Mr. Bradford turned and returned to the couch.

"Mr. Bradford, considering that I ate breakfast alone, how is it possible that you know the exact menu I was served?"

Mr. Bradford blinked. "You mean the small apple cider, Huevos Rancheros, four strips of crisp bacon, sourdough toast, multiple dollops of our finest dark cherry jam, and two cups of coffee?"

Casper said, "Ah Ha! The first time you said I had four, not multiple dollops, of your finest dark cherry preserves."

Mr Bradford's shoulders stiffened slightly. In his tenure as the manager of The Oaks, this was the first time a family member had ever questioned him in this manner. A moment went by as he paused, considering his response. Then he said, "Mr. Potts, you are correct. I did say four dollops. I felt it was important to note that we do not serve our family members an inexpensive cherry jam plucked off a grocery store shelf. No, at The Oaks we offer the finest dark cherry preserves imported from France during our breakfast service. Now if you'll excuse me, I have a very important meeting with the—"

A second surge of testosterone provided Casper with the strength to actually look the manager in the eye and demand, "I'm waiting for you to answer my question, Mr. Bradford. Why are you keeping track of what I was served for breakfast? Why is it so important that you know every item down to the four dollops of dark cherry preserves imported from France?"

Mr. Bradford's eyes widened and darted around Casper's living room, as if he had just awakened and found himself locked inside the monkey cage at The Griffith Park Zoo. Struggling to control his mounting angst, he said, "Mr. Potts, I apologize, but that information is proprietary, and as such, I'm not at liberty to provide you with a reply."

"I am sorry, but that does not answer my question."

"Mr. Potts, as I stated, I have provided you with all the information I am able to give you."

"Mr. Bradford, answer my question, or . . ." Casper hesitated because he wasn't quite sure what he was going to say next.

"Or what?"

Then, out of the blue, Casper raised his lance, spurred his horse, and charged his enemy!

"I will contact the consumer desk at KTLA TV. I will inform their Emmy winning investigative reporter that, for some unexplained reason, the management at The Oaks is tracking every item of food consumed by the people who live there."

Mr. Bradford's mouth became so dry that he could barely respond. "Are you talking about the investigative reporter that broke the story about the two Michelin star restaurant that served their guests food infested with rat droppings?"

"That's the same investigative reporter! Who knows, The Oaks might be part of a secret governmental experiment. I am positive that the reporter and his remote crew will listen to my story and any skullduggery will be aired on the eleven o'clock news. Mr. Bradford, I am giving you two choices. You can answer the reporters questions in front of a live television camera, or my questions in the privacy of my apartment."

Beads of sweat popped up on Mr. Bradford's brow as a bolt of panic shot through him, from the tips of his toes to the top of his scalp, like a shot of white hot lightning. He started to rise, as if to end the conversation, hovered, and then sat down again. "Mr. Potts, be honest. You wouldn't dare call that TV station."

Although Casper wasn't sure what he had uncovered, he had definitely hit a nerve. "I won't call them as long as you answer my questions. However, if you continue to stall . . .”

Mr. Bradford's previous erect demeanor crumpled like a cheap suit as he said, “Mr. Potts, I will answer your question as long as you'll agree to the following stipulation—you have to swear that you will never divulge to anyone what I am about to tell you. If you do not agree to my stipulation, then this discussion is over. We will both stand up. You will follow me to my office where I will return your entrance fee of $750,000, and your first month's rent of $5,897. Then you will leave The Oaks family for good!”

Casper was beginning to enjoy this game. “Mr. Bradford, I agree to your stipulation.”

Mr. Bradford said, “Mr. Potts, that is not good enough. You must raise your right hand and swear. Then I will tell you what you want to know.”

Casper raised his right hand. “What do you want me say?”

“I swear that I will never divulge to any living being what Mr. Bradford is about to tell me.”

Casper, still holding his right hand in the air, repeated Mr. Bradford's statement. A look of relief rushed over Mr. Bradford's face, as if his very existence hung on Casper's allegiance. Mr. Bradford glanced to his left and right, and then whispered, “It has to do with the daily food costs per resident. The cost of the food it takes to prepare each and every meal served, to each and every family member at The Oaks, is tracked on a daily basis. At the end of each day, I input each member's total daily food costs into a highly complex algorithm that calculates, and then updates the proposed annual rental fee for that member. In other words, if one family member eats twice the amount of food, on a daily basis then the average family member, the heavy eater will pay a higher monthly rental fee with their next rent increase to cover the excessive food consumed."

Casper said, "So you're telling me that we don't all pay the same monthly rental fee?"

"Mr. Potts, you are correct. Now, I have many things on my—"

"Not so fast." Casper's mind was creating a scenario based on his casserole lunch with Izzy and new found knowledge provided by Mr. Bradford. "Using your example of a higher annual rent due to consuming more food than the average family member, would it be possible for someone, such as myself, to reduce their annual rental fee by consuming less food?"

Mr. Bradford tugged at his collar. "In theory that would be correct, but . . . ah . . . as I said, I have an—"

"In theory? Answer this. Does anyone at The Oaks pay a lower monthly rental fee based on food consumption?"

Mr. Bradford stood up and slowly edged his way toward Casper's door. "At the present time, there is no one paying a reduced monthly rental due to lower food costs."

"Mr. Bradford, I am a man with a limited income. Today, I can afford to pay my monthly rental, but if you increase it annually, it's possible that in a few years I could be priced out of my two-bedroom apartment. If I consumed less food would you reduce my monthly rental?"

"Mr. Potts, you could downgrade your living accommodations to a one-bedroom apartment."

"Mr. Bradford, I do not consider that an alternative, and you are avoiding my question."

"But Mr. Potts, we all require nourishing food to sustain ourselves. I don't see how . . . "

As Mr. Bradford rambled on, Casper considered that prior to this conversation, he realized he had never deviating from the straight and narrow. But then he recalled those days when the City Inspector would stop by the meat market, and Mr. Delgado would tell Casper to wrap up twenty pounds of boneless rib-eye steaks for the inspector, no charge. Casper knew that what he was doing was wrong, but he did it anyway. Since he had been a child, Casper Potts thought he had aways been true to himself. But now he realized that there had been moments when he had been complicit in illicit activities. As far as he could see, a potential agreement with Mr. Bradford would be legal, if not entirely ethical, so he interrupted Mr. Bradford mid-sentence. "Mr. Bradford, from my view, all I have to do is embrace The Ladies' Casserole Club offer of a delicious, free casserole each day. That way I would only eat breakfast in the dining room.

I'm just a retired meat cutter, but I guess that the food for my dinners costs around $60.00. So I would estimate a monthly rental decrease of perhaps, $1800?"

"Mr. Potts, you are on the right track, but the wrong railroad. We are talking food costs, not the retail cost of a dinner. Depending on the entrees offered, the food costs for one dinner run around twenty-five to thirty-five percent of the total. So if we were to use your $60 dinner example, the food costs for that meal would be between $15 to $21 per meal."

Casper pondered the numbers offered by Mr. Bradford and felt a touch out of his comfort zone as he had no restaurant experience to refute them. "Mr. Bradford, if you'll agree to $25 per day then it's a short step to a monthly reduction of $750.00."

"Mr. Potts, I'm sorry, but my risk is too high." Taking a calculated gamble, he stood and turned toward the door. "Good bye, Mr. Potts."

Casper, having missed his enemy on his first charge, lowered his face mask, lifted his lance, and spurred his horse.

"Mr. Bradford, if you walk out of my apartment, I will opt out of our previously agreed-upon confidentiality stipulation and contact that investigative reporter I mentioned."

The manager stopped in his tracks and turned. Casper spotted that the cords in his neck had tightened. "You wouldn't dare!"

Direct hit! The knight in the black armor fell off his horse and crashed to the earth.

Casper responded, "I could and I would. Mr. Bradford, please understand that there's nothing personal in this. Once you reduce my monthly rental fee by $750, I will have enough discretionary income to remain at The Oaks until I die."

Mr. Bradford, feeling like he was both winning and losing, hyperventilate for a moment, and then, with a loud exhale of air, exclaimed, "Okay! If you only consume breakfast at The Oaks, at the next annual adjustment, I will reduce your monthly rental fee by $750 per month. But, Mr. Potts, you will have to put something of equal value on the line."

What is this? The black knight rises from the ground, turns and lifts his lance.

Now it was Casper's turn to exhibit trepidation as the wrinkles over his nose tensed up. "Forgive me, but I do not understand what you mean, that I have to put something of equal value on the line."

"Mr. Potts, if you don't risk anything in our little game, then it's not an equal quid pro quo."

"Mr. Bradford, that sounds a lot like gambling to me and you just told me that gambling at The Oaks is against the rules."

"Technically, you are correct, but Mr. Potts, you are asking me to reduce your monthly rent by $750. I am carrying all the risk. If you win, your rent is reduced. If you lose, your rent remains the same as it was when we began this discussion. That is patently unfair. You must risk something of equal value."

The creases above Potts' nose relaxed. "I understand now. What do you suggest?"

Mr. Bradford glanced around Casper's living room. His gaze settled on the beautiful wet bar to the right of the granite kitchen counter. "I see you have a bottle of Glenlivet Archive, a 21-year-old single malt Scotch. A single bottle of that excellent whiskey must have set you back around two hundred dollars. If you lose, you will owe me four cases of Glenlivet Archive 21. I believe that will level the risk."

Casper fought to retain his stoic expression as he quickly multiplied two hundred, times twelve, times four, and was shocked when $9600 popped up on his mental calculator screen. Then Casper did the next calculation: seven hundred and fifty, times twelve, and noted his win would save $9000, six hundred dollars less than Mr. Bradford's win. All in all, not worth arguing about because he knew in his heart that he was going to win. "Mr. Bradford, does our bet continue each year this little game is played?"

"Yes, Mr. Potts, that would be correct."

The black knight stands his ground for a moment, and then tumbles to the ground, mortally wounded.

Enjoying theI accept the challenge. Now to make sure we both understand the rules of the game, if I avoid consuming dinner at The Oaks for

12 months my rent will be reduced by $750. If I do not, you win 4 cases of the world's finest single malt Scotch. Do we agree?"

sudden rush of endorphins that were released by the thrill of victory, he exclaimed, "Mr. Bradford, as I see that you are a man who also enjoys the world's greatest single malt, and as a fellow gentleman, I will risk four cases of Glenlivet Archive 21. Now, just to make sure we both understand the rules of the game, each month that I avoid consuming lunch and dinner at The Oaks, my rent will be reduced by $750.00. If I do that for twelve months I win. If I do not, you win. Do we agree?"

Mr. Bradford paused. As bad as things were at the moment, he was still ahead of the game due to the fact that Casper Potts had shorted himself about half the true food cost savings of the average dinner along with the cost of the wait staff. "I agree. And thank you, Mr. Potts, this has been a very interesting meeting. Now I must take my leave. Oh, and again, I bid you welcome to the family at The Oaks."

As soon as the door closed, Casper sat down and took some deep breaths. Once his trembling fingers slowed down, he picked up his phone and keyed in the front desk.

"Hello, Mr. Potts. How may I help you?"

"I am looking for Izzy's phone number."

"I'm sorry sir, but by The Oaks policy, I am not allowed to give out family member's phone numbers. I would be happy to contact Mrs. Sandor's room and tell her that you would like to talk with her."

"Thank you." Casper set the phone down and noted that his stomach had finally settled down. A moment later his phone rang and Izzy exclaimed, "Casper, I am so happy you called. I was wondering if—"

"Izzy, when you were here, before we started our lunch, there was a knock at my door. Who came by to see me?"

"The person at your door was Delilah Madison. She also wanted to welcome you to The Oaks."

"Did she have a casserole in hand?"

The phone silence informed Casper that Delilah Madison had been turned away by Izzy while bearing a casserole destined for him.

Casper said, "Do you happen to have Delilah's telephone number?"

"Why?" growled Izzy.

"I want to call and thank her for stopping by."

Izzy hesitated, but begrudgingly gave Casper Delilah's phone number. Then Izzy turned on her honeyed voice, a volume of syrup large enough to sweeten a foot-high stack of pancakes. "Casper, I know what you are going to do, and playing the field is fine with me, but don't get dazzled by Del's looks. Underneath all her glamour lies a very troubled woman."

"I appreciate your concern, Izzy, but I'd rather make my own assessment of Delilah Madison."

"Suit yourself, but don't say I didn't warn you. Casper, one of these days, I'm positive you'll want a second taste of my Chicken Paprikash with Dumplings. When that day comes, just pick up your phone and give me a call. I'll be by your side quicker than you can say Hungarian spice."

Casper said, "Thank you. I will keep your generosity in mind, but the next time, if there is a next time, I would ask that you cut down on the hot Hungarian spices."

After a pause, Izzy said, "Casper, no one, not my late husband, or any other person that has eaten my Chicken Paprikash ever complained that the spices were too hot."

"Izzy, trust me, I tried to come up with a diplomatic way to tell you, but to me, but the spices were too hot."

"Okay, the next time I'll cut back the hot paprika."

"Thank you, Izzy. Goodbye."

As soon as Izzy hung up, Casper dialed Delilah's number.

A soft female voice said, "Hello?"

"Hello. This is Casper Potts. Izzy just informed me that she turned you away from my door. I hope you know that I didn't realize you had dropped by."

Del said, "Mr. Potts, I appreciate your call. Would it be possible for me to knock on your door in the near future? I could bring an outstanding southern dish called Shrimp and Grits?"

"Delilah, please drop the Mister Potts. I'm Casper to my friends."

"Casper, now that we're friends, call me Del."

"Del, what is your definition of 'the near future'?"

"Let me think. Not tomorrow because I have an important appointment."

Casper immediately warmed to the fact that Del was not throwing herself at him.

Del said, "Hold on, I'm still checking my calendar . . . ah ha, next Tuesday is clear."

Casper said, "Excellent. Does two in the afternoon work for you?"

"Sorry, two's a little early. How about two-thirty."

"Til then, goodbye, Del."

After his victorious verbal joust with Mr. Bradford, and a brief phone call to Del Madison, Casper Potts had set the wheels in motion for what was to become his great adventure with The Oaks Ladies' Casserole Club.

Worn out from the day's events, Casper sat down in his favorite chair by the picture window, picked up his edition of the *Los Angeles Times* and scanned the front page, but he found it difficult to concentrate on old news after such an exciting and victorious afternoon.

Chapter Eight

Shrimp and Grits Redux

At a time when some of the family members at The Oaks were slowly losing their mental acuity, Casper Potts was rapidly evolving from his previous role of dutiful son, dependable meat cutter, and faithful family man, into a lifestyle where he was beginning to embrace the greater the risk, the greater the reward.

It was as if Casper had become a Clint Eastwood-type macho-man who had drawn a line in the sand and then dared the manager of The Oaks, Mr. Bradford, to step across.

However, Casper's pursuit of a reduction in his future rental fees at The Oaks was not really due to a lack of discretionary funds. In fact, with the pension from the meat cutters union, Casper would receive enough income to pay the monthly rental fee, and to keep his wet bar stocked with bottles of decent wine and Glenlivet Archive 21. But the opportunity to join into a risky game, reduce his rent, and to win that game by partaking in daily casserole lunches with a flock of friendly females was too good to pass up.

So on top of living his 'golden years' at The Oaks, a beautiful abode with outstanding amenities and activities, Casper had discovered in himself a previously hidden personality trait, a genuine competitive streak that was the driving force pushing him to make the bet with Mr. Bradford.

A loud belch flowed past his lips. Izzy's casserole had been delicious, but after his large breakfast, the spicy dish, including a salad, was sitting heavily on his stomach. In fact, the total amount of food he had consumed between breakfast and lunch that day was more than he normally ingested in three meals. Casper concluded that he had to shift his normal noontime meal to a later hour—to allow him to extend his future casserole lunches all the way to breakfast the next morning.

The following day, after Casper had established his afternoon tête-à-tête with Del, he heard a soft knock on his front door at precisely two-twenty-nine.

He opened the door and stared into the lovely blue eyes of Delilah Madison. Her honey-blonde hair framed a striking countenance. She flashed a coquettish smile, "Casper, first you need to reach into my right apron pocket, pull out an extra set of pot holders, and don't get fresh."

His cheeks took on a rosy glow as he started to do as she instructed. Before he shifted his gaze down to her apron pocket however, he had to first force his eyes off the azure of her eyes.

Delilah's enticing voice continued. "Now place your strong hands under the casserole dish and take it from me."

Again, Casper followed her directions. As his eyes worked their way from her apron pocket to above the casserole dish, he couldn't help notice that the woman standing before him had been blessed with a most enticing full female form.

Del, her hands now free, slipped a bottle of white wine from her other apron pocket, and said, "Casper, place the casserole on your table. I'll open this bottle of chardonnay from Freeman Winery. I just love the nose of this Russian River Valley wine, a subtle blend of delicate stone fruit and a lemon-cream. Please, sit down. I'll pour you a glass so you can relax while I make us a little salad."

She waltzed past Casper leaving him a little stunned by her beauty, not to mention her command of the situation.

Casper turned his head just in time to admire the rear view of Delilah Madison as she disappeared into the kitchen. He said, "Just a moment, I have some lettuce in the refrigerator and —"

A soft voice with just a touch of southern drawl layered beneath her newly acquired California cadence called from the kitchen. "Casper, all the refrigerators in The Oaks are identical so I know exactly where to look lettuce, green onions, radishes

98

and . . . oh, I see you have ripe tomatoes on the counter top."

As Casper walked toward his dining table, he was pleased she found the tomato he had just purchased that morning. "Del, you can add that tomato the salad fixings you'll find—"

"That's okay. A couple of slices of this tomato will be the perfect addition my Shrimp and Grits."

Casper set the warm casserole dish on a trivet, lifted the cover and inhaled. The combination of fresh shrimp, cheddar cheese, butter, and bacon, nearly overwhelmed his olfactory system. "Del, your casserole smells very good."

"The tomato is sliced. All you have to do is set the table and then sit down. You are about to enjoy a sumptuous southern classic."

"Okay, but hurry up. I'm not sure how long I can prevent myself from digging into this dish and eating with the serving spoon."

Del pulled out a plastic container that had protected two fresh eggs from her left apron pocket and said, "Sorry, Casper, but you'll have to hold your horses another four minutes while I fry up a couple of eggs. While the pan heats up, I'll pour you some wine."

She joined him at the dining table. "I have discovered that not all white wines have enough backbone to stand up to my Shrimp and Grits. Are you familiar with the outstanding Russian River Valley chardonnays?"

Intrigued, Casper took two wine glasses from his china cabinet. "I don't believe I've ever tried a chardonnay from the Russian River Valley."

Del poured two glasses.

They clinked the glasses as Casper said, "To a very interesting lunch . . . and to the future."

Del gave Casper a long, seductive stare that nearly burned her initials onto his chest.

For the first time in a long time, Casper's heart pounded so hard he had trouble catching his breath. "Del, I don't see why you feel the need to fry up some eggs. Can't we just—"

"Relax. Sit down and enjoy your wine. When I'm finished frying the eggs, I will place one on top of each serving of the Shrimp and Grits. The sunny-side-up-egg, with its runny yoke brings the dish together and gives the grits a creamy, richer taste." Del spun around and returned to the kitchen.

While Casper sipped his wine, he heard a knock. He set down his wine, jumped up, and opened the door. There were two women, casseroles in hand, and while they circled each other they uttering growls and guttural noises as if they were two wolves waiting for an opening to strike.

Casper said, "Ladies, please, show a little propriety. What's going on here?"

The short, rounder female with the flame red hair said, "Mr. Potts. My name is Maeve Mahoney and I've made you my Irish Shepherd's Pie. I was here first and this vixen wants to push ahead of me and—"

Casper raised his hand toward the Irish woman and said, "Stop." He glanced at the other woman. "And your name is?"

"Gertrude Schwarz."

Casper noticed the casserole dish in her hand. "And you have brought a casserole?"

"Ya. It's my famous German Meatball and Spaetzle casserole."

Back in Casper's apartment, carrying a plate of sliced tomatoes in her right hand, and hot frying pan in left hand, Del walked out of the kitchen. "Casper, everything is ready."

Casper opened the door and all three ladies' gaped and gasped at each other.

Casper said, "I'm sorry, ladies', but Del Madison is already here with her Shrimp and Grits casserole."

Maeve tossed her head and exclaimed, "Shite!"

Gertrude stamped her foot and said, "Verdammt!"

Without another word, the two turned and stormed down the hall in opposite directions, Maeve to the left, and Gertrude to the right.

Del smiled. "Good! Now we can eat." She hesitated. "And after I put away all the clean dishes, who knows?"

But Casper, upset by the vision of casserole-armed, fighting females at his doorstep, had stripped from his thoughts any later happenings. He said, "Del, I cannot abide this sort of unseemly behavior to occur outside my door again. I'm truly sorry, but after we finish eating, I need to make a trip to the local hardware store. Assuming I find the items I require, could you possibly arrange for me to visit the next Ladies' Casserole Club meeting?"

A deflated Del set the tomatoes down, grabbed her glass of chardonnay, slumped into her chair and downed a rather large gulp of wine. Picking up the warm frying pan, she said, "Sorry, you'll have to talk to Izzy about that. She and I had a little falling out and I do not attend the meetings anymore." She sighed, "Well, we might as well eat before everything gets cold."

Casper lifted his fork. "Bon Appetite."

He truly enjoyed the Shrimp and Grits, but he was so distracted by the image of the bickering females he didn't notice that Del was picking at her food. They ate lunch in silence, both lost in their thoughts.

After Del had left, Casper, determined to never see a pair of bickering women outside his door again, found his tape measure and measured the width of his front door.

With the proper measurement noted down on a pad of paper, he drove to the nearest Home Depot and purchased the items he was looking for.

When he returned to his apartment, he laid a newly purchased 20"x30" white board onto his dining room table and penciled in a series of straight lines, both horizontal and vertical. Then he took a new roll of eighth-inch-wide black tape and carefully covered the penciled lines. At the base of the white board he attached a two-inch metal shelf. Finished, Casper set his creation against a wall, placed a black erasable marking pen and an eraser on the metal shelf, and voila, he had created a white board calendar with blank spaces for dates and the name of a LCC member.

Proud of his handiwork, Casper dialed the phone number for The Oaks maintenance crew. A gruff voice answered, "Yah?"

"Good afternoon. My name is Casper Potts. I just moved into—"

"I know. Just finished painting your joint. You got a problem?"

"Actually, no. I noticed that many of the apartments adorn their front doors with decorations such as plastic flowers, straw wreaths or—"

"So what do you want from me?"

For all the money Casper was paying each month, he had expected better manners from the staff. He decided to use a different tactic. "To whom am I speaking?"

"Huh?"

"Sir, my name is Mr. Potts, and you are . . .?

"Oh, I've gotcha now. Mr. June."

Casper, still not positive they were working toward a common goal, said, "Mr. June. Like the month?"

"Right. April, May, then me, June. Potts, what is it you need from maintenance?"

"Mr. June, I am looking for some assistance to attach a sort of decoration onto my door."

"Hey, why didn't you say so in the first place. Let me check my schedule . . . hum . . . okay. I'll be knocking on your front door tomorrow morning around ten."

"Thank you, Mr. June. I look forward to working with you."

Immediately after his call to Mr. June, Casper called Izzy.

Alone in her apartment with her many duties, both real and imagined, Izzy wasn't surprised when she heard Casper's voice as she placed the phone to her ear. "Casper? I didn't think you'd be back to me so soon. Are you ready for another shot at my Chicken Paprikash with Dumplings?"

"Sorry, Izzy, not yet. I nee your help to straighten out what has evolved into a full-blown scheduling crisis." Casper went on to explain what had occurred outside his apartment that afternoon.

Izzy said, "Tell me. Did you and Del have enough time after lunch to . . . ?"

Casper said, "Izzy, I am a gentleman, and as such, I will pretend you never asked me that question."

Izzy chuckled, "So now I'm led to believe that I'm working with a gentleman. Okay, so Maeve and Gertrude stirred the pot when they both showed up outside your apartment with casseroles in hand. Sorry about the brouhaha, but I can't say I'm sorry ʰat Del's plans were interrupted. Casper, there is ᵗhing a gentleman can tell me. Did Del use ᵔrimp for her casserole this time around?"

"Izzy. Be nice."

"Being nice goes against my nature. Okay, Casper, what do you want from me?"

"I would like you to call a meeting of the Ladies' Casserole Club. I believe I've come up with a solution to avoid another situation like the one that occurred outside my front door this afternoon."

"Casper, what happened is no biggie. We've had these little dust-ups before at The Oaks over the latest hottie."

At that moment, it was as if Casper was straddling the ridge line of a steeply peaked roof—with one foot on success, and the other foot on failure. If Izzy wouldn't allow him to talk to the Casserole Club membership to achieve their needed buy-in, he would have to surrender the game to Mr. Bradford and lose the 'case' of Glenlivet Archive 21. He decided to use the Clint Eastwood approach. "Izzy, this scheduling problem must be fixed or I'm going to move out. If the ladies want to retain their 'latest hottie,' then I insist that I be allowed to talk to the Ladies' Casserole Club membership."

"Calm down, Casper. If your proposal, whatever it is, will keep my club members happy, I'm all for it."

"Thank you. Now, I have one more request. I would like you to invite Del Madison to your next meeting. I don't know what happened between the two of you, but life is too short to spend our dwindling hours making enemies. Remember, we're supposed to be one big family here at The Oaks."

105

Izzy paused. "Don't tell me you're falling for Bradford's bull about our big happy family?"

"I'm just trying to—"

Izzy said, "Relax. I'll consider inviting Del to the next meeting, but you'll owe me big time." Izzy paused, and then said, "Casper, I am beginning to believe that you're not just another old dude looking for an afternoon quickie!"

Chapter Nine

Casper's Scheduling Board 1.0

The following morning, after a stellar breakfast of unfiltered apple cider, a ham, cheese, and green chili omelet, two strips of crisp bacon, two pieces of dark pumpernickel toast, five pats of Danish butter, his favorite imported dark cherry preserves, and two steaming cups of coffee brewed from The Oaks proprietary blend, Casper met Mr. June at his front door. Casper held a small black bag in his right hand. In his left hand, Mr June held a battered metal box that looked to Casper as if it had lasted through two or three Mr. Junes.

"What's in the bag, Mr. Potts?" asked Mr. June.

"My household tools." Casper responded proudly as he reached in, pulled out his prized Phillips screwdriver, handed the tool to Mr. June, and extracted four Phillips screws from his pocket and handed them to his newfound workmate. "I'm pretty sure these screws are the right size to mount the whiteboard I purchased at Home Depot."

Mr. June gave the four screws close scrutiny and shook his head. "Sorry, Potts, but these babies are too long. They'll go all the way through your door and come out the other side. Don't worry, I've got some in my tool box that'll do the job." Mr. June set his metal box down and opened the top. "And you don't want to waste your energy playing around with your Phillips screwdriver. I've got a battery powered drill that'll pop those babies into your door in seconds."

Mr. June was correct. The whole job, a task that Casper had estimated would take him more than an hour, took Mr. June no more than five minutes.

"Mr. June, how much do I owe you for the four screws?"

"No charge. All I ask is you remember the maintenance crew at Christmas time. We've got four guys who work hard more than forty hours a week, every week. Trust me, with all these apartments there's always something going wrong in this old dump."

Casper cringed a touch when Mr. June described The Oaks as an old dump. He made a mental note to find out when his apartment had been built.

"Thank you again, Mr. June. And I won't forget the maintenance crew this Christmas."

Mr. June stood back and looked at his handy work. "Mr. Potts, this ain't no kind of decoration. Just what the hell is this thing suppose to be? . . . Oh my God, you're the new dude I've heard about that's got all the women after him." He turned and counted the spaces on the white board. "Mr. Potts,

108

and I'm sure my fellow maintenance dudes would agree, good luck to you. And just between us, how do you keep your . . . ah . . . energy up."

Casper, not a hundred percent sure why the man standing next to him wished him good luck, said, "Thank you. Mr. June."

Chapter Ten

Rules at the Oaks

A few days after Casper installed his scheduling board, while Casper lingered over his last cup of coffee brewed from freshly ground beans that came from The Oaks's proprietary morning blend, he reviewed a printout of the activities offered at The Oaks that day. His gaze landed on:

Senior Strength Class

1:30 p.m.

Forty-five minutes in duration.

The first floor multi-purpose room.

Gym clothing preferred but not required.

Casper sat back and considered the fact that since he had retired from the meat market and moved to The Oaks, his physical activity had been limited to avoiding the elevator and sprinting up the two flights of stairs to his apartment.

He pocketed the activity schedule, rose from his chair, smiled and nodded to the two other men sitting at their nearby tables, left the dining area and took the stairs to his apartment. Once there, Casper called the number listed for Ms. Zeiss, the leader for the Senior Strength Class.

"Hello?"

Casper said, "Am I speaking to Ms. Zeiss?"

"You are."

"Ms. Zeiss, I recently joined the family here at The Oaks. Would it be possible for me to join your Senior Strength Class this afternoon?"

"Of course you can join. We meet three times a week at one-thirty in the multi-purpose room. And you are?"

"Potts. Casper Potts."

Casper thought he heard a sharp intake of Ms. Zeiss's breath on the other end of the call. "You're the man who just moved in a couple of days ago?"

Curious how she knew, he responded, "I did move in a couple of days ago."

"Mr. Potts, you are more than welcome. Have you ever participated in a senior strength class before?

"I have not."

"Mr. Potts, I recommend you wear sweatpants, a t-shirt and athletic shoes."

"Ms. Zeiss, please call me Casper."

"I can do that. And when we meet at the class you will see that everyone addresses me as Thelma."

"Thank you, Thelma. I look forward to meeting you at one-thirty."

Casper hung up the phone and smiled, thinking it could be beneficial for him to work up a little sweat three times a week.

As a child, teen, or as an adult, Casper had never been involved in sports. He and his wife had never played golf, bowled, or jogged, so his total sporting wardrobe consisted of a single pair of off-gray sweatpants and a pair of Dr. Scholl's black and silver walking shoes that he had purchased a few years ago at a sixty percent discount in the mall's sporting goods store.

Casper changed from his morning attire to his sweatpants, a bright yellow t-shirt, and his Dr. Scholl's walking shoes. After a quick glance in the full length mirror mounted on the wall in his bedroom, he decided he looked rather spiffy.

At 1:15, Casper sprinted down the stairs to the first floor and was moving quickly through the long hall to the multi-purpose room when a man propped up with a cane cried, "Young man, it's against The Oak's rules to run in the hall."

Casper stopped. "I'm sorry. I didn't know that rule. My name is Casper Potts and I just moved in a few days ago."

"I don't care who you are or how long you've lived here. It's still against the rules to run in the halls. If you're not careful you'll knock down the Easter decorations."

Casper said, "As I said, my name is Casper Potts. And your name is?"

"Stately, James Stately. Tell me, Mr. Potts, did you find the breakfast cereal they served us this morning a little stale?"

"I'm sorry, Mr. Stately, but I had the French Toast."

"Mr. Potts, you should avoid French Toast and eat a cup and a half of bran everyday. Good roughage you know. And that movie they showed last night. Nothing but dancing and singing."

Casper thought back to last night's offered movie. "Mr. Stately, the movie was _Singing In The Rain_. It's a classic musical with Gene Kel—"

"Humph! I went there expecting to see a good old western shoot-em-up. And another thing, the issue of Time Magazine in the library is more than a week old." Mr. Stately grabbed Casper's arm and continued his rant. "Potts, have you noticed that the shuttle bus was four, no, five minutes late yesterday?"

Casper glanced at his watch and was relieved to see it showed 1:27. He peeled Mr. Stately's fingers off his arm and said, "Mr. Stately, excuse me but I have to leave because I don't want to be late for my first Senior Strength Class."

While Casper continued toward the door of the multi-purpose room, Mr. Stately's strident voice followed him. "And another thing, Potts, I think the bridge game is fixed. The same people win each and . . ."

As Casper entered the multi-purpose room, Stately's voice faded away. While Casper made a

113

mental note to avoid Mr. Stately in the future, he scanned the room and saw forty to fifty people sitting in a large circle of chairs. He was startled to note there were only two other men in the circle. A touch surprised at the throng of womanliness, Casper noticed a gray-haired female sitting at the head of the class. She waved to him, pointed to her right, and said, "You must be Casper. There's a box against that far wall. Grab a stretch band and a couple of weights." Her eyes rapidly took note of him from his Dr. Scholl's walking shoes to the silver hair that topped his head. "I'd guess you should start with the four pound weights. If the fours are too easy, you can jump to the fives. Once you pick out your stretch band and weights, find an empty chair and sit down." Thelma Zeiss, a lifelong stickler for punctuality, checked her watch. "We'll start our first exercise routine in less than two minutes."

A quick glance around the room informed Casper that there were very few vacant chairs. One was next to that Irish woman with the red hair who had stood outside his doorway fighting with another woman and there was no way Casper was going to sit next to her.

The other empty chair was next to one of the males in the room and Casper scrambled to what looked like a tiny island of sanctuary.

After he sat down, he took a moment to look at his neighbor sitting next to him. The man's skin was shriveled like a dried prune. He was obviously long past his prime and had white tufts of hair, like small cotton balls dotting his pate. When Casper took a closer look, he noticed that a sizable paunch drooped over the man's blue sweatpants. The man stuck out a hand and said, "Hi, my name is Clint Sullivan. I'm over ninety. Ninety-three to be exact. Just move in?"

Casper said, "Yes. My name is Casper Potts."

"I remember you. You sit at the table next to me every morning. For a slim dude you pack away a lot of grub at breakfast." Clint glanced at the clock, then at Thelma, and said, "We've still got a few seconds. See that other dude who just came into the room?"

Casper looked, and said, "Yes."

"His name is James Stately. He's originally from Boston, or one of those east coast towns, and whatever you do, don't ever call him Jim, or ask him how's he feeling, or how his day going, or if he had a good sleep last night."

Casper didn't immediately respond. During his six-decades he had never lived in a community like The Oaks, a large facility with hundreds of people packed into close quarters. Therefore, he had never developed the social skills required to successfully function in the unique environment of The Oaks.

"Clint, I ran into Mr. Stately in the hall before I came in today. He did seem to be a touch cantankerous."

Clint stared at Casper for a few seconds, as if he was attempting to determine if Casper was pulling his leg. "Cantankerous? That dude is a genuine, dyed-in-the-wool, pain-in-the-ass. No matter what you say to him, he'll hurl back a negative comment. Like one day, as I passed him eating alone at a table in the dining room, I asked him if the grub was good today. He spent the next five minutes telling me, and everyone else within shouting distance, just how crappy the food was at The Oaks. Or another day, when I was about to jump into the outdoor pool, I saw him standing at the shallow end with water up to his waist and he was wearing a big hat, like he needed to keep the sun off his bald head. I said, 'Jim, are you enjoying the water?' He answered with, 'Don't call me Jim!. My name is James. And then, before I could say anything, he continued, 'I can remember when I could get a nice tan swimming in a pool like this, but now all I get are skin cancers.' That dude's a bad apple."

"Thank you, Clint, I'll keep my eye out for him."

"Casper, let me guess. Are you a recent widower?"

Casper was a little taken aback at the abruptness of the question. He had just started to get used to living without the love of his life at his side. "Ah . . .yes. How about you?"

Clint chuckled. "Not quite. You see, during my younger days, I had my own insurance agency and earned a damn good living. Let's just say I was financially secure, but my personal relationships over the years might be considered on the rocky side. I've been married three times, widowed twice, divorced once. For some weird reason, after all these years and multiple wives, I'm ninety-three, still breathing, sitting next to you and lifting weights at The Oaks Senior Strength Class."

Again Clint checked out Thelma to be sure she wasn't ready to start the class. "Casper, my first marriage happened during those passion-filled years of youth. I guess you could say I married Marylou for love and lust, although not particularly in that order. There was one problem with our marriage. My wife, Marylou, who I loved with all my heart, believed that the consumption of alcohol, in any form, was the harbinger of doom. While she abstained, her unbridled love for me didn't slow me down from drinking beer, wine, and downing my double shot of Jack Daniels each evening before dinner."

Thelma's loud voice suddenly shut down Clint's accounting of his past. "Ladies and gentlemen, we have a new member in our Senior Strength Class today. His name is Casper Potts. Stand up, Casper."

As he stood, Casper noticed the red-haired Irish lady to his far right began to hyperventilate. That seemed strange to him that she would be breathing heavily because the first exercise routine had not even started.

Thelma said, "All right. Let's get going. Ladies and gentlemen, grab your weights, stand up, let your arms hang by your side, turn your hands so your palms face forward, and lift up. Ready? One, two, three . . ."

While Casper dutifully followed Thelma's instructions, he noticed that Del was standing in front of her chair to the far left side of the group.

When Thelma reached what turned out to be her magic number of sixteen, she stopped counting. Then she said, "Keep your palms facing forward and lift your arms behind you. One, two, three . . . "

Casper watched Del go through her paces and when he heard Thelma reach twelve, he noticed the muscles in his upper arms were beginning to tire. He came to the obvious conclusion that, since he had moved into The Oaks, whatever muscle tone in his arms he once had from meat cutting had vanished.

While Thelma took the class through its paces, Clint jabbed Casper in his side, interrupting Casper's concentration on the lovely Del, and continued the story of his first marriage. "There she was, never touched a drop, and me drinking like a fish, when my Marylou died at age forty-three from what the Doc called a brain aneurysm. You know, I've spent the rest of my life wondering if a single glass of wine each evening at dinner might have helped her live longer."

Thelma cried, "Mr. Sullivan, concentrate on the exercise. You're falling behind the group."

The moment Thelma shifted her gaze in the direction of someone else, Clint turned his attention back to Casper, and said, "About a year and a half after Marylou's death, I courted, and soon married my second wife, Vera. At this stage of our lives, the passion of youth had sort of petered out. That's another way of saying that sex didn't happen very often, if at all, but Vera and I got along pretty well during the first few weeks of our marriage. Over time, however, our different lifestyles took us further and further apart. Every weekday, Monday through Friday, while I was busting my butt at my insurance agency, Vera was filling her days with five different quilts in five different quilting groups.

"So there I was, tired after a full day of jawing on the phone and the only thing Vera wanted to do was talk about quilting. What she didn't know was that before I married her, I'd play poker with my buddies three to four nights a week. That's when I figured out that quilters and poker players don't mix any better than oil and water. And I'm not including the arguments we had when she found out I wanted to spend my Saturdays at the racetrack so I could bet on the ponies. Casper, I tried real hard to make our marriage work. I offered to take Vera along with me to my poker games, or to the racetrack, but she turned me down. Looking back, I think it was her worrying about losing real money on the turn of a card, or the whims of a horse and jockey. Whatever her reason, we just drifted apart. Toward the end, Vera tried to get me to visit an art gallery, a local museum, or a performance at a local theater, but hell, none of that crap interested me, so I turned her down. By point our marriage had failed to the stage where Vera and I had moved into separate bedrooms so we only saw each other in the morning at breakfast.

One morning, when Vera didn't show up for breakfast, I went upstairs and knocked on her bedroom door. After I didn't hear anything, I opened the door and saw her lying in bed, just like she was still asleep, but she was deader than a doornail. My second wife had peacefully died in her sleep at the age of sixty-one."

Thelma yelled, "Mr. Potts, you're not keeping up with the count . . . fourteen, fifteen, sixteen."

Casper concentrated on the class instructor until she began the count for the next exercise, Heel Lifts, then he said, "Mr. Sullivan, what happened next?"

Clint sighed. "Casper, when it comes to romance, everybody knows that old farts like us follow our dicks rather than listen to the brain that's tucked between our ears. Right?"

Casper didn't think that Clint was describing him, but before he could open his mouth, Clint continued. "Hell, the truth is I was so horny, that after my first date with Judith, all I wanted to do was hop into bed with her. But Judith acted real coy, so right after the movie, while we walked back to my car, I proposed and she said yes! We got into my car and I drove to Vegas where we got hitched at the *Elvis Lives Wedding Chapel* on the Strip. I know that sounds crazy, one movie date and then a wedding in Vegas at an Elvis Presley wedding chapel. Guess what, my married life with Judith turned out just as crazy as you might think. The following morning, after our quickie wedding, and a wild night in our hotel room, we took the elevator down to the restaurant to order our first breakfast as husband and wife. That was when I discovered that besides being great in bed, Judith had some down-right-wacko ideas about food. My new bride told the waiter she wanted a bowl of strawberries, an apple, and some grapes. When the waiter said, 'I'm sorry, madam, but we don't have any fresh grapes. I could bring you an order of toast with grape jelly?' She flipped out, 'Young man, I only consume the food that all sane humans should eat— no glutens—no grains—no meat—no dairy—just fresh fruits and vegetables!' In the middle of her beating up that poor waiter, I interrupted her. 'My God, Judith, just what the hell do you eat?' She answered, 'Didn't you know? I only consume raw, uncooked, and unprocessed fruits and vegetables!' I shuddered and that was the moment I tumbled to the fact that my third marriage might have been a drastic mistake. By now, people in the restaurant were starting to stare so I pulled myself together, patted Judith on her shoulder, and told her that normally I eat a lot of meat, like a steak, a hamburger, a rack of ribs, even a couple of fried polish sausages every day! But I'd give her crazy fruits and stuff a try. Casper, after I suffered through my first breakfast of strawberries and a few pieces of raw apple, we checked out of the hotel and headed home. That first full day of my third marriage, I went along with her crazy food routine as I tried to survive on apples with the seeds and core, carrots with most of the dirt brushed off, grapes that included chewing and swallowing the seeds, and celery without the strings removed. Dinner, the final blow, a bowlful of uncooked, gas producing, Brussel sprouts. After a full day of choking down that crap, I snapped. The second morning of our marriage, while Judith showered, I went downstairs to the kitchen, fried up a pile of bacon, scrambled six eggs, threw in a fistful of pepper cheese, and whipped up a giant omelet. Then I split the omelet in half and served it onto two plates. I popped some sourdough bread into the toaster and sat down at the kitchen table to wait for Judith. My boy, I was sprinkling some little plops of bright red Sriracha sauce all over my omelet when Judith stopped at the kitchen door, recoiled, and screamed, 'Oh my God, Clint, have you lost your mind? You've cooked bacon, eggs, toast, and now you're eating it!' Then she spun around, ran back to the bedroom, packed her bag, and stormed out of the house without so much as a good-bye. Two days later I received divorce papers from her lawyer, and I never saw the crazy broad again. Judith turned out to be my last leap into the pool of marriage,"

Clint winked at Casper. "Now you know why all of the babes in this joint are after me. I've got a pile of money and I'm available! But then again, it could be my six-pack abs. Ha! Ha! Dude, you look in damn good shape. This strength class is for old farts like me who can barely get it up anymore, if you get my meaning."

Casper didn't get his meaning, but he responded anyway. "Mr. Sullivan, I'm here, like I'm sure you are, because I believe we could both use a little more exercise."

"Young fella, will you please stop calling me Mr. Sullivan. I'm Clint."

Casper smiled. "My mother taught me it is good manners to address people by their proper name. In your case, Mr. Sullivan."

"You know, Mr. Sullivan does make me sound more refined, but you damn well better call me Clint from now on or I'll kick your ass. Ha! Ha! Only kidding, Casper. Come to think of it, would you be interested in joining my Texas Hold'em game every Tuesday evening at my place? It's not a big money affair, but on a bad night, I've seen guys lose as much as fifty bucks."

"No thank you, Mr. Sullivan. I've never been much for gambling."

"Hey, I thought we agreed you'd call me Clint. How about betting the ponies? I love to bet the horses. Every morning at breakfast I go over the Daily Racing Form looking for the perfect long shot."

"Well, Clint, I'm afraid I don't gamble at cards or horse racing."

"Like I say, whatever floats your boat." Clint glanced toward Thelma sitting at the far end of the ring of chairs. "You know, there's something about the way Thelma lifts those weights that reminds me of my second wife. Hey, we'd better stop bullshitting and get serious. Thelma doesn't like us talking and she wants everybody to do the exercises together, and on her count."

Casper frowned. "Why is that, Clint?"

"Got me."

While the group followed Thelma's count through each and every exercise, Casper again checked out Del. She was dressed in a close fitting exercise outfit and he noted that all the proper places were filled out according to her ample female form. Their eyes met. She nodded and flashed a very warm smile, but before Casper could respond with his smile, he felt a tap on his shoulder.

He turned and stared directly into the face of Mr. Bradford.

"Mr. Potts, could you step into the hall? We need to talk."

"Mr. Bradford, as you can see, I'm taking advantage of one of the many activities available to residents of The Oaks."

"Mr. Potts, I am fully aware of what you are doing, but we need to talk."

Thelma, attempting to continue her exercise routine in spite of the growing interruption from Casper and Mr. Bradford, shouted, "Set the weights down on the floor and grab your stretch bands."

Mr. Bradford took Casper's stretch band from the arm of his chair and handed it to him.

Casper said, "Thank you, Mr. Bradford. Go ahead, I think I can do the exercises and still talk with you. What's so important?"

Thelma, still struggling to ignore the intruding male voices, cried, "Place the stretch band behind your back, level with your armpits, and pull forward on my count. One, two, three, four . . ."

"Your apartment door is what's important, Mr. Potts. I understand that you have mounted a large —"

Thelma's commands increased in volume, "fourteen, fifteen, sixteen," and drowned out the end of Mr. Bradford's statement to Casper. "Now place your band beneath your right foot and get ready to lift your arms up."

While the group moved the stretch band from their backs to under their right foot, Mr. Bradford said, "Mr. Potts, you had a member of my maintenance crew permanently mount a white board on your apartment front door. Concerned that the item he had placed on your front door might be against the rules here at The Oaks, the maintenance man came to my office."

Thelma glared in the direction of Mr. Bradford's voice as she started her count. "Lift! One, two, three . . ."

Casper, continuing to lift his band to Thelma's cadence, responded, "What about all those other thing-a-ma-bobs that are hanging on those other apartment front doors? Did those people receive permission from you before they attached that flotsam and jetsam to their doors?"

When she finished her count, Thelma set down her band and walked toward Casper's chair. When she reached Casper, she cried, "With your left hand, hold the band over your heart and pull your right arm up and away. Ready? One, two, three . . . "

When Casper had set his band over his heart and started to pull, Thelma flashed Mr. Bradford a cold stare that could have flash-frozen a twenty pound turkey. The moment her cadence reached the number sixteen, still glaring at Mr. Bradford, she said, "Now hold half your band over the right side of your chest and pull the band up and to the left. Ready? One, two, three . . . " Once the class started to pull their bands, Thelma lowered her voice to a whisper. "First it was Clint Sullivan, now it's The Oaks' manager, Mr. Bradford. Mr. Potts, why do you continue to interrupt my Senior Strength Class?"

Mr. Bradford said, "I apologize, Ms. Zeiss, but I felt the need to settle a minor policy difference with Mr. Potts."

Thelma glanced at her watch. "Mr. Bradford, it is currently one forty-one and my Senior Strength Class will be completed in thirty-four minutes. Short of a catastrophic fire, hurricane, or a devastating earthquake, I allow nothing to interrupt my class. At two-fifteen, once Mr. Potts has returned his band and weights, he will be available to discuss any subject you want. Or, if you care to, you can go to the box by the wall, pick out a stretch band and some weights and start exercising. I've given you two choices, join us, or immediately back away from Mr. Potts. The strength class allows the participants to build muscles and expand their lung capacity, but they only have three days a week and forty-five minutes each day to gain the fruits of their labors. That is a total of one hundred and thirty-five minutes a week of needed work and today you have caused my class to lose some of those precious moments!"

Mr. Bradford was both shocked and mortified. He had not been berated in that manner since he was in the forth grade when his teacher, Mrs. Gardner, in the middle of her lesson on personal hygiene, caught him closely examining a giant, green booger he had just extracted from his right nostril. Over his brief career as the manager of an independent senior-living complex, no one had spoken to him like that, not a single employee, much less Ms. Zeiss, a lowly contract worker. But, as an independent senior-living manager who wanted to remain in his chosen profession, Mr. Bradford was well versed on when to hold 'em, and when to fold 'em.

He nodded his head as a sign of defeat and said, "I apologize for my interruption, Ms. Zeiss."

Then Mr. Bradford turned and walked across the expansive parquet oak floor of the multi-purpose room and slumped into a chair.

After missing almost two and a half minutes of valuable workout time, Thelma barked, "Thank you, Mr. Bradford. Now everyone sit down, place your band beneath your feet and pull your band close to your chest. On my count, separate your feet and when we reach sixteen, hold your feet apart. Ready, one, two, three . . . "

While Casper followed Thelma's count, he couldn't help notice a trace of a smile that darted across her lips. With Mr. Bradford sitting by the side of the room, Casper turned his concentration back to Del. But wait, she was gone. Somehow, during Casper's dustup with Mr. Bradford, Del had left the multi-purpose room.

When Thelma reached sixteen, she said, "Now hold your feet apart . . . hold 'em . . . . just few more seconds . . . okay, relax."

The Senior Strength Class exercise routines continued until 2:10 when Thelma announced, "All right. After you place the stretch bands on the back of your chair, and put your weights under the chair, everyone standup, walk clockwise around the room and maintain a brisk pace for the next five minutes."

During the following three hundred seconds, each time Casper made the circuit around the large multi-purpose room he passed a dejected Mr. Bradford, who avoided eye contact with all the participants, especially Thelma.

After five minutes, Thelma announced, "Your heart should be beating faster than when you started. Congratulations class, you are done for the day. Please replace your stretch bands and weights in the box. I'll see you all on Wednesday at 1:30."

Many of the group called out, "Thank you, Thelma."

Clint waved as Casper returned his band and weights to the box, avoided bumping into Mr. Stately, walked over to Mr. Bradford, and said, "I believe you expressed a concern that I asked maintenance to attach a white board to the front door of my apartment."

Mr. Bradford waited until Ms. Zeiss and all the others had cleared out of the multi-purpose room before he answered, "You are correct."

"And you stated that was against the rules here at The Oaks?"

"Again, correct."

"Mr. Bradford, speaking of rules, I think you shouldn't have interrupted Thelma's Senior Strength Class."

Mr. Bradford frowned. "Who's Thelma?"

"Ms. Zeiss. Her full name is Thelma Zeiss."

Mr. Bradford shrugged. "Oh. I didn't know that."

"Now I have question, Mr. Bradford. Did all the other apartment dwellers receive your permission before they mounted those plastic flowers, pictures of kittens or puppies, religious symbols, or any of the other junk they have attached to their apartment doors?"

Casper had asked Mr. Bradford one of the many questions that he had been avoiding since he took over managing The Oaks. Personally, he thought most of the door decorations were ridiculous, ugly, or in poor taste, but since the company had no corporate policy against attaching doodads to apartment doors, and since Mr. Bradford was generally incapable of making a decision on his own volition, the door decorations remained. Mr. Bradford decided to appeal to Mr. Potts sense of male solidarity. "Mr. Potts, you are correct. No one had asked for, nor did anyone receive permission for their expressions of individuality as demonstrated by their door decorations. However, in your case, the white board is more of a utilitarian device, something functional, not decorative. I'm positive you will agree there is a major difference between a decorative bobble attached to a front door and functioning whiteboard."

Casper's heartbeat had returned to normal and his muscles had ceased to complain, all of which informed him that he would need to take advantage of future Senior Strength Classes.

"Mr. Bradford, I agree with you that my whiteboard is a utilitarian device, but I'm afraid I don't see the difference between my board and the two-foot stalk of dried wheat on the door across the hall, or the large bouquet of plastic red roses on the door down the hall. Unless you can show me a written policy that bans door decorations, and that policy is being followed by all the family members

130

here at The Oaks, my whiteboard will remain attached to my door thanks to the excellent job done by your maintenance crew."

Mr. Bradford thrust his right hand in Casper's direction. "Mr, Potts, as usual, it has been a pleasure to talk with you and although we do not always agree, please let us part as friends. Remember, the door to my office is always open."

That was the moment when Casper recalled Del's nod and smile during the exercise session. He suddenly realized that his heated discussion with Mr. Bradford had become more important than talking to the delightful Delilah Madison. Eager to find her in the crowd, Casper ignored Mr. Bradford's offer of his hand, scanned the room but she was nowhere in sight. Casper vowed to call Del as soon as he returned to his room.

As he exited the multi-purpose room, however, a bony hand attached to the arm of an elderly female grabbed the top of his sweatpants and stopped him in his tracks.

Chapter Eleven

The Drug Store Merry-Go-Round

The voice that emanated from the body that held his sweatpants exclaimed, "Young man, my name is Elizabeth von Thurn und Taxis. For the sake of brevity, you can drop the und Taxis and in the future you will address me as Miss von Thurn. I am fully cognizant of the fact that I don't know you, nor do you know me, but I understand you own a motor vehicle. Am I correct?"

He wanted to ask her why she felt she could grab his sweatpants. And how did she know he owned a car? But being a perfect gentleman, Casper said, "Yes. I do have a car."

"And what is the model?"

"A late model Toyota Camry. Why is the model of my vehicle of concern to you?"

"Some years ago, a gentleman agreed to drive me and it turned out that his motor vehicle was a pick-up truck. During my ninety-two years on this earth I have never ridden in a pick-up truck and I never will. So is your motor vehicle a pick-up truck?"

Casper tried to pull his body away from her hand but her grip remained viselike. "As I told you, my car is a Toyota Camry. Trust me, it's a very comfortable sedan."

"I am disappointed it is not a Cadillac!"

"Ms. von Thurn, is there a reason that you do not take The Oaks shuttle to wherever you need to go?"

She snapped, "Young man, I am not a Ms. In fact that title offends me. In the future you will address me as Miss von Thurn, or not at all. What is your name?"

"Casper Potts."

Miss Elizabeth von Thurn unlocked her grip on Casper's clothing and tilted her head back, as if attempting to bring his face into focus. "Your name rings a bell. Are you a member of the restaurant committee?"

"The what?"

"Ah, then you are. Mr. Potts, at the next meeting of the committee, I want you to express my strong complaint concerning the quality of the yogurt that was served to me for dessert at today's lunch. Mr. Potts, I understand that everyone has different tastes when it comes to the world of yogurt, but why this establishment would consider serving a plain, American yogurt, when there are many, many outstanding Greek-style yogurts, some with fruit, and they are all available at a reasonable cost. Today's dessert was a complete failure and someone needs to be held accountable!"

"Miss von Thurn, I'm sorry, but I am not on the restaurant committee, or any other committee here at The Oaks. I will, however, pass on your complaint to Mr. Bradford the next time I talk with him."

"Complaining to that wet dishrag will accomplish nothing. Moving on to the reason I detained you, I need to do some important drug store shopping. Could you drive me?"

"Right now?"

"Of course right now! Mr. Potts, do you think I would ask you to drive me to the drug store if it wasn't of vital importance?"

The urgency in her voice indicated to Casper that the woman was on some sort of a vital mission and she was not to be deterred. "Of course not, Miss von Thurn." He glanced at his watch and saw he still had time to help out this poor old lady. "I have just enough time if we can catch the elevator and go down to the basement where my car is parked."

"Mr. Potts, I have never descended into the bowels of this structure on that contraption and do not intend to do so. You will pick me up at the front door."

Casper, a bit taken aback by the old lady's abruptness, responded meekly, "Of course, Miss von Thurn. I'll be at the front door entrance in ten minutes."

Chapter Twelve

A Mysterious and Enticing Perfume

Casper ran up the stairs to his apartment, and between the missed hoped for encounter with Del, his skirmish with Mr. Bradford, and his pending rendezvous with the baffling Miss von Thurn, his head buzzed with excitement. But the moment he entered his living room, his olfactory organs shifted into high gear as he detected a subtle citrus scent followed by sweet vanilla. My God, he thought, that's The One by Dolce & Gabbana! The identical perfume I had given to my wife, Margaret, last Christmas. He pulled out his wallet and extracted the note she had given him so he wouldn't accidentally purchase the wrong perfume. There it was, in her handwriting, DOLCE & GABBANNA, The One Eau De Parfum, 2.5 Oz.

Casper didn't believe in ghosts, but as a single tear slipped down his right cheek bone, he whispered, "Margaret, are you here? Hello?"

Getting no answer, he walked through his apartment to see if he could pin down the aroma.

Casper picked up his phone, keyed in 0 and the front desk receptionist answered. "The Oaks, how may I help you?"

"This is Casper Potts. I just walked into my apartment and someone wearing The One perfume, by Dolce & Gabbana, entered my apartment while I was participating in the Senior Strength Class."

"Mr. Potts, just a moment . . . that might have been your cleaning lady. Let me check the schedule . . . ah yes, your apartment is on her schedule today for cleaning. Nothing to worry about. A cleaning lady was supposed to be in your apartment."

He inhaled more of the lingering vanilla. "To tell you the truth, I had forgotten all about the cleaning service. How often is my apartment cleaned?"

"Once each week. According to the schedule, your apartment is cleaned each Wednesday afternoon between one and three."

"Thank you." Casper set the phone down and it immediately rang. "Hello?"

"Casper, Izzy here. I have set up the LCC meeting. It's tonight at seven in the multi-purpose room. Do you know where that is?"

"Yes, I do."

"I had so many women wanting to attend that the library wasn't going to be large enough to hold the crowd. That's why it's been moved to the multi-purpose room. Okay, this is how the meeting will go down. I'll call the meeting to order, introduce you, and then you'll be on your own. Just between us, what the hell is going on?"

"Izzy, you'll find out soon enough. Thank you for setting up the meeting. By the way, did you invite Del?"

"I made sure she got word of the meeting. That's all I'll say. See you at seven."

Chapter Thirteen

Drug Store Discount Coupons, Ad Infinitum

Between the intriguing and lingering aroma of the enticing perfume that remained in the air, and his unexpected call from Izzy, Casper's promise to pick up Miss von Thurn at the front door had almost slipped his mind. "Oh my God!" he exclaimed to himself as he sprinted out of his apartment and down the stairs to The Oaks' underground parking facility.

No more than a minute and a half late, Casper drove his car up to the front door of The Oaks where Miss von Thurn paced back and forth in front of the main entrance. Her expression looked angry and anxious to Casper.

Moving quicker than he had in years, Casper jumped out of his car, ran around to the passenger side, and opened the door for Miss von Thurn.

After Miss von Thurn was seated, but before she buckled her seat belt, she stared at Casper for a long moment, as if she was having trouble focusing in on him. What she saw was not an active, independent senior adult, but another unruly student in her elementary school fourth grade class. She leaned forward, looked directly into his eyes, and said, "Young man, sit down at once in your assigned seat and face the front of the class or I will be forced to send you to the principal's office!"

Casper, taken aback at her strange, off-the-wall remark, countered, "Pardon me, Miss von Thurn, what did you just say to me?"

Miss von Thurn took a second, long look at her driver. "Ah, Mr. Potts. You left me standing outside The Oaks, in the hot sun, for nearly twelve minutes. Do you run late for all your important appointments, or do you have a valid excuse to convince me that your tardiness was an unexpected aberration on your part?"

As Miss von Thurn spat out the word 'tardiness', a spark of recall fired in Casper's head. Miss von Thurn sounded exactly like the reincarnation of Miss Myrtle Winesap, Casper's third grade teacher. As he buckled his seat belt, he stammered, "No, Miss von Thurn, normally I am a very punctual person, but because of your unexpected request to drive you to a drug store, I had to make some changes to my plans for the afternoon and that cost me a couple of extra minutes."

"Mr. Potts, now I have to correct you again. You used the singular for drug store, as if we were only going to stop at a single drug store."

Casper's mind raced back to their previous conversation and he was positive that she had said drug store. But the expression of frustration on his passenger's face told him it was not the time to argue with her. "I apologize, Miss von Thurn, my hearing is not what it used to be. Am I to understand that your drug store itinerary will include more than one stop?"

"You are correct. In fact, we will visit three drug stores today."

"May I ask why?"

"You may not," she snapped. "The first store you will drive me to is the CVS on Vine just south of Hollywood Boulevard."

While Casper made his way through the heavy traffic caused by the myriad of rental cars that choked Hollywood Boulevard, he noticed that Miss von Thurn was shuffling through a handful of coupons that had previously been neatly stacked on her lap. He smiled. "Are you looking for some real bargains?"

"That is none of your business, Mr. Potts." And as if suddenly unaware of his presence, she muttered, "For the life of me, I do not understand why all my drivers feel the need to delve into my private life."

As Casper's vehicle moved Miss von Thurn closer to her first drug store, she suddenly said,

"Mr. Potts, don't think I'm not grateful to you, and the other drivers who have helped me on my quest."

And what was Miss von Thurn's quest? Casper would discover the answer to that query much later.

Today, as he drove through the streets of Hollywood on what was beginning to look like a fool's errand, Casper's demeanor slipped from a bright, sunny, outlook to a dark, smog-filled Los Angeles frame of mind.

After a couple of left and right turns, his car rolled into the CVS parking lot. As he pulled on the handbrake, Miss von Thurn turned toward him and stated, "You wait in the car. I will return in a few moments."

Ten minutes later, Miss Von Thurn returned to Casper's car, set a small paper bag on the floor next to her feet, and said, "The next drug store is the Rite-Aid on Sunset about a mile west of Vine."

The two rode in silence until Casper drove into the Rite-Aid parking lot. Again, Miss von Thurn said, "Mr. Potts, you will wait in your vehicle. I will return in a few minutes."

Casper whiled away the moments by attempting to figure out what Miss von Thurn could be buying that made the items so important these visits had to be made immediately. He was about to lean over and peek into the bag she had left on the floor of the passenger side when the door popped open.

Miss von Thurn set the second paper bag on the floor by her feet, next to the first, and said, "The last one is a Walgreen's on Fairfax next to—"

Casper interrupted, "I know, next to the Farmers Market. Miss von Thurn, I don't want to pry, but I couldn't help notice that when we started out you had many coupons, and that the stack has been reduced with each drug store visit."

"You are very observant, Mr. Potts. I find that a commendable characteristic."

Casper waited in vain for a further explanation. Then, in a valiant attempt to gain a little camaraderie with his passenger, he said, "Miss von Thurn, your name interests me. Are you of German origin?"

"I am pleased you asked, Mr. Potts. I can trace my ancestry back to the 16th century lineage of the Thurn und Taxis family name. My antecedents are among the noblest and wealthiest in Germany. The von Thurns have resided at St. Emmeram Castle in Regensburg since 1748."

"Very impressive. And what exactly does the 'von' stand for?"

"Generally, the von is a particle added to a surname, or family name, to signal the nobility of a family."

"So if I understand what you just told me, the 'von' indicates nobility and that you are a direct descendent of noble German aristocracy."

"Excellent answer, my boy, you learn quickly and retain what you have learned. I will see that you receive a high mark on today's final examination."

"I'm sorry, Miss von Thurn, I think you must be confused. What final examination are you talking about?"

She hesitated, sat back and rubbed the temples of her forehead with her bony right hand. "No, Mr. Potts, it is you who is confused. Now, once I have completed my shopping at Walgreen's, you will return me back to The Oaks. Oh, in case I forget, thank you for your assistance today. You have made a valuable contribution toward the security of your nation."

"You're welcome, Miss . . ." Casper caught himself the instant before he blurted out the name of his old third grade teacher, Miss Myrtle Winesap. "Miss von Thurn!"

Chapter Fourteen

Casper Meets With The Ladies' Casserole Club Membership To Explain His Scheduling Board-1.0

Casper returned home with just enough time to shower and shave. When he approached the multi-purpose room at 6:55 pm, he immediately noticed how many women were entering. While he stood at the door to the large room, he recalled an earlier conversation with Mr. Bradford in his apartment. "Mr. Potts, are you aware that most of the women here at The Oaks are active?"

Casper responded, "Active? In what way?"

"Mr. Potts, by 'active' I mean all sorts of activities, but some activities come with a large caveat, and the Ladies' Casserole Club is the best example of my caution. In that unsanctioned organization of . . . ah . . . unattached females, most are actively seeking more than a shared casserole lunch with a male family member. In almost all cases, they are searching for male companionship and they seldom have matrimony in mind, if you get my drift."

At first, Casper did not truly get Mr. Bradford's drift, but after his shared casserole lunches with Izzy and Del, and the shocking confrontation between two women outside of his front door, he now fully understood Mr. Bradford's warning.

But an evolving Casper Potts, taking pleasure in his new role as the best looking rooster in the barnyard, plus his foray into gambling as measured by his monumental bet with Mr. Bradford, caused him to hide his glee as he counted more than fifty females seated in their chairs and more jockeying for seats.

After Izzy introduced Casper, he paused for a moment as he stood before the sea of femininity, then he said, "Members of the Ladies' Casserole Club, I thank you for the opportunity to meet with you this evening. First and foremost, I am honored that your membership has chosen me to be a recipient of your world-class casseroles. The reason I asked Izzy to bring you together tonight is simple. We need to work together to avoid a repeat of the scene that happened not long ago when two of you fine Ladies', casseroles in hand, appeared simultaneously at my apartment door. I have a solution that will keep this sort of situation from happening in the future. My proposed fix?" Casper noticed that many of the women had pulled out note pads and were writing down his every word as he continued, "I have installed a white board on my front door that will have spaces for thirty dates and names. Why the number thirty? I have previous commitments outside The Oaks each Saturday and Wednesday, so the thirty boxes are the equivalent of six, five day calendar weeks. At the base of the white board there will be a shelf with a marking pen and an eraser. Does anyone have any questions so far?"

He glanced around and saw no hands had been raised.

"Okay, I have filled in the dates for the first six weeks. You, the members of the Ladies' Casserole Club, can pick the date if you want to join me in my apartment to share your casserole. All you have to do is write your name in the empty space. Now do you have any questions?"

The Irish lady with the orange-red-hair jumped up. "So if I write in my name, Maeve Mahony, into an empty box, you say that day will belong to me to serve you my Irish Shepard's Pie?"

"Yes, Maeve, that is what I propose."

Maeve pointed to her right and continued, "And that vixen, Gertrude Schwarz, will have to find another day to stuff her German Meatballs and Spaetzle down your throat?"

Before he could answer, Casper saw Gertrude leap up and start pushing her way down the full aisle of women toward Maeve. He turned and said, "Izzy, I'm done here.You better get involved before those two hurt each other."

Izzy jumped up and yelled, "Maeve, Gertrude, stop this instant or you'll be placed on probation and don't forget what being on probation means. Each week I will email Casper the name, or names, of any member who's on probation and he's agreed to not allow that member to write her name on his scheduling board. Got it, ladies'? Probation equals no casserole lunch with Casper Potts. Now, as we've taken care of all of the club's business, this meeting is adjourned."

As Izzy and Casper watched the throng leave the multi-purpose room, she whispered, "Casper, when will you be ready for another try at my Chicken Paprikash With Dumplings?"

In spite of Izzy's obvious rough edges, Casper found he was enjoying her straight-forward manner. She wasn't a Del by any measure, but he did appreciate her taking command at what could have been a bad situation!

He smiled. "Izzy, as soon as I return to my apartment I will write in your name in the last box."

"But that means I'll have to wait six weeks!" Izzy pondered her options for a moment, and gave Casper a playful punch on his arm. "Sweetie, at my age, waiting that long will seem like an eternity, but don't worry, six weeks from now, I'll be knocking on your door for a second try at my famous casserole and just for you, I'll tone down the spice a touch."

Chapter Fifteen

The Scheduling Board-1.0 Works!

The evening after the Ladies' Casserole Club meeting, as Casper was unlocking his front door, two females approached. A woman with champagne blonde tresses he did not recognize said, "Mr. Potts, just where are the dates you promised would be on the scheduling board?"

A bit taken aback by the rapid response, Casper said, "I apologize. I'll fill those dates in right now." He grabbed the marking pen and filled in the empty spaces with numbers. "Now, that I have completed my responsibility, who wants to fill in their name?"

The champagne blonde grabbed the marking pen and wrote Judith Evens in the first empty space. She handed the pen to the other woman and she scribbled Margo Shield in the second empty space. With a smile, Margo set the marking pen on the shelf that Casper had designed for exactly that purpose.

Judith said, "Mr. Potts, I will see you tomorrow with my Zucchini Pizza Casserole. Do you have a preferred time?"

Casper said, "Two thirty would be perfect."

"I'll be here at two thirty and get ready to be dazzled!"

"And I'll be here with my Farmer's Pork Sausage Scramble the following day," said Margo.

The two women giggled, turned, and disappeared down the hall.

Casper suddenly recalled his promise to Izzy. He took the marking pen in hand and wrote her name in the last space, and noted 'light on the spice'.

After they left, Casper looked at all the empty spaces and recalled Mr. June's comment, "Thirty times in six weeks? Mr. Potts, and I'm sure my fellow maintenance guys will agree, all I can say is good luck to you. And just between you and me, I hope you have a way to keep your . . . ah . . . energy up."

Only after he opened the apartment door and walked into his living room did Casper begin to realize the magnitude of what the Ladies' Casserole Club expected of him.

Chapter Sixteen

Casseroles Ad Infinitum

Many weeks later, after partaking in a multitude of casserole lunches, and with the scheduling board filled with names, Casper considered his growing concern over what was expected of him as the recipient of all these meals. He was no longer as naive as he was during his first few casserole encounters.

His guilelessness had begun to vanish when he saw the overwhelming attendance at the Ladies' Casserole Club meeting, and the eagerness of Judith and Margo to sign up on the newly installed scheduling board. Those actions, plus sly winks and nods from many of the single females as he passed them in the hall after breakfast, helped Casper fathom that there could be much more on his afternoon agenda than the casual sharing of a favorite casserole dish.

So after partaking in his first four casserole, and with his next six weeks planned out, Casper decided it was time to codify a personal list of principles, or criteria, that he would need to follow for all future casserole lunches.

First—In Casper's mind, once a member of the Ladies' Casserole Club brought her dish into his apartment, there was a high probability that more was expected of him than the simple sharing of a meal between two consenting adults.

Second—Although Casper understood that his first conclusion could be somewhat chauvinistic, if any sort of activity were to follow a scheduled lunch, he would have to be attracted to the member of the Ladies' Casserole Club, somewhere along the line of his smoldering feelings toward Del.

Third—If Casper did experience a physical attraction, but also experienced a lack of . . . ah . . . energy, and was not able to follow through as intended, he would need to devise some sort of "rain check" system.

Finally—As a true gentleman, under no circumstances would Casper ever discuss, or divulge any details of his casserole lunches with anyone, and that included Mr. Bradford!

Casserole luncheon rules now firmly set in his mind, Casper left for the Senior Strength Class.

Prior to the start of the forty-five minute session, he said hello to Clint Sullivan who took the chair next to him. As the exercises progressed, he scanned the room and was disappointed to note that Del was not part of the group that session. He made a mental note to call her this afternoon.

When the exercise group dispersed, Clint Sullivan cornered Casper and whispered, "I saw that crazy female talk to you last week. You know, the one with that weird German name?"

Casper said, "Do you mean Miss von Thurn."

"Yup, that's the one. What did she want you to do?"

"Drive her to the drugstore. Why do you ask?"

"Potts, I'll bet you five bucks you took her to more than one drugstore."

"No bet, Clint. I drove her to three drug stores. How did you know that, and why do you think driving her to drug stores makes her crazy?"

"She's strong-armed every dude in this joint who owns a car. The broad sits around her apartment all week, goes through stacks of newspapers and cuts out drugstore coupons. Then she cons a nice guy, like you, to drive her around town so she can buy all her bargains."

"Clint, I'm sorry, but I see nothing wrong with someone trying to be thrifty."

"Hey, she buys all sorts of crazy things. Things she doesn't need. I know because I checked out one of her paper bags the day I drove her. Three brands of men's deodorant. Small jars of instant coffee. Travel tubes of toothpaste. A large box of colored pencils. All sorts of junk like that."

"Thanks, Clint. I'll try to avoid her if she asks again."

"Don't worry, she'll ask again. She usually grabs a guy's arm after the strength class. And that babe

152

has a grip of steel. And Potts, don't forget about my Texas Hold'em party. "

"I'm not much of a card player, Clint."

"I understand, but promise you'll join my Texas Hold'em game once before I die."

"I will," called Casper as he headed toward the stairs. But in his heart, Casper knew that throwing away his hard earned money on a game of chance was not a part of his DNA. "But give me a call to remind me. Okay?"

Clint said, "Hot damn, you're a tough nut to crack. Don't worry, Casper. I'll make sure those Texas Hold'em sharks leave a couple of bucks in your wallet."

"I appreciate that, Clint." As Casper walked down the hall festooned with Mother's Day decorations, his thoughts shifted to Miss von Thurn and her drugstore trips until he opened his front door. Once again, the sweet aroma of The One perfume filled the air. Casper left his apartment and reentered the hall. He moved to his left and then his right, sniffing the air. There was a heavier scent to his left so he walked down the hall to the next apartment door and placed his ear as close to the door as he dared. He heard the whine of a vacuum.

Casper knocked.

The noise of a vacuum continued.

The second time he knocked so hard that he bruised a knuckle on his right hand.

153

This time, the vacuuming noise stopped. In a moment the door opened a crack and a female voice said, "Yes."

Casper said, "Excuse me. My name is Casper Potts. I live next door and I want to ask you . . . ah . . . " It suddenly dawned on Casper that he didn't have a clue of what he wanted to ask.

The door opened further and Casper could finally gaze upon the appealing countenance that belonged to the lady who was wearing The One perfume.

Casper stammered, "Good . . . Good afternoon. As I said before, my name is Casper Potts. And your name is?"

Her coal black hair framed features that exhibited a few wrinkles near her dark eyes but otherwise her brown skin was smooth and flawless. She stepped into the hallway and Casper was pleased to note some slips of gray strands through her black hair.

"My name is Paloma Franco."

Casper was delighted to see that she was about the same height and weight as Margaret had been before her unexpected death. He took a second to look into her eyes and was astonished to see they were a beautiful, deep brown.

Paloma began to blush under Casper's gaze. "What are you staring at?"

"Your eyes. I've never seen such a lovely color."

She frowned, "Mr. Potts, I have already cleaned your apartment. Did I do something wrong?

"No, Ms. Franco. On the contrary, you did an excellent job. I just wanted to meet you." Casper inhaled and Paloma's perfume filled his nostrils. "And to tell you that your perfume, The One, was my wife's favorite."

Paloma blinked and turned her head, as if she were taken by surprise by his remark. "My perfume? Your wife?"

"Yes. I'm sorry but you are the only person I know, besides my wife, who wears The One."

Paloma said, "You are married?"

Casper looked down at the carpet. "No. I was happily married for nearly thirty years when my wife, Margaret, was taken away from me by a stroke."

Paloma's expression softened. "A stroke? I'm sorry to hear that." Then she looked in the direction of Casper's apartment. "Wait! You are the man that lives in that apartment. The one with that board on his door!"

"Yes, I am," said Casper, as he suddenly realized that he had become the man with that board on his door.

Paloma glanced back at Casper's door. "I'm sorry your wife died, Mr. Potts, but I'm not the kind of woman who can be seen talking with a man like you. I need my job. Please leave me alone so I can go back to my work."

"But Paloma, I only wanted to discuss the perfume you're wearing."

Paloma turned, and as she walked back into the apartment she was cleaning, she said, "Good bye, Mr. Potts," and then slammed the door.

Casper stood in the hall, now alone but curiously pleased at the resolution of Paloma Franco. Obviously, she was a proud and moral woman, nothing like some of the members of the LCC, and that difference piqued Casper's interest. He vowed that from this day on he would figure out a way to spend more time with Paloma Franco.

Chapter Fourteen

Paloma Franco—Casper's Housekeeper

Paloma was fully aware that her perfume—The One, by Dolce & Gabbana—was attractive to men, and she had been warned by Mr. Bradford to be careful of the man with the board on his door. That's why she reacted so abruptly when Casper asked her about her perfume. However, as Paloma grew older and wiser, she had learned there was often much more to a person than a face, a name, or the fact that her boss had warned her about that man with the board on his door.

Paloma Franco was a third generation Latina born and raised in Los Angeles, a city that prided itself as a true melting pot of cultures. But in reality, those cultures—African-American, Asian, Latino, and Anglo, to name some but not all— generally remained separate due to skin color, language, education, and the monetary value of the homes in their neighborhoods.

Paloma's barely educated father emigrated from Mexico to Southern California where he worked at a cemetery running a backhoe to dig graves. When burial excavations hit a lull, he worked with the groundskeeping crew to cut grass, trim weeds, and pluck the dead flowers from the grave sites. Her mother stayed at home to cook, clean house and raise the family's two children, Paloma and her younger brother, Carlo. Both parents had raised their children to follow the doctrines of the Roman Catholic Church and to always be courteous to their elders.

But Paloma, beyond her mother's stark admonition, 'whatever you do, don't trust boys', hadn't received any other practical guidance as she struggled her way through puberty. In fact, apart from her mother's general warning about boys, she grew up pretty much on her own.

In spite of her good grades throughout elementary school, Paloma had to fight with her father to remain in high school after her quinceañera. This was the celebration of her fifteenth birthday, an age when according to hispanic tradition, many fathers felt their daughters had reached childbearing age and were ready for marriage, not for more education.

As soon as she graduated from high school, Paloma moved away from her parents and brother into an apartment in Boyle Heights with a girlfriend. To pay her bills, she got a full-time job sewing women's blouses in the garment district in East Los Angeles.

A year after Paloma left her parents and their constant reminders of church doctrines, she met a handsome latino named Ramon at a local restaurant. He flashed his dark eyes at her and promised that his love for her was eternal, and that once she married him, he would give her children, money, and happiness.

In Ramon's case, a man whose name meant 'Wise Protector', one promise out of three wasn't bad. He did marry her and give Paloma a child, a daughter named Teresa. But soon after Teresa was born, and a few days before the apartment's rent was due, Ramon vanished from Paloma's life, leaving her without a husband, a fatherless daughter, and no roof over their heads.

Paloma wanted to return to her childhood home, to her parent's protection, but she did not want to give her father the satisfaction of knowing her decision to marry Ramon was wrong. She convinced her mother to help raise Teresa while she spent the next eighteen years working twelve to sixteen hours a day cleaning houses.

The hours were long and the days off few, but Paloma knew she had done the right thing because her daughter, Teresa, was now completing her second year at the Los Angeles City College Registered Nursing program. Even Paloma's mother proudly announced to her friends that her granddaughter would soon become a Registered Nurse!

When Paloma spotted a newspaper ad for a cleaning lady position at The Oaks, a job that would pay her enough to work only eight hours a day, with health insurance benefits, she jumped at the opportunity.

But there was another reason why Paloma reacted the way she did to Casper's seemingly innocent question concerning her perfume.

She had worked too many sixteen hour days, in too many houses, over too many years, to ignore Mr. Bradford's warning concerning the man with the strange board on his door, even if that man did seem to be polite. And, she had to admit, very handsome.

Even though their encounter in the hallway had been very brief, Paloma couldn't help but smile when she recalled that the handsome man with the white board had chosen her out of all the female gringos who lived at The Oaks.

Chapter Seventeen

Casper Ponders His Path Forward

As the weeks slipped by, Casper's vivid memory of his ephemeral visit with Paloma, and of her perfume, and of her reaction to his scheduling board, was beginning to impinge upon the pleasure of sharing a favorite casserole with a Ladies' Casserole Club member during their afternoon tête-à-tête in his apartment.

At his Senior Strength Class, he briefly exchanged pleasantries with Clint Sullivan, while the whole class followed Thelma's instructions, "Go behind your chair and stand on one leg and be sure to hold onto the back of your chair if you need to."

As Casper stood on his right leg, memories of Paloma's perfume flooded his thoughts. While maintaining his balance, he noticed Del standing on one leg directly across from him not thirty feet away. Eyes locked, he smiled and she returned his smile, but her smile seemed more perfunctory. Not sure what to do next, Casper glanced around the circle of seniors and saw they were doing their very best to duplicate a flock of one-legged flamingos.

A few moments later, after Thelma called out, "Thank you. See you the day after tomorrow, and don't forget to put your weights and bands away," Casper headed in Del's direction but he was blocked by Clint Sullivan.

"Casper, that Thelma babe really does work us hard. I'm not worried but my old heart feels like it's ready to jump right out of my chest."

Clint's comment caused Casper to forget about Del and ask, "Do you want me to call for help?"

Clint smiled and Casper was surprised to see he had no teeth. "I'm fine. My Doc told me that prostate cancer will get me long before my ticker stops. Did that German babe ask you to drive her again?

"Not yet."

Clint turned and headed toward the exit. "See you in a couple of days and we'll get another chance to stare at all these good-looking babes go through their paces. Bye."

Casper glanced around but Del had left and he was thinking about calling her. When he walked into the hallway, a familiar steel hand grabbed his arm.

"Ah, Miss von Thurn, I trust you are having a good day."

"Mr. Potts, I need you to drive me."

"To a drugstore?"

"No! Three drug stores. Just like the last time."

Casper decided to test out Clint Sullivan's theory. "Miss von Thurn, I am running a little late so I only have time to drive you to the CVS Drugstore in Hollywood."

Her grip relaxed and she stood back, as if she were seeing Casper Potts in his true form for the first time. "Mr. Potts, I cannot only go to one drugstore." She reached into a small purse. "I have all these coupons that must be used."

"But Miss von Thurn, I'll have more time next week and then you can use the coupons."

An angry expression flashed across her face. "They all have expiration dates. By next week many of the coupons will be worthless." She spun around and muttered, "Men, not one of you understand." And marched away from Casper who made a mental note to thank Clint Sullivan for his sage insight at the next exercise class.

He reached his apartment in time to take a quick shower and get ready for his scheduled Ham Hocks, Andouille Sausage, and White Bean casserole.

Later that afternoon, upon the completion of his sumptuous meal, and gallantly escorted a sweet lady named Lola across his threshold, Casper closed his apartment door and poured himself a glass of Cabernet. He sat down in his favorite chair and tried to understand why he had reached the point where he spent much of his waking hours dreaming of Paloma and her perfume when all the casserole ladies were constantly at his side.

In fact, Paloma had filled his thoughts to the point that he was considering suspending his agreement with the Ladies' Casserole Club and canceling his bet with Mr. Bradford.

With renewed courage bolstered by a couple of sips of wine, he decided what he really needed to do was to talk with Paloma again, to discover if he could develop a relationship between them. He recalled that at the conclusion of their first, very short meeting, she had slammed a door in his face. But there was something about the way she looked at him as the door closed that made him feel if he approached her in just the right way, a kind, gentlemanly way, she would at least agree to talk with him.

But how could he turn this situation around?

Casper poured himself a second glass of cabernet. He considered calling Izzy, making up a story about a friend who couldn't figure out how to approach a woman and ask her advice. He was sure, however, that she'd figure out he was talking about himself, not a friend. He searched through his mind for anyone else who could help him solve his dilemma.

Hold on! How about his old friend, Mr. Jack Lasco, at the meat market? He was the man who had taught Casper that one of the most important aspects of a meat cutter's success was learning how to properly schmooze the female customers.

Casper set his wine glass down and dialed the meat market's phone number.

"You have reached Delgado's, purveyors of the finest meat in the Los Angeles basin. Jason speaking."

"Hello, Jason, Casper Potts here. Is Mr. Jack Lasco working today?"

"Hi, Casper. I guess you didn't hear, but he quit about a week after you left. The scuttlebutt I heard was he had to head off for parts unknown to get away from an angry husband. You'd think a dude who's older than you would be cooling his jets by now. Can I help you with anything else?"

Casper considered that other than Mr. Jack Lasco's on-the-job training, and listening to his daily banter with the female customers, he really didn't know much about Mr. Jack Lasco's life outside the meat market. "No thank you, Jason. Goodbye."

Casper hung up the phone, and as he lifted the glass of cabernet to his lips, he realized that The Oaks was now his family. There had to be someone in those four hundred people who could assist him. Suddenly, the friendly face of Mr. June, the maintenance man who had helped him install the white board, popped into Casper's mind. He downed his wine, grabbed the phone, and dialed the extension for maintenance.

After three rings a voice said, "Maintenance. June here."

"Mr. June. This is Casper Potts. The man whose scheduling board you helped install."

"How could I forget? How's it going Potts?"

"Just fine, and thank you for asking. Mr. June, I have a favor to ask of you. Do you have time to stop by my apartment?"

"Let me check my job board."

"What do you mean, your job board?"

"You know, Potts, that's kind of a funny question. Down here in the basement we've got a big white board with little boxes, just like you've got on your front door, except my job board lays out the work we've got to do, while your board lays out . . . hey, my white board says I'm not scheduled for anything. I'll grab my tool box and be up to your place in five. Bye."

Casper set his phone down, closed his eyes, sat back, and while he waited for Mr. June to appear at his door, he tried to figure out exactly what he was going to ask him when he arrived.

He jumped up when he heard a loud knock and let Mr. June, tool box in hand, into his apartment.

Mr. June glanced around and said, "It's amazing what a couple coats of paint can do to spark up an old place. Okay, I've brought all my tools, what do you need?"

Mr. June's comment about the condition of Casper's apartment was his second remark concerning the age of The Oaks. Casper said, "I have something to ask you, but first, I'm curious just how old is The Oaks?"

Mr. June closed his right eye, as if that was the key to unlock his memory. "I've been here ten years, my guess is thirty, maybe thirty-five years. Why?"

"Because everything looks so new."

"Like I said, it's amazing what a coat of paint will do. And the management upgrades the kitchens every five years. Once you put in a fancy granite counter top, a new oven and cooktop, it's weird how an updated kitchen can take ten, fifteen years off an old apartment."

Casper was a little bothered that all his $750,000 entrance fee had bought was an upgraded kitchen and a new coat of paint, but that was not why he had wanted to talk with his maintenance friend so he filed his concern away.

"Mr. June, what I am about to discuss with you must be held in strictest confidence. Do you agree to my stipulation?"

Mr. June cocked his head and scrunched his eyes. "Stipulation? What's a stipulation?"

"It's sort of an agreement by you to keep what I'm going to tell you a secret between us."

"Secret? Okay, I guess I agree. Potts, I'm a busy man. Cut to the chase."

"Mr. June, I'm . . . I'm looking for help . . . It is my fondest wish to talk with one of the house cleaning staff. Her name is Paloma Franco and—"

Mr. June's jaw dropped with amazement. "Potts, with all the broads you've got coming in and out of this apartment every day, bringing you all those casseroles, and themselves, you're asking for my help to chase after one of the Mexican housemaids?"

Casper's chest puffed out in anger. "Mr. June, the reason I invite the ladies to bring their

167

casseroles to my apartment is strictly confidential and will remain that way, and as a fellow gentleman, I would expect you to honor that. Now, will you help me?"

"I will, but I need to warn you up front that I don't think I'll be much help."

"Why is that?"

"You see, all the maids, and waiters are Mexican, and the Mexicans in this joint pretty much stick together. Me, and the other maintenance guys in the basement are white. I can nose around, but I probably won't get much. I know we all work for The Oaks, but it's really like we're working in two different countries, if you get my drift."

Then Mr. June's eyes shifted back and forth until his eyebrows jumped. "Wait, I've got it. The waiters are all Mexican. That's where you want to start looking for help."

Casper smiled and thought, why hadn't he thought of that? His waiter at breakfast, Julio, was obviously from Mexico and if all the Mexicans stick together, as Mr. June insinuated, then Julio was the man who could help him. "Mr. June, thank you for stopping by, and for your excellent advice."

Casper walked to his door, opened it, and before Mr. June exited into the hall, the maintenance man said, "Potts, sorry I couldn't do more for you. Hey, how about I check to make sure your toilet is flushing properly. Or I carry a supply of dried lemon peels in my tool box. How about I run a fistful through your garbage disposal?"

"Mr. June, my toilet and garbage disposal are just fine, and thank you for advice concerning the waiters. I believe you've pointed me in the right direction."

Chapter Eighteen

Julio Santana, The Waiter That Looked Mexican

Casper was right on one account. Julio did look Mexican, but actually, Julio Santana was born on the island of Kauai, near Nawiliwili Bay, in America's fiftieth state of Hawaii. So why did Mr. June and Casper think Julio was Mexican?

In 1960, Julio's Portuguese grandfather, Julio Santana, immigrated from Portugal to Hawaii where he fell in love with, and married a beautiful Hawaiian wahine named Okana.

In 1962 their brand new son was named Kauai to honor the Hawaiian island paradise where he was born.

In 1985, Kauai married a lovely Hawaiian wahine named Hana who had come from a diverse cultural mix of Hawaiian, Japanese, and Chinese.

In 1996, their son was born and they named him Julio to honor his grandfather's Portuguese roots.

Julio Santana's beautiful brown skin was not from being Mexican, but an amalgamation of Portuguese, Hawaiian, Japanese, and Chinese DNA. And you also know that Julio's surname, Santana, was not Mexican, but Portuguese.

In 2016, Julio Santana flew across the Pacific Ocean and arrived in Los Angeles to attend UCLA. There, he soon learned from his fellow Bruin classmates that becoming a member of the waitstaff at The Oaks was a coveted part-time job with four-hour shifts each day, seven days a week.

The first four-hour morning shift started at 6:30 a.m. and consisted of breakfast set up and serving breakfast to the second largest gathering of The Oaks diners each day, only exceeded by the evening dinner crowd. After breakfast, the morning shift bussed the dirty dishes and set the tables for lunch.

The next four-hour shift began at 11:30 a.m. and consisted of serving lunch to a smaller group of consumers of food, followed by bussing the dirty dishes and setting the tables for dinner.

The final four-hour shift started at 4:00 p.m. and entailed the serving meals to the largest crowd of diners each day.

Julio liked the morning shift because, after setting the tables for the breakfast service, he would usually have a few minutes of free time to study. Then, after serving breakfast to The Oaks family members, and setting the table for the lunch crowd, he would study or head back to classes in Westwood.

The management of The Oaks was fully aware that the college student waiters were taking study breaks between their setting up and serving duties, but they understood that getting and keeping a young, well groomed, waitstaff was more important than worrying about a few employees taking study breaks. And they took pride in the fact that in their small way, The Oaks was assisting disadvantaged students achieve their goals of a college degree.

If, however, the truth were to be known, The Oaks' management's singular objective was not completely altruistic. The corporation's only goal was to be sure no member of the waitstaff was scheduled to work more than twenty hours a week, thus circumventing the requirement that it offer the waitstaff benefits, such as health insurance, 401(k), vacations, sick pay, etc.

But The Oaks corporate motivations, both charitable, and not-so-charitable, did not bother Julio. He had found a solid part-time job with one free meal each shift, occasional time to study, plus the sporadic muffin he stuffed into his pocket when Mr. Bradford's back was turned.

The morning after Mr. June suggested Casper talk to one of the Mexican waiters, Casper entered the dining area ten minutes after the room opened. He glanced around and spotted Julio serving breakfast to Clint Sullivan who sat alone at a table located along the west wall of the dining room. It's strange that the two men who shared a Senior

Strength Class together wouldn't share a table at breakfast but each day they ate alone.

Why?

One morning, soon after Casper joined The Senior Strength Class, Casper said to Clint Sullivan who sat two tables away. "Clint, would you care to join me for breakfast?"

Clint took a bite of bacon and said, "Nah. I need to study my Racing Form. Casper, I'm looking for a 'locked-in' ten to one shot and been shut out for a week. I'm not the kind of company you're looking for in the morning."

Casper glanced across the dining room at the only other occupied table. Mr. Furchak, who according to Clint was stone deaf and almost blind, sat with his back to Casper and Clint Sullivan holding his Wall Street Journal about an inch from his coke bottle bottom thick glasses.

So after that first morning, Casper sat alone at 'his' table and consumed his prodigious breakfast.

The morning following Casper's discussion with Mr. June concerning the ethnicity of the waitstaff, Casper spotted his Mexican waiter and sat down at one of the tables within the waiter's area of responsibility.

When the waiter approached to take Casper's order, Casper smiled, and exclaimed in a warm tone, "¡Buenos días! ¿Cómo está usted?"

In perfect anglo English, the waiter responded, "Pardon me. I . . . I don't understand what you just said."

Casper was a touch nonplused by the waiter's response because he had used his best high-school Spanish he could recall. Momentarily stumped, Casper said, "If you don't understand Spanish, do you speak any other language?"

"Beside English, I speak a little Hawaiian."

A puzzled Casper countered, "And why do you speak Hawaiian?"

"I speak some Hawaiian because I was born in Hawaii. Presently I attend UCLA and work part-time here at The Oaks waiting tables. What did you say to me in Spanish?"

"What I said, using my limited Spanish, was 'Good morning. How are you?'"

"In Hawaiian you would say, 'Aloha kakahiaka. Pehea `oe?'"

"Interesting! Young man, what is your name?"

"Julio."

"My name is Casper Potts, and as we are now on a first-name basis, in the future please address me by my first name, Casper."

"I know who you are, Mr. Potts, I would like to do as you ask, but the waiters have been instructed by Mr. Bradford to address the guests by their proper name."

"Do what you must, but when we are alone, as we are now, you can call me Casper."

"Okay, Casper, hat ever you say. Now, are you ready to order breakfast?"

Casper hesitated. Should he confess to Julio that he thought he was Mexican, and as a Mexican, he would be able to approach Paloma Franco easier than he, an obvious anglo, could?

Or, should he lie to Julio and make something up?

Eventually he decided to tell his waiter the truth. "Julio, I recently met a woman who works here at The Oaks cleaning apartments. Her name is Paloma Franco, and for reasons that are hard for me to understand, she seems to be afraid of me."

Julio frowned. "Casper, I don't really know you, but you seem like a cool dude. You must have done something to make her feel that way. What happened?"

Casper recounted the story of detecting a lingering perfume in his apartment. How he tracked the perfume, and Paloma Franco to the apartment next door while she was inside cleaning the place.

And how she seemed so defensive followed with her declaration that she was not that type of woman.

And how she slammed the door in his face.

Julio was about to say something when both he and Casper heard the sound of a man clearing his throat.

Mr. Bradford said, "Julio, it looks to me like Mr. Sullivan is in need of a coffee refill."

Julio snapped to attention. "Yes, sir." And sprinted toward the kitchen to obtain a carafe of hot coffee.

Mr. Bradford edged closer to Casper's table. "Is there anything I can do, Mr. Potts? If you have a question concerning The Oaks, my door is always open to you. You will find that I can answer most any question much easier, and quicker, than our waitstaff can."

"No questions, Mr. Bradford. I was just discussing Julio's class schedule at UCLA with him. Personally, I think he's carrying a heavy load, perhaps too heavy, but he's confident he can do it." Casper was beginning to trust his newfound ability to make up believable fabrications on the fly, a talent previously unknown to him in his past life as a simple butcher.

Mr. Bradford frowned. "I don't understand. Whose class schedule?"

"Julio's. The young waiter who was about to take my breakfast order before you sent him away."

Mr. Bradford glanced in the direction of the waiters exit. "Oh, one of our young Mexican waiters. Enjoy your breakfast, Mr. Potts."

Mr. Bradford pulled out a small note pad, glanced again in the general direction of the kitchen, jotted down a few notes, turned and marched out of the dining room.

The moment Mr. Bradford exited, Julio returned to the dining room, and Casper's table. "Casper, I really need this job, so I think it would be better if I just served your food."

"But, Julio, I need to talk to you. Do you get a break?"

"Yes. Fifteen minutes after the breakfast service closes. Around 9:30."

Casper was not used to all this thrilling activity and his heart rate increased with his anxiety. He scribbled his apartment number on a napkin and handed it to Julio. "After your shift is over, meet me at my apartment. I'll make it worth your time, just hear me me out."

Julio took a step back and visually checked out Casper Potts from the top of his white hair to the soles of his athletic shoes. "Casper, I hope you're not going to try any kind of funny business because I was Lihue's middle weight wrestling champion in high school."

"No, no, my boy. I'm just looking for a quiet place where we can talk without Mr. Bradford interrupting."

Julio glanced at the apartment number and nodded. "I'll be there. Got any cold beer?"

Casper's heart slowed down as he said, "Do you have a favorite brand?"

"Yes. Newcastle Brown."

"I'll buy you a six-pack and you can take home what you don't drink."

"Casper, I knew you were a cool dude. Mahalo!"

Casper smiled. "Mahalo to you, too."

Chapter Nineteen

Casper Sets The StageFor His Meeting With Paloma Franco

Casper was so excited over his pending meeting with Julio that he trimmed his usual enormous breakfast down to a glass of tomato juice, three slices of sourdough toast, six pats of butter, imported dark cherry preserves, and two cups of coffee.

Anticipating success, he left the dining room, took the elevator down to the underground garage, jumped into his car and made the quick round-trip to the closest Seven-Eleven store where he purchased a chilled six-pack of Newcastle Brown. He was back in his apartment, placing the six-pack onto his granite counter top, when he heard a light knock around 9:35.

He opened the door and there, as promised, stood Julio.

Casper said, "Welcome."

Julio didn't respond and stood his ground.

To Casper, Julio did not act like the same young, relaxed man he had talked with at breakfast. Julio remained in the hallway, rocking on the balls of his feet, as if he was ready to make a quick escape if needed.

A touch confused at Julio's obvious concern that he had laid some sort of nefarious trap inside his apartment, Casper said, "Julio, please come in."

Julio said, "Look, I know I'm only an ignorant freshman at UCLA, but I'm not an idiot. Dude, I'm not gay, and I don't care how much money you offer me, you're talking to the wrong man."

Casper, somewhat perplexed by Julio's insinuation, said, "Julio, I don't know what I've done or said to make you think about me this way. Please come in."

Julio did a quick double take at the white board attached to the front of the door and his fears slowly dissipated as he realized wasn't walking into some kind of a kinky setup. But, before he entered Casper's apartment, he glanced over both shoulders, to make sure that the ever present Mr. Bradford wasn't hiding around the corner.

As Julio stepped into Casper's apartment, he wagged his finger at Casper Potts. "Now I know who you are. You're that dude I've heard about with all the casserole ladies."

Casper said, "Come, come, we have much to discuss in a short time."

179

Julio said, "I've got about ten minutes. Give me a bottle of Newcastle Brown and tell me what it is you want me to do."

While Casper popped the cap off Julio's bottle of beer, he explained, "I want to meet with a woman who cleans apartments at The Oaks. Her name is Paloma Franco. Our meeting should take place outside the confines of The Oaks, in a location where she will feel comfortable and we can talk without Mr. Bradford popping up unexpectedly. Somewhere, anywhere, a public place like a park, a restaurant, or even a Dodger's game. I don't care! Wherever Paloma would feel safe meeting with me."

Julio asked, "And why did you pick me to do this job?"

"Because you're Mexican!"

After a swig of beer, Julio said, "Dude, like I told you before, I'm Hawaiian, not Mexican, and the Mexicans do stick together, so I'll have to figure out a way to break through their tortilla curtain."

Silence settled in Casper's apartment while Julio took a second, then a third gulp of beer. "Okay, Casper. I'll try to set up the meeting but with the following caveat. What you're asking me to do won't be easy. Around The Oaks, everybody knows you as the old dude who cons single women out of a free meal, and God knows what else! So convincing Paloma Franco that you just want to talk is going to be a really tough sell. One that's going to cost you a couple more six-packs of Newcastle Brown."

Casper was a little taken aback at Julio's description of his reputation at The Oaks. He briefly considered telling Julio why he needed the Ladies' Casserole Club members to provide him a casserole each day, and the details of his bet with Mr. Bradford, but he knew if that information ever got back to Mr. Bradford, he would cancel the bet and end the game.

Finally he said, "Julio, I'm counting on you to convey to Ms. Franco that, as a gentleman, my intentions are honorable. My boy, if you require a full case of Newcastle Brown to get my point across to her, so be it."

Julio drained the beer from the bottle, grabbed the five remaining bottles sitting in the now damp six-pack holder, and said, "As soon as I have things set up I'll hand you a note with all the details while I serve you breakfast in the morning, but you have to stop talking to me while I'm close to you or pouring you more coffee. I can't afford to lose this job and I think I'm already on Bradford's shit list."

Julio opened Casper's door, looked both ways, and said, "The coast is clear. And don't forget, we can't talk like normal people while I'm serving you breakfast. And that reminds me, Casper, I don't know how you stay so trim. Without question, you stoke down more food at breakfast than any other person I've ever seen. When you add in your daily casserole lunch followed up with a full-blown dinner each evening, I don't see why you're not getting fat like damn near all of the people that live here."

"It's very simple, Julio, I exercise all those extra pounds away by attending the Senior Strength Class in the multipurpose room three times a week. Mahalo."

As the front door latch clicked shut, a shiver of excitement marched down Casper's backbone, a physical indication of just how action-packed his life had become since he had moved into The Oaks.

Chapter Twenty

Tragedy Strikes At Breakfast

Ever since he made his arrangement with Julio, Casper's days seemed to slow down at The Oaks. It was as though the final determination of a meeting with Paloma had taken on more importance than all the other aspects of his life.

Each morning, when he approached the dining room, his heart pounded with anticipation, only to be disappointed as Casper eagerly scanned the dining room for a note on his table, a subtle nod of Julio's head, any indication that his waiter had successfully set up a rendezvous with Paloma Franco.

Also, during those long days of waiting for a sign of success from Julio, Casper had begun to notice Mr. Bradford always seemed to be lurking close by—down the hallway along Casper's route to the Senior Strength Class—on the far side of the dining room as Casper consumed his prodigious breakfast, or casually passing him in the hallway outside of his apartment.

If spotted, Mr. Bradford would give Casper a perfunctory nod and scurry away, but in Casper's mind, he had become a target of the manager's continuous observation.

One morning, Casper's seemingly endless wait for an indication from Julio was interrupted by a terrible tragedy that quickly turned into a three ring circus.

On the morning in question, as usual, the same three men were seated in the dining room around seven-fifteen eating their breakfasts.

Along with Casper, there was Clint Sullivan, Casper's Senior Strength Class partner and Texas Hold'em entrepreneur, who sat alone at a table no more than fifteen feet behind Casper's table.

Also, in the dining room sat Mr. Furchak, a man who Casper had never met, ever talked with, or heard utter a single word. Mr. Furchak commandeered a plush booth at the far side of the dining room.

As usual, the heads of both Mr. Sullivan and Mr. Furchak were buried in newspapers. In Mr. Sullivan's case, he was pursuing the Daily Racing Form with pencil in hand, and Casper noted that Mr. Furchak was, as usual, completely engrossed in his Wall Street Journal.

Casper had just consumed another outstanding breakfast. He sat back, took a sip from another perfect cup of coffee and was somewhat lost in thought about Paloma when he heard an unusual gurgling sound. He glanced over his shoulder just in time to see Mr. Sullivan tumble off his chair and crash to the carpet. Casper jumped up and yelled, "Mr. Furchak, Mr. Bradford, Julio, come quick! Mr. Sullivan seems to be in some sort of trouble."

At the moment, none of the three responded.

First, Mr. Furchak was totally deaf and his head was buried in his Wall Street Journal.

Second, Mr. Bradford was lying in bed inside his personal apartment nursing a bad cold.

Third, at the precise moment Casper cried for assistance, Julio was standing in the noisy kitchen adding coffee to the decorative serving carafe used for refills in the dining room.

Casper reached Mr. Sullivan and felt his wrist for a pulse. There was none. Oh my God! He's dead!

Casper recalled Mr. Sullivan's doctor's incorrect prediction that his patient would die from prostate cancer before his heart gave out.

Casper let go of Mr. Sullivan's wrist and the arm hit the carpet with a final thud just as Julio reentered the dining room with a container of fresh coffee.

"Julio, Mr. Sullivan just died. My goodness, does this sort of thing happen often?"

"Not usually during the breakfast service, but yes, I've heard from the other waiters that people buy the farm in the dining room all the time. But what would you expect? Casper, unlike yourself,

The Oaks is a place where most of the residents are waiting to die."

Casper was shocked at Julio's depiction of The Oaks population of active seniors. He said, "I don't want to disagree with you my friend, but according to Mr. Bradford, The Oaks is an establishment for active seniors. I read their ad in the *Los Angeles Times* and did not see one word about death, or people dying."

"Sorry to burst your bubble, Casper, but that ad in the LA Times won't bring Mr. Sullivan back to life. What the hell are we going to do now?"

"I don't know."

Julio was pacing back and forth, as if he was considering running back into the kitchen to hide. "Casper, we have to do something quick before the morning breakfast rush starts."

Casper grabbed a table cloth off an empty table and said, "We could drag him over by the drapes, cover him with this table cloth, otherwise somebody's bound to notice him lying on the floor in the middle of the dining room."

Julio's expression was beginning to show the strain of the situation. He cried, "Casper, it's almost eight o'clock. Other people will be arriving in minutes. We need to get this corpse out of the dining room. RIGHT NOW!"

Casper glanced over Julio's shoulder to the other side of the dining room and spotted a wheelchair sitting against the wall. "I've got an idea! Julio, parked behind you. Get that wheelchair."

Julio turned and said, "But that chair belongs to Mr. Furchak and he's still eating his breakfast in booth seven."

"Get the wheelchair! We both know that Mr. Furchak is as deaf as a post and mostly blind, so between his breakfast and his Wall Street Journal, he'll never notice his chair is gone. Besides, we're not going to steal his wheelchair, we're just going to borrow it for a couple of minutes."

While Julio ran to the wheelchair, Casper leaned down and rolled Mr. Sullivan's lifeless body in the table cloth and when the wheelchair arrived, the two lifted the table cloth into the wheelchair.

Julio's voice rose as he said, "Okay, okay, now what are we going to do?"

Casper glanced at Mr. Furchak. His nose was still buried in his Wall Street Journal and hadn't noticed a thing. "Calm down, Julio. We're going sit Mr. Sullivan in Mr. Furchak's wheelchair and push him down the hall and into Bradford's office just like we do that every day."

As the two pushed Mr. Sullivan's body toward Mr. Bradford's office, Julio said, "After we get to Bradford's office, then what?"

Casper grinned. "My boy, I don't know what you're going to do, but I'm going to run back to my apartment as fast as my legs will take me."

Julio couldn't suppress a nervous giggle. "Casper, I'm just a poor college student, so if I lose my job over this, I'm going to be pissed."

Casper opened Mr. Bradford's door and a wave of relief flowed over him when he saw the office was empty. They pushed the wheel chair inside, closed the door, unwrapped Mr. Sullivan's body, and placed him upright in the wheelchair. Casper took Sullivan's lifeless hands, wrapped the fingers on the arms of the chair, bowed his head and considered his former Senior Exercise Class pal for a moment.

Julio nudged Casper's ribs. "Casper, wake up. We've got to get out of here!"

"Julio, Clint Sullivan was a good man and the least we can do is give him a moment of respect." Casper spoke in a somber tone. "Clint, I regret that I never made it to one of your Texas Hold'em games and I promise I will go to the next one that comes my way. And you were right about two things. First, there are some good looking women in the exercise class, and second, Miss von Thurn is nuttier than a fruitcake." Then Casper said, "Julio, can you slip this table cloth into the dirty linen bin?"

Julio took the the makeshift shroud and said, "No problem."

Casper said, "Now, before you head back to your post and me to my apartment, we need to get our stories straight. First, and I know this to be a fact because my wife died of a massive stroke in our house and a police detective told me that when someone dies anywhere other than a hospital, the police are required to investigate the death. So when I'm asked by the police what happened, I'll tell them that just after I finished my breakfast my coffee cup was empty so I asked my waiter, Julio, for a second cup."

"I've got it," said Julio. "I'll tell the cops that my refill container was empty so I had to return to the kitchen to get more coffee for Mr. Potts."

Casper said, "Then I'll tell the police that after you left, Mr. Sullivan got up from his table, and for some strange reason, climbed into Mr. Furchak's wheelchair and wheeled himself out of the dining room. I thought that was an odd thing for Mr. Sullivan to do, but he was a man known for doing odd things."

Julio said, "And when I returned to pour Mr. Potts more coffee, Mr. Sullivan was gone, along with Mr. Furchak's wheelchair. I asked Mr. Potts what had happened. He shrugged and told me that Mr. Sullivan had left in Mr. Furchak's wheelchair."

"Julio, I'm positive we'll be fine as long as we both stick to that story."

"You know, Casper, I like your style. Mahalo. "

"Mahalo to you too, Julio."

Julio pushed Bradford's door open and glanced down the hall, "Hey, we've got to get out of here. I'm heading back to the dining room."

Casper smiled, "See you tomorrow morning at breakfast.

"That's assuming I'm not in jail."

"Julio, just stick to your story."

Julio nodded and as he walked into the dining room, he heard Mr. Furchak yell, "HEY, SOMEBODY CALL THE COPS. MY WHEELCHAIR'S BEEN RIPPED OFF."

Julio said, "Calm down, Mr. Furchak,. I'll try to find Mr. Bradford."

Mr. Furchak said, "WHAT DID YOU SAY? DID YOU HEAR ME? I JUST TOLD YOU THAT SOMEONE STOLE MY WHEELCHAIR! THOSE THINGS ARE EXPENSIVE. THEY DON'T GROW ON TREES YOU KNOW."

"I know, Mr. Furchak."

"WHAT?"

Julio, knowing that responding to Mr. Furchak was like trying to empty the ocean with a tea cup, turned and ran down the hall to the reception desk. "We've got a major problem in the dining room. Do you have any idea where Bradford is?"

"That's Mr. Bradford, not Bradford to you. Concerning your question about his availability, he is feeling under the weather today."

Julio said, "Well, he'd better get out from under that cloud because Mr. Furchak is screaming that someone just stole his wheelchair.

The receptionist grabbed her phone, keyed in a number, and Julio watched her lips move for a moment and then hung up the phone. "Don't move. He'll be right here."

Inside of three minutes, Mr Bradford showed up. He was not wearing his usual suit and tie, but instead was decked out in a pair of navy blue

190

sweatpants and sweatshirt that looked as if he had just pulled them off the shelf. With a nasally voice he said, "What's going on?"

"Mr. Furchak told me that someone just stole his wheelchair."

Mr Bradford reached into his pocket, pulled our two tissues, folded them, held them to his face and failed in an attempt to stifle an explosive sneeze. After he wiped his nose clean, he turned and marched into the dining room where Mr. Furchak was yelling, "SOMEBODY CALL THE COPS."

Mr. Bradford said, "Calm down, Mr. Furchak, I'm here now and will take care of this."

Mr. Furchak said, "WHAT?"

Mr. Bradford moved closer to Furchak's ear and yelled, "Mr. Furchak, I'm here now." He patted Mr. Furchak on his shoulder to calm him down. He turned toward Julio and said, "Boy, did you see anything."

"No sir. I was in the kitchen filling my coffee carafe when I heard Mr. Furchak yell that somebody stole his wheelchair. Mr. Bradford, he's right about the wheelchair being gone. Mr. Furchak used that wheelchair to get here this morning and it's not where he left it."

Mr. Furchak grabbed Mr. Bradford's arm, pulled him closer and yelled. "BRADFORD, I DON'T THINK YOU HEARD ME. MY WHEELCHAIR HAS BEEN STOLEN. THEY'RE VERY VALUABLE. THE DAMN THING COST ME NEARLY FOUR HUNDRED DOLLARS. IF I

191

DON'T GET IT BACK SOMEBODY'S GOING TO
HAVE TO BUY A NEW ONE AND IT AIN'T
GOING TO BE ME."

Bradford said, "Boy, go find Mr. Furchak one of
the spare wheelchairs that we keep in the utility
room so he can get back to his room."

Mr. Bradford pulled his arm from the old man's
grasp. "I did hear you, Mr. Furchak." Mr. Bradford
took out another tissue from his pocket, blew his
nose, and continued, "Okay, after you get Mr.
Furchak a spare wheelchair and a hot cup of coffee,
I want you to look around for his wheelchair. I have
to go to my office because I've run out of tissues."

Mr. Bradford walked down the hall and opened
the door to his office and nearly fainted. There,
sitting in Mr. Furchak's wheelchair, was Clint
Sullivan. He grabbed his wrist and it felt cool and
he detected no pulse. No doubt, the man was dead.

The fever from his cold was wearing Mr.
Bradford down, but he picked up his phone, dialed
911, and when he heard a response, said, "My name
is Bradford. I'm the manager at The Oaks, the
active senior community in the Hollywood Hills.
One of the members of our family just died and—"
He listened for a moment and then continued, "The
body happens to be sitting in a wheelchair that
belongs to someone else. Would it be okay if I lift
the body out of the—no?—fine. I'll leave the body
where it is and let one of your people take it out.
When they arrive, just tell the receptionist to direct
them to my office where the body will be waiting."

He set the phone down just as his office door popped open and there was Mr. Furchak sitting in a wheelchair being pushed by Julio. He yelled, "BRADFORD, THAT'S MY WHEELCHAIR RIGHT THERE IN FRONT OF YOU. TELL THAT MAN TO GET UP AND GET OUT OF WHAT'S RIGHTFULLY MINE."

"I'm sorry, Mr. Furchak, but Mr. Sullivan is dead and the police won't allow me to take him out before they arrive."

"DEAD YOU SAY! BRADFORD, YOU WILL HAVE TO SANITIZE MY CHAIR! HOLD ON, I DEMAND YOU BUY ME A BRAND NEW CHAIR. NO MATTER WHAT YOU DO, YOU'LL NEVER BE ABLE TO REMOVE THE STENCH OF DEATH FROM THE OLD ONE. DO YOU HEAR ME?"

Mr. Bradford sat back, pulled out a tissue and for the moment cleared his nasal passages. "Yes, Mr. Furchak, I heard you."

Mr. Furchak leaned closer. "WHAT?"

Mr. Bradford, his head pounding with fever, closed his eyes and sunk down into his soft leather chair.

193

Chapter Twenty-one

Texas Hold'em

The evening after Clint's sudden death, Casper was forced to take stock of his life since his move to The Oaks, and he wasn't happy with what he saw.

Since childhood, he had always taken the less risky path, the route that would get him what he needed to live. But since meeting many of his new-found friends at The Oaks, he now realized that there was more to life—even a 'bucket list' of items he wanted to do before he died.

The next day Casper called Phil Gray, one of the men Clint had told him had participated in his weekly Texas Hold'em game.

"Mr. Gray?"

"People call my dad Mr. Gray. If you're selling life insurance you got ten seconds and then I'm hanging up."

"I'm not selling anything!" Casper shouted. "Pardon my yell. My name is Casper Potts. I live here, at The Oaks, and I was a friend of Clint

Sullivan's. Before Clint died he suggested I sit in on one of his Texas Hold 'em games. Now that Clint's not with us anymore, is there still going to be a Texas Hold'em poker game every Tuesday evening?"

"Sullivan's not with us? Say it like it is. The man's dead! Potts? Are you that guy on the second floor with that scheduling board on your front door?"

"Yes, I am."

"Tell me. How's that the board working out for you?"

"Mr. Gray, I called—"

"Right. We'll talk about that board later. Okay, you asked about the poker game. Yes, it's still on every Tuesday at seven o'clock, but we've moved the game to my apartment, number 317. If you want to sit in, bring at least forty bucks and expect to lose every penny."

With the excitement of beginning a new adventure, Casper asked, "will you hold me a spot in your next game?"

"You've got it, Potts."

The next Tuesday evening, after fighting through a large amount of trepidation, Casper tucked two fresh twenty dollar bills into his wallet and walked up the stairs to apartment 317.

The door opened and a man almost as wide as he was tall smiled. "Hey, I've seen you before. You were walking into the multi-purpose room for that exercise class."

"I apologize, Mr. Gray. I've never noticed you working out with the rest of the group."

"Hell, I didn't say I ever went into the multi-purpose room. Just said I saw you going in. Now, tell me, what do you know about Texas-Hold 'em?"

Casper reached into his back pocket, pulled out his wallet, and extracted two twenties. "Absolutely nothing. In fact, I've never played any form of poker. I played Gin Rummy with my wife, and Fish with my mother, but beyond that, I'm a complete novice concerning card games."

Phil Gray grabbed Casper's money as if he was an alpha wolf pouncing on a fresh kill. "There's a cooler on the floor next to the table. Grab a beer while I get your chips. Don't worry, I'll introduce you to the other guys when they get here. And, Potts, don't plan on winning anything tonight. Just consider your forty bucks as tuition for your Texas Hold'em education."

Two hours later, and forty dollars lighter, Casper returned to his apartment to go to bed. As he pulled on his pajama bottoms, he smiled and said, "Clint, if you can hear me, I want you to know I sat in the Texas Hold'em poker game. Can't say I'll ever go back, but you were right, now and again, a man's got to be willing to take a risk!

Chapter Twenty-two

Eggs Florentine Casserole And The Scheduling Board Fracas

To Casper's surprise, the tragic death of Mr. Sullivan created little more than a one line mention in The Oaks Press, a single sheet of paper delivered daily under each apartment door.

And, as Casper had predicted, a police detective interviewed the only people who were present in the dining room at the time of Mr. Sullivan's death— Mr. Furchak, who proved that he was nearly as blind as he was deaf and, Julio, and Casper.

Mr. Furchak either didn't understand the detective's questions, or he couldn't hear them because his only response to each question was a muffled grunt and his eyes never left his Wall Street Journal throughout the interview.

Casper was next. He told the story that he and Julio had agreed upon. The detective thanked Casper and then turned his attention to Julio.

Julio recounted his story. The detective nodded, picked up his notebook and left The Oaks.

In fact, the whole police investigation was as Julio had so aptly stated earlier, "After all Casper, you do live in a place where the people are waiting to die."

Many, many days passed since Casper and Julio's wheelchair caper in the dining room and he still hadn't received anything concerning Julio's attempts to set up Casper's desired rendezvous with Paloma Franco. His life settled back into his previous pattern of a large, lavish breakfast each morning, a casserole lunch late each afternoon five days a week, and his dinners outside the confines of The Oaks each Sunday at DuPar's, and each Thursday at El Cholo's restaurant.

One Wednesday afternoon, as Casper walked along the hall decorated with Halloween pumpkins and witches, and still in the glow of his Senior Strength workout, he stopped and stared at his white board mounted on his front door and felt better about himself. His innovative invention had single-handedly dampened the unrest among the members of the Ladies' Casserole Club and a semblance of peace had settled over the unsanctioned club at The Oaks.

But Casper's fragile self-assurance was about to take another hit. While the apparent tranquility among his casserole providers seemed genuine, a few of the club membership were locked in a state of growing angst. It was as if they had become active

198

volcanos where their molten magma was rapidly bubbling to the surface to eventually blow the top off Casper's brilliant white board scheme!

The unanticipated eruption happened that same uneventful Wednesday afternoon, a few moments after the likable Miriam Gardner had served Casper a generous helping of her locally famous Eggs Florentine Casserole.

As Casper lifted a fork to his mouth, Miriam said, "I usually make my casserole with the customary eggs, spinach, and cheese, but this time I included a hefty dollop of spicy pork sausage, because as we all know, a man as busy as you are requires a generous portion of protein in his diet."

Once the spicy sausage hit Casper's tongue, the powerfully seasoned pork attacked the roof of his mouth! At that moment, he realized that Miriam's definition of a hefty dollop of spicy pork sausage had been woefully understated as most of his taste buds went numb.

While he worked to choke down his first bite of peppery pork, they were both startled by a loud commotion coming from the hallway outside of Casper's front door.

Casper, thankful that he could stop stuffing his mouth with the fiery sausage, jumped from his chair, ran across his living room, and opened the door.

Startled by Casper's unexpected appearance in the doorway, two females, and Mr. Bradford, froze as if they had suddenly become members in an old fashioned tableau of historical figures. What Casper saw was the two women battling over the white board eraser, while Mr. Bradford, standing about five feet away from the fight, had been snapping pictures with his phone.

Casper frowned. "Ladies, what is going on here?"

Mr. Bradford responded, "Mr. Potts, I warned you that your scheduling board would come to no good. As you are in violation of The Oaks's recently modified front door policy, I demand you immediately remove that abomination from your front door."

Casper said, "Please, Mr. Bradford, I had addressed my question to the two ladies."

Maeve, an Irish lady with bright orange-red-hair, still clutching one half of the eraser, cried, "I caught Gertrude Schwarz erasing my name from my space on the board." She pointed to a rectangular space filled with a black smudge. "Mr. Potts, that's where my name was. I had reserved that date to serve you my Irish version of Bubble and Squeak."

While Casper listened to Maeve extol the virtues of her casserole, he couldn't help but wonder why women of a certain age felt the need to dye their hair. In Maeve's case, the color of her hair was a hue that was unmatchable in nature, an orange-reddish tint that could never be found anywhere on the earth.

And Gertrude's blonde hair might have been natural when she was twenty, but her twenties were long gone and the result of her twice monthly trips to The Oaks beauty salon were tresses with a strange straw-like shade. That hue might possibly have enhanced the beauty of a young movie star, but certainly not a woman of Gertrude Schwarz's age.

The Germanic blonde continued to pull on her half of the eraser. "Maeve, I did not erase your name. Your name covered two spaces and that was a clear violation of the white board rules. I was in my rights to clear one space so Mr. Potts would have the opportunity to sample my Schnitzel and Kraut Casserole."

Casper, struggled to use his calmest, and most soothing tone said, "Ladies, please hand me the eraser."

By now, the doors on either side of Casper's apartment had popped opened and curious heads were protruding into the hall.

The two females had suddenly become aware that they were the center of attention in an embarrassing situation. So they stopped arguing, lowered their heads, and quietly handed Casper the eraser.

"Thank you, ladies. I now see that I will have to make a few modifications to my scheduling board. I will contact Izzy and ask her to assemble the Ladies' Casserole Club membership as soon as I have come up with a solution to the problem you have uncovered. Until that time, no one will be allowed to write her name on the scheduling board. Do you understand?"

The two females nodded, glared at each other and parted with Gertrude scooting down the hall to Casper's right, and Maeve heading left.

With the unexpected show over, the heads from the adjoining apartments receded, and their doors slammed shut.

Casper stared at his adversary and said, "Mr. Bradford, you must be getting desperate. It looks to me like you created this situation."

"Not so, Mr. Potts. Earlier today I just happened to walk by and noticed that Ms. Mahoney's name had covered more than one of your dated spaces."

Casper said, "And then you just happened to call Ms. Schwarz to inform her of Ms. Mahoney's grievous error?"

Mr. Bradford, a man who was never comfortable when he was being cornered, seemed to shrink a little.

Casper said, "And then you just happened to be outside my apartment to take photos of the women's argument?"

"Well . . . I . . ."

Casper, using his best imitation of *Dirty Harry's* tone, growled, "Mr. Bradford, hand me your phone," and was a bit surprised when Mr. Bradford did as he, or perhaps it was *Dirty Harry*, had demanded.

Mr. Bradford's phone in hand, Casper opened the Photo App and permanently deleted all the photos that Mr. Bradford had taken during the fracas. He returned the phone and said, "Mr. Bradford, your desperate actions tell me that you are getting close to making a decision concerning my annual rental rate. I fully understand you would like to win our bet, but until this moment, I was positive that our agreement was one between gentlemen, and as such, I would have never considered you would do anything dishonorable. However, if in the future you persist in this egregious manner, I will be forced to contact the local television station we previously discussed."

Casper turned, walked over his threshold and slammed the door.

He looked into the agreeable face of Miriam Gardner and smiled. "Miriam, I know you have waited many weeks to share your casserole with me, but I think we both have had enough excitement for one day. I will contact you shortly with another date."

Miriam stood by his door with her casserole dish still full of eggs, spinach, Swiss cheese, and spicy pork sausage. "Casper, while you were in the hall I tasted my Eggs Florentine and, I'm embarrassed to admit that I had added way too much spicy sausage. I promise to do better next time."

Casper nodded as he opened his front door. "Miriam, I am confident that you will. Until next time, good afternoon."

Chapter Twenty-three

Casper And Mr. June Upgrade Scheduling Board 1.0

The moment Casper closed the door, he rushed to his coffee table, grabbed the phone, and called The Oaks's maintenance department located many flights below his apartment.

"Maintenance. June here."

"Mr. June, this is Casper Potts. I have just discovered a design flaw with my scheduling board system that I had not anticipated."

"Sounds interesting. Are you looking for my help?"

"I am."

"You know Potts, that scheduling board of yours is getting to be the best part of my day. I'll be knocking on your door in a jiffy."

True to his word, there was a loud rap on Casper's door within five minutes after he had hung up his phone.

Casper opened the door and Mr. June, tool box in hand, stood there with a big smile pasted on his face.

June glanced at the board and said, "Board looks okay to me. What's the problem?"

Casper explained what had happened between the two women in the hallway, but he left out the part that Mr. Bradford played in the scene.

"Mr. June, I had never considered that anyone would accidentally erase one of the names that had been written in one of the spaces."

"Potts, in my experience, you can never underestimate what anybody, particularly the broads in this joint, are capable of doing. Just between you and me, I'll bet the erasure wasn't an accident."

"Mr. June, I strive to look for the best in people, so I am pretty sure in this case it was an accident."

"Who cares. Accident this time, on purpose the next. It doesn't make much difference, if you get my drift. Now, to solve this problem we're going to have to do some powerful cogitating. You don't happen to have an extra beer laying around do you?"

"I'm sorry, I don't drink beer. Would you care for a glass of wine?"

"Sure. Wine's not my thing, but any alcohol is better than nothing. My wife tells me that when I drink too much wine I belch a whole lot, and when I go to bed, I . . . hold on, Potts, I think I just figured out a way to fix your board."

"Great!"

Casper started to sit down when June said, "But don't let that stop you from getting me that glass of wine."

Casper said, "Red or white?"

"Make it red. My wife tells me that white wine makes her gassy. God knows, you don't want a gassy wife."

After Casper left the living room, June called toward the kitchen, "Potts, have you ever been to Sweden?"

"No I haven't. When I was a child I grew up in Anaheim, in Orange County, but since then I haven't left Los Angeles."

"Those places are not even fifty miles apart. Is that really as far as you've traveled?"

"I'm afraid so."

"That's too bad. My wife thinks travel broadens the mind, but I think all it does to me is broaden my butt from sitting on those seats at the airport, but that's another story. Anyway, the wife likes to travel, so every year she plans a trip somewhere for me and her, usually out of the country. She does everything, airplanes, car rentals, hotels, apartments, all that crap. So all I have to do is go with her and see what she thinks is the important stuff to see. A couple of years ago we were staying in an apartment in Stockholm, Sweden. I told you that sometimes my wife rents an apartment, right?"

On the conscious level, Casper was listening to Mr. June's chatter. On another level, he was wondering why a maintenance man at The Oaks had traveled all over the world while the closest thing he had come to traveling was mingling with the tourists at The Los Angeles Farmers Market. Slowly, Mr. June's question trickled into his brain. "Yes, Mr. June. I recall that you told me about your wife renting an apartment in Sweden."

"Not just any old city in Sweden, Stockholm! So, there we were, in this apartment on one of those islands that make up Stockholm when my wife decided it was time to do some laundry. So—"

Casper said, "Mr. June, I would love to hear all about your trip to Stockholm, but I have to solve my scheduling board problem."

"Cool your jets, Potts, I'm getting to that. So the wife hands me a basket filled with dirty clothes and we go down to the basement where they had one giant washing machine and a couple of dryers. Oh, what I forgot to tell you was there were about fifty apartments in that building and what me and the wife didn't know was each apartment had been given a little round thingamajig with a key inside."

Casper said, "A thig-ama-what?"

"Hard to visualize, right? Okay, picture this. You've got fifty apartments and they all got baskets of dirty clothes. There's only one big washer, and they all want to use that washer on Saturday morning. I'm not great with math, but even I know that fifty doesn't go into one. How did they fix that?

The dudes that owned the apartment took a piece of plywood, drilled in sixty-two holes in it, one for each day of the month, morning and afternoon, and then they mounted sixty metal locks on the back side of the plywood board. Potts, you with me so far?"

Casper closed his eyes to envision a piece of plywood with sixty-two holes, but that was about as far as he got. "I guess I am, but Mr. June, you need to slow down. Everyone is not as capable as you are when it comes to solving complex, technical engineering problems."

"Right. Okay, now the dude that runs the apartment supplied each apartment renter a little round thing, I call it a thingamajig with a key inside. Let's say me and my wife want to wash our clothes the next morning. We pick up our little round thingamajig with a key inside, go down to the basement, but we find that apartment 16 already had their little thingamajig in the hole for tomorrow morning and that it was locked in place and the key was gone! My wife checked the plywood board and found the next open time for the washer was the follow day in the afternoon. She put our thingamajig into that hole, turned the key, and just like that, nobody in that fifty-unit apartment complex could use the washer tomorrow afternoon because nobody could unlock our thing and put in theirs."

It was as if a light clicked on in Casper's head. "I see it now. We build a new board along with the required number of properly engineered locking devices. Once that project has been completed, I will offer each member of the Ladies' Casserole Club a locking device that includes their personal key. From that day forward, when a member picks a day for her casserole date, she will insert the device into the desired date on the new board, lock it in place, and remove the key. That way no one can move that device, right?"

"You got it, Potts, and I like the term, 'properly engineered locking device' better than my thingamajig. Now, the parts to do this job are going to run more than a few bucks. Are you ready to spend some money?"

"I am! Any idea how long it will take us to build the new board?"

"Not really. First, I've got to do my normal maintenance stuff, but as long as I can keep myself under Bradford's radar, maybe a week to get the parts and another week to assemble the board."

Casper said, "What do you require from me today to get our project off the ground?"

"Give me a hundred bucks. It may run a little more, or it may cost less, but a C note will get this show on the road."

Casper pulled out his wallet, handed June two fifties, and said, "Thank you, Mr. June. If not a glass of wine to celebrate, how about a wee dram of the world's finest single malt?"

"That's Scotch, right?"

"You are correct."

"I can't imagine a good Scotch will cause me any gas. A glass of whiskey sounds good. Potts, no matter what other people say about you, you're not a bad guy."

My goodness, Casper pondered, just what are people saying about me!

Chapter Twenty-four

Del's Dilemma

Seven days passed, and Casper had just said goodbye to his latest casserole lady when his phone rang. He quickly decided that during all his years on earth, his days had never been so packed with this much excitement. He took a big breath to clear his head and answered the phone on the fifth ring. "Hello?"

"Good afternoon, Casper. This is Del. Are you free?"

Del had been Casper's second casserole lady at The Oaks, and the first female whose striking features had caught his eye. Before Casper could respond with his immediate availability, or lack thereof, Del continued, "I'm about to make a life-changing decision and feel the need to discuss my options with a man of your vast business experience."

Casper, puzzled as to why Del had thought his weighing and wrapping ground beef equated to vast business experience, responded, "Del, I'm pleased you've asked for my opinion, but I've had a very trying day. Just what sort of life-changing decision are you considering?"

"All I will say over the phone is it's big and I have to come to a decision within the next twenty-four hours."

"My goodness! What has happened?"

"As I said, the details will wait until we meet face to face. Are you available right now?"

"Give me thirty minutes to clean up," said Casper.

Del said, "Fine. See you in a half an hour."

Casper carefully listened for the click that indicated that Del had hung up, then he dropped his phone into his pocket and sprinted to the dining room table. In one fell swoop, he swept the dirty dishes into his arms, ran into the kitchen and gently placed the soiled plates in the sink. Then he grabbed his favorite black bag tool kit, and raced back to his front door. He unzipped the tool kit, pulled out his trusted ratchet screwdriver with the Phillips head and removed the four screws that fastened the four corners of his now obsolete scheduling board to his front door.

Casper had just pushed the board into his closet when the door bell rang. He ran his fingers through his hair, took a deep breath, and opened the front door.

Outside his apartment stood the beautiful Del. Casper smiled. "Please come in."

Del entered, sat down on Casper's couch, and said, "What happened to the fancy board that used to be attached to your door?"

"I took it off."

"Are you stopping your daily casserole lunches?"

"No, the old sign-up process was flawed so I've developed a new concept."

He looked closely at Del and her attractive face expressed a certain concern. Casper wondered if she was ill, or angry at someone, or was there something else wrong? His heart skipped a beat. What if Del had dropped by to ask him if he wanted to expand their casserole relationship into something more? As good as that idea sounded, he wasn't sure he was ready to make that sort of a commitment.

Their eyes locked for a second, and then Del spoke to break what had turned into the awkward silence. "Casper, it's been many, many months since we lingered over my Shrimp and Grits Casserole."

"You're right. It's been some time now," said Casper, still not sure where Del was going with this conversation. "And?"

"I feel as if you've been avoiding me."

Casper tried to understand her accusation. "But, Del, I haven't been avoiding—"

"How about that day you walked by me when I was sitting under the hair dryer in the beauty salon?"

"I'm sorry. I've been going through a lot these days. I guess my mind was somewhere else."

"Humph. How about that afternoon in the Senior Strength Class?"

Casper's mind raced back to the day. "You mean the class when Mr. Bradford cornered me and—"

"All I know is that during one of the exercise routines, I smiled at you and I thought you had acknowledged my smile. After the class was done, I rushed over to join you but you were more interested in talking with The Oaks manager than me."

"Del, I wasn't more interested in talking to—"

"And then the day that old man died, when we passed each other in the hall outside the computer lounge. I smiled and said 'hi', but you walked right by me without any sort of an acknowledgement."

"Oh that morning! I apologize, but I was in the dining room when Clint Sullivan died and—"

Del sighed. "See, you have been avoiding me!" Del hesitated, pulled out a white handkerchief from her breast pocket and dabbed it under her right eye. Then she continued, "But I'm sure our budding relationship is strong enough to put that behind us. Casper, in my humble opinion, you are the only man at The Oaks worthy of my trust. I need your input on a problem of a personal nature."

"You want my input with a personal problem? Del, I'm not sure that I'm the person to—"

Del sighed. "Casper, you're not listening to me. I said, need, not want your input. But before we go into that, you could offer me a glass of wine."

Casper's heart skipped a beat. Did she just say need? What does she mean by need? "I do have some wine. You have your choice of cabernet or chardonnay."

"If the chardonnay is properly chilled, at least two years old, and the grapes were harvested from the Russian River Valley in Sonoma County, a glass would hit the spot."

Del's remark concerning the proper serving temperature and the vineyard designation of a wine, had displayed an egocentric side of her character that Casper had never noticed before. He said, "I can only hope I have a chardonnay that meets your high standards." And he walked into his kitchen.

From her place on the couch, Del tossed a verbal response in the direction of Casper's last remark. "Good."

Casper scanned the white wines slumbering in his well-stocked refrigerated wine storage rack and discovered a nice chardonnay, two years old, from a small vineyard off of Westside Road along the Russian River Valley. He poured the wine into two glasses and returned to Del's side.

She took the glass, swallowed more than what he would describe as a polite sip, and said, "Casper, I've given The Oaks more time than I had planned and unless something changes, I am moving out!"

Then she lifted her glass and drained the remaining wine.

Casper watched Del chug-a-lug a glass of his expensive chardonnay as if she was someone dying of thirst and had just discovered a canteen filled with lifesaving water. He said, "Del, I would love to help you, but I have absolutely no idea what you are talking about."

Del stared at Casper as though she were attempting to measure the validity of each word he had just uttered. Suddenly, her expression telegraphed that she had experienced a eureka moment that seemed to explain the reason for his unexpected ignorance.

"Casper, it's time I laid my cards on the table. As you may or may not know, my married name was Madison." She paused and again the threat of silence settled into Casper's apartment. "I see that my deceased husband's name means nothing to you."

"I'm afraid not," said Casper after he downed the remaining chardonnay in his own glass. "Should it?"

Casper stood and poured more wine as Del pondered his question.

"I think I should start at the beginning, Casper. My husband, Jaden Madison, was a direct descendent of James Madison."

Casper was actually impressed. "The same James Madison who helped write the Constitution and the Bill of Rights?"

Del proudly lifted her chin. "And he was also the fourth President of the United States, from 1809 to 1817."

Casper had no idea as to the lineage of the Potts family name but he was absolutely positive that there was not one President of the United States among his ancestors. "Del, I'd be proud to have a relative who had been a President, but what does that have to do with you wanting to leave The Oaks?"

"I'm getting to that." she snapped. Del took another large slug of wine and continued. "I guess I'm overly proud that my husband, Jaden, and I were both born in Savannah Georgia. We are true Southerners to the core of our very being. I met my husband at Savannah's annual Christmas Cotillion Débutante Ball, where, as a débutante, I was presented."

Casper, still a touch confused as to where this conversation was going, said, "I'm sorry. You were presented? I don't understand what you mean by presented."

Del, in spite of Casper's obvious ignorance of Southern tradition, forged ahead. "I find it hard to believe you don't understand presented. Casper, at the Cotillion, I was presented to the fashionable society of Savannah."

Casper didn't initially reply to Del's explanation, mainly because he still didn't know what to say. As a product of Southern California, he had grown up in an area where that form of high society did not exist. Finally he said, "And that dance is where you met your husband?"

Del was getting a bit exasperated. "My goodness, Casper, it's hard to get through to you. The débutante ball is not just a dance. In fact, the Christmas Cotillion, in Savannah, Georgia, was first held in 1817 and it is the oldest, and most revered débutante ball in the United States. A Cotillion is an occasion that can change the path of a young woman's future. I know it did mine." She hesitated, and then continued, "Casper, you seem to lack the understanding of what I consider to be the finer things of life. Where were you born?"

"Right here in Southern California. Anaheim, to be exact. That's a little town less than forty miles from where we sit, and today is best known as the home of Disneyland."

Del said, "My goodness, that is too bad. But I can live with that. Now, my husband, Jaden, was a better than average provider, and when he died in a tragic accident on the Hollywood Freeway, he left me a large fortune."

"Del, I'm sorry to hear about your husband's unfortunate accident."

"Casper," Del moved closer to him. "What I'm trying to say is that I'm a very lonely woman and I'm asking you to move in with me so my dreary life at The Oaks will take on some meaning."

"Del, I don't think I'm ready to make that kind of a—"

Del cut him off. "Once my deceased husband's estate was settled, and our mansion in the Hollywood Hills was sold, I was a very, very wealthily widow. However, as the escrow days counted down, I found myself with less than thirty days away from being declared homeless."

Casper stifled a smile as he imagined Del, standing by the exit to the Safeway grocery store parking lot, decked out in a a fancy designer gown, a pair of high-heeled shoes, and a flashy bag while holding a cardboard, hand lettered sign that proclaimed:

HOMELESS!

PLEASE!

ANYTHING WILL HELP!

But his ridiculous mental picture was just about as absurd as the direction this discussion was headed. He shook his head to clear his mind and said, "But I thought you were happy living here! You told me that you'd found a little piece of heaven in your luxury three bedroom casita."

"But Casper, therein lies the rub. From the day I walked through the front door, The Oaks was just one of my many possible solutions, albeit a temporary one. If I fell in love with the facility, I would live out my life in my casita. If not, I have more than enough money to find a more opulent place to live. A home where all my meals are prepared by real gourmet chefs, not the hacks we have working in The Oaks kitchens. Luxurious amenities such as a walnut paneled library with hundreds of bestsellers, or top class outdoor furniture by the pool, not chairs made out of plastic. And the most important item on my list, I would be surrounded with a higher class of people. In a few words, a place that would better suit my societal status."

Casper's mind reeled at Del's defining The Oaks as a facility. That meant that she viewed his apartment, the place for which he had spent three-quarters of million dollars on an entrance fee, as if it was nothing more than a public toilet! He composed himself for a brief moment, and then he said, "I see now that you're not happy with your life here at The Oaks. Have you decided when you're going to move out?"

Del's expression suddenly turned from the cold wrath of winter to the warm sweetness of spring. "Casper, that's where you come in. I could tell from the moment that we met that you were a man of good breeding," Her tone turned frosty, "Even if you were born in Southern California. Casper, I know in my heart that you will understand my dilemma and come to my rescue. All we have to do is make a short drive to my attorney's office where he will draw up a detailed prenuptial agreement, and then on to the City Hall where we will get married."

Casper nearly dropped his glass of chardonnay. "Prenuptial agreement? Marriage? I don't want to burst your bubble, Del, but I'm not the man you think I am. I'm just a high school graduate. I'm a retired meat cutter. A very good meat cutter, but I'm much closer to a skilled craftsman than your mental picture of the man you think you want to marry. I paid for my entrance fee at The Oaks from the sale of my house and my wife's life insurance. Finally, my wife was never a débutante nor did we meet at the Anaheim Cotillion or any other dance."

Del's sunny expression vanished as quickly as it had appeared. "A retired meat cutter? I was sure that your wealth and superior bearing came from good lineage."

Casper's anger began to bubble up as if he were a volcano about to erupt. "Del, I did come from a good family so I fear your definition, and my definition of 'good lineage' are not quite the same. Concerning my breeding, my father was a mortician and my mother was a librarian. As far as I know, or care, none of their ancestors were passengers on the Mayflower when that boat landed at Plymouth Rock. Or helped write the Constitution. Or was elected President of our country."

Del opened her mouth as if to respond, but Casper held up his hand. "I'm sorry, Del, but it's my turn now and I'm confused. What have I done that made you feel that I would understand your dilemma and want to marry you?"

Del jumped up and started to head toward Casper's front door. "I'm afraid if you don't understand my needs by now, it's far too late."

Casper, concerned that any move he made in Del's direction could be misconstrued, remained in place.

"Del, at this point in my life I'm not ready to get married, and it's not just you. I did not set up the casserole lunches to find a suitable companion. At this time, I'm not interested in anyone—" But Casper stopped mid-sentence as he recalled his so far futile attempts to pursue the elusive Paloma and his cheeks flushed a touch as a sign he misspoke.

Del stopped at his front door and turned. "Casper, I would appreciate it if you would keep this little discussion between us."

"You have my word on that, Del. Not a single word will ever leave this room."

"Ah! I was mistaken. You must be a man with a modicum of breeding. And after I move, can I rely on your continued discretion?"

"Del, I would never make a disparaging remark about you to anyone here at The Oaks. I value your friendship. I just never felt that I was ready to think about marriage, must less—"

"Goodbye, Casper. I still feel that we would have made the perfect couple and I'm seldom wrong concerning matters of the heart. Ah! What our lives could have been!"

She spun around, stormed into the hall, and slammed the door behind her.

Chapter Twenty-five

The Locking Keyboard—Scheduling Board-2.0

After the door closed, Casper sat down in his favorite chair, still a little stunned at Del's offer of a pre-nuptial agreement followed by marriage, when the ringing of his phone brought him back to the present. "Hello?"

"Potts, June here. I've finished your new board, and if you have a couple of minutes, this would be a good time for me to bring it upstairs so you can give it a look-see."

Casper sat up. "Mr. June, I have the time, and I bought some beer last week so we can celebrate. I hope you like Newcastle Brown."

"Potts, there ain't a beer made that I don't like. Some I like better than others, but I'll drink them all. See you in five."

Casper said, "Excellent."

He hung up the phone and walked into his kitchen, opened the refrigerator and admired the thirty-six bottles that he had purchased to celebrate with Julio upon the completion of his task. He pulled out a cold bottle and a chilled glass, popped the top, and poured the dark liquid into the frosted container. Casper had just set the beer down on his dining table when he heard the knock. He opened his front door and Mr. June stood there with his tool box in his left hand and the new scheduling board for Casper's Casserole Ladies' tucked under his right arm.

"Mr. June, please come in."

June did as Casper asked and his eyes immediately settled on the glass of beer that graced Casper's dining table. "Potts, you didn't need to pour the brew into a glass. Hell, if I recall, Newcastle Brown comes in a bottle, which is made of glass, so it's all the same to an uneducated guy like me."

"Mr. June, I hope my new board works as good as it looks."

"Thanks, Potts."

"You're welcome. Please sit and enjoy your celebratory beer. I'll pour myself a glass of wine and join you."

June sat down, and by the time Casper had returned to the table, the beer had vanished from the glass. Casper set his glass of wine down, returned to the kitchen, popped the top off a second bottle and returned to the table. June took the filled bottle and drained approximately half of it in one gulp.

"Thanks, again, Potts," was followed by a deep belch. June stood, lifted the new board up and said, "I made this baby the same size as the old board so we can reuse the old screw holes in your door."

June grabbed his tool box and pulled out his power drill. Casper set his wine glass down and started to stand up when June said, "Drink your wine, Potts, I've got this. While I'm mounting the board to your front door, you might open one more of those Newcastle Browns. I forgot just how good a beer that is."

June walked to the front door and placed molly bolts into the four screw holes, then he lifted the board and slipped the top screws into the molly bolts. "By the way, Potts, the total for the whole assembly, plywood, sixty-two locks, and two hundred and fifty lockable inserts, comes to one-hundred and fifty-three bucks. Sorry, but I left the receipt in the basement."

"Mr. June, two hundred and fifty lockable inserts? Doesn't that sound like a lot to you?"

"I don't think so. I checked with the babe behind the desk and she told me that presently there are one hundred and ninety-two members in the Ladies' Casserole Club. You'll need one lockable insert for each member, and when you add in membership turnover, two hundred and fifty inserts seemed like a good number to start with."

Casper considered Mr. June's logic for a moment, shrugged his shoulders, pulled out his wallet and was pleased to discover six twenties. "Mr. June, I

225

don't need a receipt. My goodness, I trust you! Presently, I have a hundred and twenty dollars in my wallet. Will that make us even?"

"When you add in the hundred clams you gave me to start this operation, I'd say we're more than even."

"No labor charge?" asked Casper.

"Nah! We'll let Mr. Bradford pick up the labor charge."

Casper chuckled as June's drill zapped in the two top screws. He popped in the two lower screws and inside of sixty seconds he had finished mounting the new board. He replaced his tools into his tool box, and returned to Casper's dining table to down his third and final beer.

After June turned over to Casper the two hundred and fifty lockable inserts, he grabbed his tool box and said before he closed Casper's door, "And don't forget, as far as Bradford's concerned, you and I have never talked about anything. In fact, we've never even met. Right?"

"As you wish, Mr. June."

After Casper stared at the box of lockable inserts for a moment, he picked up his phone and dialed Izzy's number.

She said, "Hello, Casper. Are you ready for another taste of my excellent Hungarian cuisine?"

"Not yet, Izzy."

"But . . . okay, what do you want?"

"Izzy, I need to talk with the membership again. Mounted on my front door is the ultimate solution to all future scheduling problems."

"Don't you think I need to see your solution before I gather all the Ladies?"

"Excellent idea. Come anytime."

Izzy said, "I'll be there in five minutes."

True to her word, Casper heard another knock on his front door in just under five minutes. He opened the door and Izzy stood in the hall, staring at his door. She shook her head and exclaimed, "How in God's name does that thing work?"

Before Izzy arrived, Casper had taken one of the lockable inserts from the box on his dining table. He handed an insert to her and said, "I'll show you. From now on, that little thing I just gave you belongs to you, and you alone. Please note on the side of the insert is a number one. Let's say you wanted to give me the opportunity to sample another of your outstanding Hungarian casseroles. All you have to do is select an open date on the new board, place your insert into that date, turn the key, take the key out of the insert, and your number one will reserve that date until you arrive at my apartment. And Izzy, once you have locked your insert into your selected date, and your key has been removed, no one, and that means no one, can move or change your date. To put it simply, you are locked into a casserole luncheon with me."

Izzy's mouth dropped. "Casper, this scheduling solution is brilliant, absolutely brilliant! But you're going to need a whole bunch of these inserts. The last I checked, we have around a hundred and ninety members."

"I knew you had a large membership in the club, so I had two hundred and fifty of them made."

"Casper, as I said, brilliant. Now, let's go inside your place and . . . ah . . . celebrate!"

Casper, now fully aware of Izzy's endless double entendres, said, "Okay, but I only have time for a glass of wine. Nothing more, I'm sorry to say."

"Damn, you can't fault an old gal for trying. Okay, I'll settle for a glass of vino."

Casper escorted Izzy into his apartment. "Red or white?"

Izzy said, "Hell, whatever you've got open."

Casper poured two glasses of chardonnay, handed one to Izzy, and said, "That's funny. When I asked that same question to Del, she responded with a specific vintage year, a vineyard designation, and questioned if I knew how to properly chill a white wine."

"Casper, please don't ruin our moment by bringing that woman into this conversation. At least she won't be bothering us much longer."

"Ah . . . Did you just say that Del's planning on leaving The Oaks?"

"I did, and I say good riddance."

"Izzy!"

"Casper, that woman walks around this place like she's got a broomstick stuck up her you-know-what. The real reason that Del wants to leave The

Oaks is because she thinks the people who live here don't meet her high standards. She lives in her own little dream world where she's still a debutante in Georgia. Frankly, no one in Los Angeles gives a rat's ass about Savannah's high society."

Casper said, "She did mention to me that she and her husband were very rich when he died in a terrible car accident."

"That woman is a real piece of work. Casper, my husband was her husband's lawyer and he knew everything there was to know concerning the dealings of Jaden Madison. And don't mention any ethical gobbledygook that claims that what you tell your lawyer will remain private. Both Jaden and Timor are dead so I won't get into any trouble for telling you this.

"When it came to investing, Jaden was like the guy who fell into a tank full of starving piranhas. My husband, Timor, told me that Del's husband started out his marriage with nearly a hundred million that he inherited and all that was left when he died was their multimillion dollar mansion in the hills above Hollywood. More than once, Timor called him a loser who couldn't find his ass with both hands and a road map. Granted, the sale of the mansion netted Del five to six million bucks, but that's nothing when compared to the ninety plus million that Jaden left on the table. If I was Del, I'd be happy that Jaden died before he figured out a way to lose the rest of family fortune."

"Izzy, when I was a child, my mother taught me that one shouldn't speak ill of the dead."

"Casper, that's the sort of the thing I like most about you. After all these years you still have a touch of innocence about you. Thanks for the wine. I'll set up the meeting, let you know the time and date, and be sure to bring all of these things with locks.

Casper chuckled, "I guess we could call them thingamajigs."

Chapter Twenty-six

Paloma Will Meet You!

The following morning, as Casper ambled through the nearly empty dining room, he noticed that his waiter, Julio, seemed to be hovering around his table, almost to the degree of ignoring future needs of Mr. Furchak, the only other Oaks family member present in the dining room.

Casper sat down and said, "Good morning, Julio. What looks good on today's breakfast menu?"

"Good morning, Mr. Potts. This morning I'd order the Paloma Franco omelet."

Casper's stomach dropped nearly as far as his eyelids jumped. He glanced around to be sure Mr. Bradford wasn't close by, and said, "Sounds interesting. Do you have further information concerning the ingredients of the Paloma Franco omelet?"

Julio set a small pad and pencil on the table. "Perhaps you'll need a pencil and paper to jot down those ingredients."

It took Casper a moment to calm himself down so he could use the pencil without his hands shaking. "Thank you, Julio. And what are those items?"

"First, you take some Guisados. Mix it with 1261 Sunset Boulevard, and top it off with a dollop of Echo Park."

"How do you spell that first ingredient?"

"G-u-i-s-a-d-o-s."

After Casper scribbled Guisados and the address, for a second time he glanced around to check for Mr. Bradford. Then he whispered, "And the day and time?"

Julio leaned over Casper's table and responded in a low tone, "Tomorrow, twelve -thirty for lunch. She will be there with her aunt whose name is Tia Consuelo as her dueña. That was the only way she would—"

Mr. Bradford's voice suddenly cut through the air from the far side of the dining room, "Julio, Mr. Furchak's coffee cup is empty!"

"Of course, Mr. Bradford," cried Julio as he scampered across the room.

Casper then wrote Julio the following note and tucked it under the salt shaker.

Thank you my friend. Walk by my apartment later this morning and pick up the brown bag I will set out for you by my door. Inside the bag you will find two six-packs of Newcastle Brown. My feeble attempt to repay you for your extraordinary work on my behalf.

Casper

Later that day, a very nervous Casper decided that to calm his angst, he had to make a practice run to Guisados, the location of his meeting with Paloma the following day. But he was so concerned that he would become lost in the maze of Los Angeles streets that he decided to use his iPhone's GPS and let the the gentle voice of Siri guide him to his destination.

From his earlier trips with Miss von Thurn on her drug store runs, he knew the route from the The Oaks to Hollywood Boulevard and once he reached the Avenue of the Stars, he felt some comfort when he heard Siri's voice say, "Continue east on Hollywood Boulevard."

As each block took him further away from his comfort zone, Casper's knuckles turned whiter from his tight grip on the wheel while his vivid imagination conjured up a scenario where he and Christopher Columbus were on the same journey, both attempting to see beyond the horizon. Columbus on the deck of the La Niña, trusting he would discover land before food and water ran out, while Casper was hoping to locate a restaurant named Guisados in the unexplored territory of Echo Park.

When Siri said, "Turn right at the signal onto Western Avenue." Casper was immediately brought back to reality.

Three blocks later, Siri said, "At the next signal, turn left onto Sunset Boulevard."

Now that he was on the same street where the restaurant was located, Casper's vise grip on the steering wheel relaxed a touch and his anxiety reduced a notch. After ten minutes of tense driving, Siri's voice directed, "In three hundred feet, turn left."

A moment later, as Casper pulled into the small Guisados parking lot, Siri declared, "Arrived. 1261 Sunset Boulevard!"

Most Angelenos might question why Casper, a man in his sixties who had lived in the city of Los Angeles for almost half a century would require a GPS driven voice to guide him the meager six miles from The Oaks to a restaurant located in the Echo Park neighborhood. The reason was pathetically simple. Casper was, like many adult men, a total creature of habit.

Before his wife died, he had grown up and lived for nearly fifty years inside a ten-block area close to the intersection of Third and Fairfax Avenue where he attended Fairfax High school, worked for more than three decades at Delgado's Meat Market in the Farmers Market, and occasionally attended church.

One of the few times Casper ventured out of the area where he felt at ease was when his boss, Mr. Delgado, invited Casper and his wife to join the Delgados at their favorite Mexican restaurant, El Cholo's. The foursome had so much fun at that first dinner, the weekly drive to El Cholo's lasted for the next twenty-two years. However, during those twenty-two years that Mr. Delgado drove his car the four and a half miles to El Cholo's, Casper sat in the back seat and never once took note of the route Mr. Delgado took, therefore, Casper's initial drive toward Echo Park, near downtown Los Angeles, was, in his view, the equivalent of him having to hack his way through the thickest jungle in the Brazilian rain forest. To calm his trepidation, he required the assistance of iPhone's Siri to find his way to Guisados in Echo Park.

Those who live in, or who have visited the Los Angeles area, might know that El Cholo's original location is also situated close to the downtown center. But as Casper had never driven in the direction of downtown Los Angeles, or Echo Park, he was also completely ignorant as to the history of the two locations.

The history of Los Angeles began in 1781 when the Governor of Spanish California allowed 44 Mexicans to take up residence next to a Southern California river and he named the settlement, El Pueblo Sobre el Rio de Nuestra Señora la Reina de los Angeles del Río de Porciúncula. For obvious reasons, something had to be done to a village name that long, so it was shortened. Some sixty years later, the first census counted 141 people living in the small community named Los Angeles.

California became the 30th state in 1850, the same year that Los Angeles was incorporated as a municipality.

Forty-two years later, the Echo Park community was named when the City parks superintendent, Joseph Henry Tomlinson, heard echoes during the construction of Echo Park Lake and the name Echo Park stuck. By 1918, Echo Park became a popular location for filming silent movies but city leaders barred the Keystone Kops from shooting future comedies by the lake because too many flowers were being trampled, thus the budding film industry moved to Hollywood.

The latest census shows the majority of people living in Echo Park are Latinos but the community is diverse as actor Steve McQueen, opera diva Marilyn Horne, and actor Leonardo DiCaprio have all lived there.

Along with Casper's lack of historical knowledge, or of the successful citizens of Echo Park, there was another legitimate question that bothered him as Siri's voice took him to his desired destination. Why did he feel the need to drive to Guisados the day before he would meet Paloma at the same location?

Casper, with the exception of the Casserole Ladies, had never felt as comfortable around women as he had with other men, such as his fellow meat cutters. His discomfort manifested itself in small ways, but generally, he would become a little tongue-tied when faced with a new female. The following day he would finally have some time with Paloma and he wanted their moments together to be better than their last disastrous meeting in the hallway outside his neighbor's apartment. He decided that being familiar with the site of their meeting would give him some much needed confidence.

And there was that 'other' woman that Julio had mentioned—Paloma's dueña—the Tia Consuelo who had Casper's very being in a state of total confusion.

What exactly did a suitor do with a dueña? Should he greet her? Could he just ignore her and act as if she wasn't there?

Casper already had enough anxiety concerning his rendezvous with Paloma to have to worry about how he should handle her dueña.

That morning in his apartment, Casper had gone online and checked a Spanish/English dictionary. A dueña was defined as: *"An older woman acting as a governess and companion in charge of girls, especially in a Spanish family; a chaperone."*

In other words, the dueña's job was to be sure her charge, Paloma in this case, and her male suitor, Casper, both behaved in an appropriate manner and nothing untoward would occur during their first meeting at the restaurant.

As his brain nearly overflowed with questions and doubt, Casper pulled into the last vacant spot at Guisados's parking lot.

He entered the building and was surprised to find the interior cluttered with people pushing toward an order counter. At first glance, Guisados had a few tables by the front window, but to Casper, this restaurant seemed to be more of a takeout place. While he stood in the crowd that inched toward the counter, attempting to absorb the cacophony of sight and sound, a young man approached him, smiled, and asked, "Lunch?"

Casper nodded.

"In the outside patio?"

Again Casper nodded and the man led him around the crowded main room and into an outside patio with tables shaded by a roof. At the far end of the covered patio was water bubbling down a rock face. Casper was pleased with his choice of the patio because the area was calm and quiet, much more conducive to a face to face meeting.

The waiter pulled a chair away from a table for two, and said, "Menu?"

Casper, who had worked hard on his limited Spanish the previous evening, responded, "Si, por favor."

The waiter smiled, handed him a menu, and said, "Vuelvo en seguida."

Unfortunately, Casper's overnight Spanish lesson hadn't reached the level where he could translate 'Vuelvo en seguida' into 'I'll be right back', so not sure what to do next, he checked out the menu and was surprised to discover that all the restaurant served were tacos. In fact, at the top of the menu there was a line that stated in bold letters, InTacosWeTrust.

The waiter returned. Casper asked, "Are all your tacos very hot?"

The waiter shook his head. "No sir. Pretty much a Gringo level of heat except for our Chiles Toreados." The waiter pondered for a moment. "That taco will melt the enamel from your teeth."

The waiter's graphic description of what would happen if he consumed a Chiles Toreados taco shook Casper to his core. During all the times he and his wife had eaten at El Cholo's Mexican restaurant in Los Angeles, never once could he recall ever being told that a dish at El Cholos might destroy the enamel on his teeth. He forced a tight smile. "Sounds a touch spicy for me. Could you recommend two of your favorite tacos that are guaranteed not to remove my tooth enamel?"

"Yes, sir. Uno Camarones and uno Pescado, and for your drink I would recommend Jamaica. That's an excellent tea made from the hibiscus flower."

Casper thought for a moment, and then decided nothing ventured, nothing gained. Feeling more multicultural than he had ever been in his life, he nodded. "Thank you. Your suggestions for lunch sound excellent."

The waiter scuttled away.

After he had completed his outstanding meal and drained the last drops from his glass of Jamaica, Casper decided that the tacos from Guisados were very likely closer to the true Mexican culture and El Cholo's food was more of an Americanized version.

He glanced at the check and was surprised to discover that the total came to twelve dollars. He placed fifteen dollars under the bill, pushed himself away from the table and returned to his car. As he started the vehicle, he verbally congratulated himself on having the courage to make this reconnaissance trip. "Casper Potts, you drove yourself all the way from Hollywood to Echo Park, had lunch at Guisados, and are now returning to Hollywood on the same day. I'm now beginning to comprehend why the life of Christopher Columbus was so exciting!"

Chapter Twenty-seven

The Meeting With Paloma And The Dreaded Dueña

The following day, Casper's heart pumped faster, his stomach tightened, and trickles of sweat dripped down his forehead as each mile brought him closer to the Echo Park location of Guisados. After months and months of patiently waiting, Casper's much anticipated meeting with the lovely, and elusive, Paloma Franco was about to take place.

As planned, he arrived fifteen minutes early for his appointed meeting, parked his car, and entered the restaurant.

Inside, the crowded space was just as busy and chaotic as his previous visit, with a large crowd lined up next to the ordering station. Some of the lunch patrons stood along a counter, while others sat eating their tacos around small, crowded tables.

As happened the day before, a man holding a clipboard approached and asked, "Lunch in the patio?"

Once again Casper nodded, and the man led him past the line of customers and opened a door to the outdoor patio. Casper glanced around and was relieved to see that Paloma had not yet arrived. He said, "I'd like that table next to the palm with the two chairs." Still not sure what to do with the dueña, he continued, "On second thought, I'll need a third chair."

The man led Casper to the table, pulled out a chair for him to sit on, and grabbed a third chair from an empty table to Casper's right.

Casper sat down and looked up through the palm fronds. The water trickling down the rock wall created a perfect setting for his much anticipated assignation with Paloma. He leaned back and locked his eyes on the door that Paloma would use to enter the patio.

A waiter appeared. He smiled and nodded as if he remembered Casper from the previous day. "Menu, Señor?"

Casper considered ordering a Jamaica to sip while he waited, but decided that might be considered impolite to his guests. He said, "Not right now. I'm waiting for the rest of my party."

The waiter started to pick up the menu and Casper said, "You can leave the menus. I'm sure they will be here in—" Casper stopped mid-sentence as the door opened and Paloma entered the patio. His heart skipped a beat. Standing in the doorway, wearing something other than her housekeeper's uniform, she was even more beautiful than he remembered.

Paloma glanced around, saw Casper and walked toward his table.

He said to the waiter, "They are here. Just leave the menus and I'll signal you when we are ready to order."

The waiter nodded.

Casper jumped up and flashed his most personable smile to Paloma. Then, for the first time, he noticed an elderly woman dressed in gray standing behind his guest of honor. Paloma turned toward the woman in gray and said, "This is Tia Consuelo." Paloma lowered her eyes a touch, as if a bit embarrassed that she, a woman in her late forties, felt the need to bring her aunt to a lunch with a man in a public place. "Mr. Potts, Tia Consuelo will be acting as my dueña."

"Paloma, please do not call me Mr. Potts. Would you rather I address you as Mrs. Franco?"

"But I cannot do that."

"Please. We are here today to meet and talk like friends. Please call me Casper."

Paloma shook her head. "I don't think Mr. Bradford would let me call you Casper. One of the rules for all employees at The Oaks is to address all guests by their proper name."

"Paloma, look around you. We are not at The Oaks. We are sitting in this outdoor patio at Guisados and we are about to order our lunch."

Paloma hesitated, as if she were afraid that Mr. Bradford might be lurking behind a palm tree. "Okay. Today, at Guisados I will call you Casper, but when we see each other back at The Oaks, you will be Mr. Potts again."

Casper grabbed a chair, and like the true gentleman he was, assisted Paloma to be seated. Then he pull out a second chair for Tia Consuelo, the dreaded dueña in gray.

Paloma cried, "No, no, Casper. Tia Consuelo does not sit at our table. She must be seated at the table close by. That is the proper arrangement for a dueña. Tia Consuelo is not here to eat lunch, but to protect my . . . it is difficult to translate a dueña's job into English because her task is part of my culture . . . she's here in case you threaten my honor."

Casper glanced at the woman. She had to be in her mid-eighties. He mentally shrugged his shoulders, and moved Tia Consuelo's chair to the adjoining table.

The old woman sat down and started to peruse the menu.

Casper returned to his table, sat down, handed Paloma a menu, and said, "Would you care to order?"

"I don't need the menu. I know I want a Mole Poblano and a Chiles Toreados."

Casper said, "But the waiter told me that a Chiles Toreados taco would melt the enamel from my teeth."

Paloma laughed and Casper was captivated by her dimples. "Casper, that's what Jorge tells all the gringos. The Chiles Toreados is hot, but I've been eating them for years and look!" She pointed and showed Casper her perfect teeth. "All my enamel is still here."

Casper was so enamored by Paloma's smile that he didn't answer her for a few seconds. "I can see that, and Paloma, just in case no one ever told you this, you have a beautiful smile."

Paloma glanced at Tia Consuelo and the dueña was totally engrossed in the menu, so Paloma gave Casper a coy nod along with a warm smile and said, "Thank you for noticing."

The waiter suddenly appeared. Paloma said, *"Buenas tardes, Jorge. Uno mole poblano y chiles toreados."*

"¿Tia Consuelo?" Asked Jorge.

"El mismo."

The waiter nodded, and said, *"¿Y lo mismo que ayer para el gringo?"*

Casper picked up the word gringo and asked, "Was he talking about me?"

Paloma said, "He was! Jorge asked me if you want the same tacos you had yesterday. My goodness, you didn't tell me that you've been to Guisados before."

"Paloma, yesterday was my first time . . . I came because I was worried about finding the place . . . and I wanted to get an idea of what to order today, and—"

245

Paloma looked at Jorge. *"Mismo que ayer."*

"What did you tell him?"

"The same order as yesterday."

The waiter left and Paloma looked over Casper's shoulder to see what Tia Consuelo was doing. Tia was dipping a chip into salsa and looked as if the chips would keep her busy for some time. She lowered her voice and said, "Casper, did you really drive all the way to Echo Park yesterday just to be sure we'd both be comfortable?"

"I did."

"That's more than sweet. Are you trying to woo me?"

Casper didn't respond for a moment because, until Paloma had asked him that specific question, he wasn't exactly sure what he was trying to do. He glanced over his shoulder at Tia Consuelo and she was completely engrossed in her basket of tortilla chips and salsa. "Yes, I guess I am trying to woo you. Paloma, I know it's Saturday and you don't work again until Monday. I'd like to order you a Jamaica to go along with your tacos."

She frowned, "How do you know I don't work until Monday?"

"I hope I'm not moving too fast, but I checked your work schedule at The Oaks."

Paloma stared at Casper as if she had the power to see into his true intentions. Then she said, "I usually have beer with my tacos, and I guessed you would like a beer too." Paloma reached into her large purse and pulled out two bottles of beer. "So I brought along two Modelo Especial."

"I didn't see beer listed on the menu."

"It's not, but you can bring your own beer if you want."

Casper said, "Then it's a Modelo Especial for me. Paloma, would you let this gringo have a tiny bite of your *chiles toreados* taco?"

"I will, but the bite will be mostly tortilla with just a little bit of the sauce. I don't want to send you to the hospital."

"Thank you."

A few moments of awkward silence passed before Jorge served their tacos, two frosted glasses for their Modelo Especial, and a large order of Jamaica for Tia Consuelo.

Once the waiter left, the three dove into the delicious fare.

Later, with Casper's mouth still tingling from from his tiny sample of the *chiles toreados*, he said, "Paloma, thank you for the taste of that hot taco, but Jorge was correct. That taco's much too spicy for the average gringo."

He checked to see if Tia Consuelo was eating or listening, and she was still eating. "Now, I have a question for you. Is there a movie theater in Echo Park that shows first run movies?"

"I don't know. Why?"

"Assuming my bite of your Chiles Toreados taco doesn't send me to the local emergency room, and if you are free the rest of the day, I would love to take you to a movie. We could go see a movie in Hollywood."

Paloma glanced at Tia Consuelo. She was concentrating on her food at the moment, so Paloma was on her own. She said, "Casper, I've always wanted to go to that theater that has the hand and foot prints in concrete of the old movie stars."

"I read about that theater. It used to be called Grauman's Chinese Theater. Now it's called the TLC Chinese Theater."

Paloma jumped in. "Do you want to go?"

"I do. We'll head to that theater and pick out the movie we want to see when we get there."

Paloma said, "I've never been to a fancy movie theater in Hollywood."

"Neither have I," said Casper. "All we have to do is take my phone, put in the address of the theater, and a nice voice will tell us how to get there."

"After the movie, could we go out for a hot fudge sundae? I haven't had a hot fudge sundae in years."

Casper pulled out his phone, keyed in hot fudge sundaes, scanned a listing of 'The Best Hot Fudge Sundaes In Los Angeles' and exclaimed, "There's a Ghirardelli's on Hollywood Boulevard and they make one of the top rated hot fudge sundaes in LA."

"Wow! Doesn't get much better than that."

"Paloma, so we're on for a movie and a hot fudge sundae."

"When you say it that way, it sounds like we're going on a real date."

"I guess it does."

Paloma said, "To tell you the truth, I haven't been on a real date for decades."

Casper smiled as he recalled the fun times he and Margaret had going to the movies. "Then I think it's past time for both of us. I can't imagine a date has changed that much. We go to a theater. We buy some popcorn, watch the movie. Later we enjoy a hot fudge sundae. Then the man drives his date home."

Paloma looked at Casper. "And that's all the man would expect from his date?"

Casper said, "It is, assuming that man is a gentleman, and Paloma, as a true gentleman, you have my word."

Paloma blinked back tears of joy. "Thank you. I guess we're going on a date. I'll tell Tia Consuelo that I will take her home after she finishes her lunch."

"Sounds perfect. I'm parked in the parking lot. I'll wait in my car while you drop off Tia Consuelo. Then I'll follow you to your place and we can drive to Hollywood in my car. Paloma, I have a feeling that this will be our first of many dates."

Paloma hesitated. Casper's offer of a date had interrupted her initial plan. She wanted to discuss the subject of Casper's involvement with The Oaks Ladies' Casserole Club. She also wanted him to explain that strange board he had mounted on his door. But she decided that if this date worked out, there would be plenty of time for those questions later. She realized that for the first time since her husband had abandoned her and their daughter, she had someone who might actually be part of her life, someone who was both fun and acted like a gentleman, someone who seemed to care for her as a person.

But the memory of the callous way her ex-husband had treated her impeded her ability to fully trust Casper. In fact, on any first date, Paloma wasn't ready to give any man, not her ex-husband, not even Casper Potts who proclaimed to be a gentleman, the address of her apartment.

She said, "Sounds great, with one minor change. After I drop Tia Consuelo off I'll meet you back here, park my car, and then you can drive us to the movie in Hollywood!"

Chapter Twenty-eight

Dating Bliss! Or Blunder?

Following their first date, an encounter that included a movie and a hot fudge sundae at Ghirardelli's on Hollywood Boulevard, Casper had pulled his car opposite Paloma's parked vehicle.

Paloma took a long look into Casper's eyes and she could see he was ready for most anything that would, or could happen next. But a single evening with Casper was just not enough for her. She still had many question to pose. She still didn't know this man well enough to trust him. Yes, he had treated her with respect, and as promised, had behaved throughout the evening as a true gentleman. However, there was that strange board mounted on his apartment door with the locks, and all those stories she had heard from the other cleaning ladies about the women who took their casseroles to him and then spent hours inside his apartment. Almost every day of the week!

Paloma was not an educated woman, but she did not require a Ph.D. to understand that she had been treated abominably by the father of her daughter. It was going to take more time, and more dates, and more gentlemanly behavior on Casper's part for her to trust him enough for her to let down her self-imposed barriers.

After Paloma unbuckled her seatbelt, Casper had to settle for a farewell peck on his forehead.

When Paloma had planted her reserved sign of affection above his eyebrow, she said, "Casper, I haven't had that much fun in years. Thank you." Before Casper could respond, she continued, "Now, it's time for me to go home. I have a busy workweek ahead of me. Good night."

As she stepped onto the pavement, Casper, obviously struggling to find the right words, finally said, "I do hope we can do this again. Maybe next Friday?"

Just before she closed the car door, she hesitated, and then said, "I'll think it over and leave you a note after I clean your apartment."

Casper nearly burst into tears with relief. He opened his door and walked toward Paloma. "I could skip the strength class next Wednesday and wait for you in my apartment. Then you could give me the news in person."

Alarm bells went off in Paloma's head.

The two of them alone in his apartment?

No!

"Casper, under no circumstances will I allow you to come inside your apartment while I'm there. It would be improper for the two of us to be together and alone. As I said a moment ago, I'll leave you a note on your kitchen counter."

"Okay, I'll wait for the note. But just in case you agree to a date, do you want to go to another movie?"

A little lost in the afterglow of an evening filled with a movie and a hot fudge sundae, she said, "I'm not sure. Do you have a suggestion?"

"How about dinner first and then a movie?"

"Dinner?" Paloma was starting to feel uneasy again. Logically, she knew she was in control, but she didn't feel comfortable being pushed by a man, any man, into a decision before she was ready. "No dinner unless I pay my share of the bill."

Casper could see that his question concerning dinner had made Paloma uncomfortable. "Paloma, I just asked you for a date next Friday and I agreed that you'll leave me a note in my apartment on Wednesday with your answer. But if you pay for half of the dinner bill, that really isn't a date. Did I do, or say, something wrong in the last few minutes that upset you?"

"Casper, you haven't done anything wrong, but you need to realize that it's been years since I dated. I just need to slow everything down."

Casper nodded when he found out that he wasn't the problem. "I think I understand."

Paloma, however, was sure that no man would ever completely comprehend how her life had changed after the father of her child had abandoned her. Paloma's existence had been nearly destroyed

253

by the man she had once loved, trusted, and had welcomed to her bed.

From the moment she acknowledged that Ramon had abandoned her, Paloma's very limited social life had strictly followed the old adage, once burned, twice shy.

She was flattered that Casper Potts, a rich, white gringo who lived at The Oaks, the very place where she cleaned apartments, wanted to take her on a date, but that was a part of her quandary. What did he really want from her? Just sex or a real relationship? Would he, like Ramon, toss her away after getting what he wanted? Standing on the sidewalk outside of Casper's car, Paloma found herself at a point in her life where a crucial decision could be made that would have a far reaching consequences on the rest of her life.

For more than a few seconds she mentally wavered back and forth. She wasn't getting any younger and Casper seemed to be an authentic gentleman. But how could she be sure he wasn't just another Ramon?

As Paloma tried to resolve what seemed to be an unsolvable dilemma, Casper said, "If your note says yes to our date next Friday, do you want me to pick you up at your home, or meet here, at Guisados?"

Paloma said, "Casper, I told you I will leave you a note. "

"I apologize, but, if you do say yes, I need to know where I'll meet you. The only place I know is here, Guisados in Echo Park."

She snapped, "And if my answer is no date, you will have all the information you need."

Casper, obviously unnerved by Paloma's anger, calmly said, "Paloma, I had more fun tonight than I've had in years and I let my enthusiasm overtake common courtesy. Please ignore my boorish behavior."

Paloma said, "If my answer is yes, you can pick me up outside of Guisados. But not here, the Guisados in Boyle Heights."

Casper said, "Boyle Heights? Why Boyle Heights?

"Because that's where I live."

Casper frowned, "Then why did we meet here, in Echo Park?"

Paloma said, "The truth?"

"Absolutely."

Paloma smiled, "Because I wasn't sure I could trust you."

Casper said, "And now you feel like you can trust me?"

"At least for now. She smiled and blew him a kiss. "Good night, Casper."

Casper said, "Good night, Paloma."

He waited for her to enter her car, and after she had clicked her seatbelt, he made sure her car started before he began his return trip to The Oaks. As he wended his way through downtown Los Angeles, Casper found himself unable to concentrate on two things. First, the answer he would see on the note she would leave him next

Wednesday. Second, he hoped Siri will be able to help him find Boyle Heights, wherever that was.

Chapter Twenty-nine

Victory And Then Loco Moco?

The following Wednesday, after his first date with Paloma, Casper walked past the Thanksgiving decorations that proclaimed the most anticipated family event event of the year. He ran up the stairs to his apartment with the hope of arriving before Paloma had finished cleaning his place.

He entered, detected Paloma's perfume that lingered in the air after her departure, and ran to his kitchen counter. Her note stated yes to the movie (her pick), and yes to dinner (his pick). She would be waiting for him at six and reminded Casper to pick her up outside of the original Quisados in Boyle Heights.

"Boyle Heights," Casper mumbled to himself. "Where is Boyle Heights?"

He ran out of his apartment, listened at the door of the apartment next to his and heard the noise of a vacuum. He knocked on the door and when Paloma answered, he said, "I don't know how to find Boyle Heights. Can you help me?"

"Casper, you just drive southeast from here. I do it everyday."

He said, "But I've never driven there."

Paloma said, "Don't worry. I'm sure you can you find your way to Boyle Heights. You found Echo Park!"

"I guess you're right." But Casper's was struggling with his old fear of leaving his comfort zone. "I'll put the Boyle Heights Guisados address on my iPhone and pick you up Friday night at six. Sorry I interrupted you. See you Friday."

Feeling both ignorant and unsophisticated, Casper walked down the stairs and into the Internet room where The Oaks had furnished six desks and computer screens. He typed in Boyle Heights and opened the first web site that appeared.

Eight years after the incorporation of Los Angeles, Andrew Boyle, a veteran of the Mexican-American War, purchased 22 acres on the bluffs that overlooked the tiny town of Los Angeles.
In 1875, Andrew Boyle's son-in-law subdivided the area and named the district Boyle Heights in honor of his father-in-law.

Casper scrolled down the information until he spotted:

By the year 2010, Los Angeles, the little settlement by the river with a population of 141 had grown to

258

3,800,000, and Andrew Boyle's twenty-two acres, the community now known as Boyle Heights, had a population of 100,000 with 95% of the citizens of Hispanic or Latino descent that included Congressman Edward R. Roybal, the Mayor of Los Angeles, Antonio Villaraigosa, and Anthony Quinn, an Academy Award winner for his roles in *Viva Zapata* and *Lust for Life.*

Casper, now realized that for him to feel relaxed driving all the way across downtown Los Angeles, an unknown area so vast, he would need to make a dry-run to the Boyle Heights location before his Friday night date.

The next day, after placing 2100 E Cesar E Chavez Ave into his iPhone, and following Siri's explicit directions, he pulled into an on-street parking spot about a half-a-block from Guisados.

He got out of his car, dropped a couple of quarters into the parking meter and walked to the corner entrance. He entered and saw that the inside was similar to the Echo Park location, except there was not a patio, and the walls were covered with original paintings.

A lady behind the counter said, "Can I help you?"

"No thank you," said Casper as he smiled and returned back to the street.

Pleased with his success, Casper walked to his car with the knowledge that his Friday night date could proceed smoothly now that he knew what it took to navigate the nine mile distance between Hollywood and Boyle Heights.

Elated, Casper spent the rest of the day trying to select the best possible restaurant, while he wondered what movie Paloma would choose.

The evening crawled by but when Friday finally did arrive, Casper woke at five, forty-five minutes earlier than he normally got out of bed. As a child, his early start to the day had allowed him to never be tardy for school. As an adult, his expeditious start got him to work on time at Delgado's Meat Market. Although his earlier awakening was unusual, he was too excited to go back to sleep so he jumped out of bed anticipating his pending dinner and movie rendezvous with his newfound female companion.

After a quick shower and shave, he dressed and was walking to the kitchen when he noticed an envelope that had been slipped under his front door. Could this be from Paloma informing him that their date had been cancelled? Anxiously, he opened the envelope and was startled to see a typewritten note from Mr. Bradford on a page of The Oaks letterhead.

Mr. Potts,
Enclosed is your new Oaks monthly facility fee for the next twelve (12) months that will become effective on the first day of next month.

As you will note, following our agreed upon verbal contract, I have reduced your monthly facility fee by $750.00 per month.

Yours,

R. S. Bradford

General Manager, The Oaks

P. S. The $750.00 monthly reduction will be voided if any part of our verbal agreement becomes public knowledge.

Casper while read the note a second time he couldn't hold back a smile. It hardly seemed possible that a year had passed so quickly, but with the exciting life he now led very little surprised him anymore.

Casper entered his kitchen and checked the calendar. There it was! It had been nearly twelve months since he had moved into The Oaks. A broad, victorious grin pasted itself across his face as he realized that many months had passed since he and Mr. Bradford had agreed upon their secret pact. As Casper stared at the fortunate missive he was holding in his hand, a piece of paper worth nine thousand dollars annually, his chest puffed out as he considered how he had forced himself to confront a true fire-breathing dragon, and today, he held confirmation that he had slain the beast.

But after a moment of delight, he considered how poorly Mr. Bradford must have felt having to reduce Casper's rent for the next twelve months. Casper had always considered himself a good sport.

261

In grammar school, win or lose, he would shake the hand of the opposing kick-ball team's captain and with a smile exclaim, "Good game."

Although his victory over Mr. Bradford was not without a certain amount of joy, he had also suffered his share of defeat. He pondered his alternatives for a moment, and then walked over to his wet bar, took a brand new bottle of Glenlivet 21 Archive and slipped it into a handsomely decorated paper bag.

With a positive lilt to his pace, Casper left his apartment and hopped down the stairs to the dining room anticipating his usual sumptuous morning meal.

He glanced around the dining room and as expected, other than Mr. Furchak whose head, as usual, was buried in his Wall Street Journal, the rest of the space empty. Casper sat down at his table by the window and was pleased to see Julio approaching with carafe in hand, ready to pour Casper his first cup of coffee.

"Good morning, Mr. Potts. Did you sleep well last night?"

"Like a veritable log in a primeval forest, Julio."

Casper glanced around, didn't see Mr.Bradford looming anywhere, and said, "Why did you address me by my last name? And where were you the past four days?"

Julio glanced over his shoulder and whispered, "I can't ever be sure Bradford's not hiding somewhere behind a curtain. I took a few days off

262

for finals. How did your date with Paloma work out?"

"Ah, the date. It worked so well that we are going on a second date tonight. Julio, I feel like a young man again. Paloma is everything I'd hoped for and I owe it all to you. If you hadn't set up our first meeting, none of my present happiness would have happened."

Julio smiled and took a little bow. "All that comes with the standard breakfast service at The Oaks. Now, do you want me to bring you your usual Friday omelet?"

Casper stiffened. "My usual Friday omelet! My God, have I become that predictable?"

"I'd say you have been in a bit of a rut. During the past few months, every Friday you've ordered the green chili and jack cheese omelet."

"Julio, I am shocked to discover I have allowed myself to fall into such a predictable routine."

Again, Julio glanced around. "Casper, about a month ago you told me that each Wednesday you went for dinner at Dupar's, and every Saturday you ate dinner at El Cholo's, and that you've followed that routine for many, many years. Now don't kill the messenger, but in my humble, college student opinion, based on the evidence, I think that you fall into ruts pretty easily."

Casper pondered Julio's remark for a moment, and then exclaimed, "My God, you are correct. Now, tell me, if you were back home in Hawaii, what was your favorite breakfast?"

The young man smiled. "I was born and raised on the garden island of Kaua'i, not on the big island of Hawai'i. My favorite breakfast? Every Sunday my mom would fix each family member an individual bowl of loco moco."

"That sounds interesting. Exactly what is loco moco?"

Julio got a faraway look in his eyes. "loco moco starts with a giant scoop of rice into a bowl, then lay on a hot, fried hamburger patty and top the hamburger patty off with two fried eggs, sunny side up. Finally, Mom would smother the whole bowl with a thick brown gravy."

"My boy, that sounds like something I'd like to try, but Hawaii is a long way from here."

"Casper, sit tight. I'll bet you a six pack of beer that I can get the chef to whip you up some loco moco."

"Sounds great, Julio. If you can do that for me, you know where you can pick up your beer."

"Great." And as Julio disappeared into the kitchen, Mr. Bradford seemed to materialized out of nowhere.

"Mr. Potts. I trust you have received my note concerning the monthly facility fee adjustment here at The Oaks?"

"I did, and I am very pleased with the results of our little agreement—"

Mr. Bradford jumped ever so slightly, as if a tiny lightning bolt had penetrated the top of his head and shot to the bottom of his flat feet. He quickly scanned around the effectively empty dining room and in a whispered voice, he said, "Mr. Potts! You are not allowed to mention our little agreement outside the confines of your apartment, and never in the presence of another resident or a member of the staff!"

Mr. Bradford stood back, took a deep breath, and poured some coffee into Casper's cup. "Just so you and I are on the same page, if anyone—anywhere—for any reason—ever mentions our little agreement, you will find you and your furniture on the street faster than you can finish that cup of coffee."

Casper lifted up his shoulders, as if to give Mr. Bradford the impression of strength, but at the same moment, his stomach tightened with trepidation. Casper took full measure of his opponent, and then, with a hint of anger in his voice, said, "Mr. Bradford, the City of Los Angeles has laws and ordinances that protect renters from unlawful evictions. Besides, there's no physical way you could evict me and my furniture from my apartment before I have finished my coffee."

"Don't be too sure of yourself, Mr. Potts. During the past months I have received more complaints from residences concerning what goes on in your apartment five days a week and have compiled a large dossier on you. You might want to review the morals clause in your rental agreement."

Morals clause? That statement quickened Casper's pulse. Mr. Bradford was right. He had never really read his rental agreement. In fact, most of the *homo sapiens* who populate the earth have never read the fine print of any rental agreement, or the middle pages of their sales contract when they purchased a new car, or the one hundred thousand words that claim to explain the dangers of downloading their smart phone's latest operating system update.

While Casper Potts was no different then ninety-nine point nine percent of his fellow humans, that didn't mean that Mr. Bradford had him between a rock and a hard spot.

He was pretty sure that Mr. Bradford was bluffing about the morals clause, but without first reviewing his rental agreement, he couldn't be sure. Under the circumstances, he decided to take a different approach. He reached down and lifted up the bag that contained the bottle of Glenlivet 21 Archive. As he handed the bag to his opponent, he said, "Mr. Bradford, please accept this as a token of my gratitude toward your following through on your obligation concerning our little game."

Mr. Bradford's eyes lit up when he pulled the bottle of whiskey out of the bag. "Mr. Potts, I appreciate your symbol of sportsmanship and I will enjoy every drop."

"Now, Mr. Bradford, if you will excuse me, I'm waiting for Julio to arrive with my breakfast."

"And what have you ordered today?"

"I don't know. It's a surprise."

"Mr. Potts, I will leave you to enjoy your morning repast."

"Thank you, Mr. Bradford."

Coffee pot in hand, Mr. Bradford walked across the room toward Mr. Furchak's table where Mr. Furchak waved him away without pulling his head from the *Wall Street Journal*.

As if his morning rounds were completed, Mr. Bradford placed the coffee pot on an empty table and left the dining room.

A few moments later, Julio appeared and set before Casper a steaming bowl of loco moco. Julio said, "Dive in before it gets cold."

"Thank you, Julio."

"Casper, back home when someone is served a bowl of loco moco, you smile and respond with *mahalo*. I'll stop by your place to pick up my six-pack of Newcastle Brown in a couple of hours."

Casper flashed his friend the biggest smile he could muster. "*Mahalo*, Julio!"

Chapter Thirty

Drugstore Redux

A few months following Clint's unexpected death in the dining room, Casper had just concluded his Wednesday Senior Strength Class where he had found it difficult to concentrate on Thelma's counts. After forty-five minutes of low impact exercise, and not really focusing on his surroundings, A distracted Casper walked out of the multipurpose room and directly into the vise-like grip of Elizabeth von Thurn.

As she pulled a startled Casper Potts toward her, she said, "Young man, the free world is again in desperate need of your assistance!"

While Casper unsuccessfully attempted to pry her boney fingers from his arm, he said, "Miss von Thurn, I am sorry, but I am not free this afternoon as I have a previous engagement."

"And what, pray tell, are you going to do that is more important than the security of The United States of America?"

In truth, Casper had told Miss von Thurn a little white lie. He was free to do anything until the early evening so he could have helped her that afternoon; however, driving Miss von Thurn to multiple drug stores was not one of the items he had planned on doing.

Casper's major problem was that he had been caught off guard by her demand, and under the baleful glare of Miss von Thurn, he could not come up with a plausible excuse.

She said, "I will meet you at the front entrance in five minutes, and this time, do not keep me waiting in the hot sun!"

Following a quick sprint upstairs to his apartment to pick up his car keys, Casper beat her five-minute deadline with a good twenty-five seconds to spare. He placed his Camry in park, leapt out of his car, and ran around his vehicle to open the passenger door for Miss von Thurn.

As she buckled her seat belt, she said, "Are you familiar with the CVS drug store on—"

"Yes, Miss von Thurn. I took you there sometime ago."

"Young man, I hope you do not plan on accompanying me inside the store as I will not be seen in public with a man who dresses so poorly."

"But you didn't give me enough time to . . . never mind. Miss von Thurn, what exactly are we doing today that could affect the security of our country?"

Casper's question seemed to interrupt Miss von Thurn's count as she shuffled through her stack of coupons. Her eyes widened as she said, "Our boys overseas eagerly await my packages!"

"Our boys? Overseas? Packages? Exactly where are our boys? And what items are in the packages?"

"Young man, I know the youth of your age only think about girls, rock and roll, and baseball, but you should occasionally read a newspaper. Our boys need all of our support. Don't you understand? The Communist horde have our troops trapped and are about to drive them into the sea."

Casper turned off his Camry and thought back to the 1950's. Rock and roll had just started and the Korean war was raging. Was it possible that Miss von Thurn was trapped in some sort of mental time warp? He said, "Miss von Thurn, are your packages for our troops fighting in Korea?"

"My, my, you are not as dense as you look. Over the years, I have purchased hundreds of needed items for our boys and wrapped them up in packages for those who are protecting our freedom in that God-forsaken war zone."

Casper said, "Miss von Thurn, I commend you on your vital work. Perhaps I can help you."

"Young man, I was sure I could count on you. After I finish making today's purchases, you can assist me by helping me wrap the packages."

Casper decided to contact Izzy once he returned to The Oaks and ask for her advice on how he should deal with Miss von Thurn. Satisfied that he was doing the right thing, he drove his slightly muddled passenger to three drug stores where together they purchased twelve travel razors with shaving cream and twelve toothbrushes with toothpaste.

After Casper had returned to the front entrance of The Oaks, he said, "Miss von Thurn, it's almost time for dinner. I don't know about you, but this shopping trip just exhausted me. I'll carry the bags to your apartment and then you can wrap each package up for shipment at your connivence."

"Bless you, young man. I was worried that I was the only one who was tired. See you in the morning."

Once Miss von Thurn had entered the front door of the Oaks, and the door had closed behind her, Casper pulled out his cell phone and called Izzy.

"Casper, is that you?"

"It is. Izzy I have a favor to—"

"I'm still waiting for you to give me a second chance to prepare my Chicken Paprikash with Dumplings for you. Once you do that I will do anything you ask. And I mean anything."

"Izzy, I promise you'll get another opportunity. Now, I just drove Miss von Thurn to three drug stores and—"

"Casper, you may not know this, but that old broad is nuttier then a pecan pie. Last time I talked

271

to her she wanted me to help her write a letter to President Truman to tell him not to worry."

"President Truman?" asked Casper. "Worry about what?"

"His election against Dewey in 1948. She wanted me to tell Truman he had the election locked up."

Casper smiled. "Izzy, you have to admit that Truman did beat Dewey in 1948, so her advice was —"

"Hell, Casper, anyone can look brilliant predicting the outcome of a past election."

A touch of frustration at Izzy's habit of interrupting him in the middle of his sentence caused Casper's vocal volume to increase. "Izzy, will you please stop breaking in while I'm talking?"

"Sorry."

Satisfied, he continued as if unabated by Izzy's previous intrusion. "I am aware that Miss von Thurn's mental acuity seems to be locked somewhere in the 1950's. I called you to see if you could suggest an idea to help us let her down gracefully."

"What do you mean, let her down gracefully?"

Casper explained his previous drives to the various drug stores and concluded with, "I have a feeling that Miss von Thurn has a closet full of packages to send to our troops fighting in Korea. You and I both know the Korean War has been over for decades, but we do have armed forces spread around the world. What do you think about—"

"I don't think, Casper. I do! I'll call a meeting of the Ladies' Casserole Club and give my members something beneficial to do with their idle hours."

A smile crossed his lips as he realized that Izzy was no more aware of her practice of interrupting conversations than Miss von Thurn was conscious that she lived in the twenty-first century.

"Thank you, Izzy."

As Casper drove his car to his assigned slot in the underground parking facility he wondered if gently nudging Miss von Thurn into reality was going to be more work then he had anticipated.

Chapter Thirty-one

Date—Numero Dos

After Casper's unplanned trips to three drug stores with Miss von Thurn, and his phone call to Izzy, he glanced at his watch and shouted out loud. "Oh my God!"

He only had thirty-five minutes to shower and shave or he'd be late for his second date with Paloma.

As he dashed toward his bathroom, he ripped off his clothes. Following a sixty-second shower, and a rapid run over his face with his electric razor, he sprinted down the stairs to his Camry in time to back out of his assigned parking slot only four minutes behind his planned departure.

While Casper drove east, he kicked himself for agreeing with Paloma to meet her outside of Guisados. That meant if Paloma arrived before he did, she would have to wait for him on the sidewalk and place herself at risk of being accosted by an unsavory character.

Casper's stomach tightened into a knot as he fought through the Friday rush hour gridlock that impeded his forward progress through downtown Los Angeles. Eventually, Casper reached Boyle Heights and spotted Paloma standing on the sidewalk near the Guisados front entrance.

He double parked. Waited for a vehicle to pass. Opened his door. Jumped out. Ran around his car, and sprinted toward Paloma's sidewalk location.

With a grim face, he said, "Paloma, I apologize for being late and making you stand on the sidewalk to wait for me!"

She smiled. "Don't worry. It was only a couple of minutes."

Before Casper could respond, the two were startled by a loud blare from a car horn. The honk was followed by a string of Spanish that Casper didn't understand, but he guessed that it contained many words not used in polite, mixed company.

While the horn continued to blast, Casper took Paloma's hand, led her down the curb and helped her into his car. Once she was seated, he closed the passenger door. Only then did he make eye contact with the driver trapped behind Casper's double-parked car who continued to hit the horn button.

The two pseudo-combatants glared at each other for a split-second. Then Casper walked around his car, entered, belted himself in, and pulled away from the confrontation as the horn-honker cried, *"Tu madre es una estupida."*

As he headed his vehicle in a westerly direction, Casper asked Paloma, "Did you hear what he said?"

Paloma attempted to stifle a smile, but she was not completely successful. "I did."

"Would you translate it for me?"

"I can, but it won't make much sense. He said 'your mother is stupid'."

Casper pondered for a moment. "You're right. That doesn't make any sense because my mother was not a stupid woman. Why would he say that?"

Paloma sighed. "I'm ashamed to admit it, but that's what many hispanic males do. The man in the car couldn't think of a nasty thing to call you, so he did the next best macho move to insult your mother's intelligence."

Casper decided that he had much to learn about the hispanic culture. "Paloma, this gringo admits that he doesn't know much about your customs. For example, last week you felt the need to bring your aunt along when we met at Guisados."

"But that was before I knew that you were a gentleman."

Casper said, "I'm pretty sure there are not too many woman in LA who would ever think about taking an aunt along on a first date."

"Our meeting at Guisados was not a first date! I had only agreed to meet you, and to get to know you, that's all!"

"And over tacos you found out that I wasn't an ogre." Casper continued with a grin. "Later, after you took your aunt home, when we went to a movie and a hot fudge sundae, is it okay if I call that a date?"

Paloma smiled back. "I guess you're right. But enough discussions of cultural differences. Where are we going for dinner?"

"Du-par's at The Farmers Market. After the tacos at Guisados, you might find the food a little bland, but Du-par's has been a favorite of mine for years. I hope you will like it. How about the movie you picked out?"

"It's a movie made in Italy and it's showing in a small art theater in Hollywood."

"Made in Italy? What's the title?"

"*La Dolce Vita.*"

"I've heard of that movie. What's it all about?"

Paloma hesitated. Ever since that waiter, Julio, asked her to meet with Casper, she had harbored concerns about Casper's reputation at The Oaks. Everyone, employees and those who lived at The Oaks, were aware that Casper was the man with that board mounted on his front door, a device that seemed to have been designed to control the flow of women into his apartment. As much as she enjoyed Casper's company, she had arrived at a point in their budding relationship where she had to figure out an approach, subtle, or not so subtle, to find out just what went on with those women in his apartment. She had heard rumors of women

277

spending their afternoons in his company. Was this the right time to confront him? Paloma had picked one of Federico Fellini's most famous movies, *La Dolce Vita,* the story about a man who struggles with his love of many women. She decided that after the movie, while eating a hot fudge sundae, might be the ideal time to let the plot of the movie set up her questions to him concerning his present lifestyle.

Paloma said, "The movie's about the absurdity of life along with the usual insanity of all Federico Fellini flicks."

Casper nodded, but he didn't really understand what Paloma was talking about as he had never seen a Federico Fellini movie. In fact, he realized that he had never seen a movie in which the actors spoke a language other than English. Not sure how to respond, he offered, "It sounds to me that you've seen a lot of foreign films. Will I have to read subtitles?"

"Yes, but don't worry, the movie's very visual."

Casper said, "Then you've already seen this film?"

"Yes, I have. During the years my daughter was going to college, she took me to many of the movie series that were shown on campus for the students. I'm happy that my daughter invited me. Each session we would see great films by Ingmar Bergman, Fellini, even Woody Allen."

Casper thought about his daughter's four years at UCLA. She never once invited him to a college film series, but he had a daytime job butchering and selling meat. "My daughter produces TV shows."

Paloma said, "Really? Would I know which one?"

"Actually, it's more than one show. She's the Potts of Potts and Panns Productions."

Paloma laughed. "I've seen some of her shows. In my case, my daughter is a Registered Nurse, and me, her mother cleans people's apartments. Your daughter is a big time TV producer and you . . Casper . . . I don't know what kind of work you did before you came to live at The Oaks."

For a fleeting moment Casper considered fabricating a tale about owning the meat market at The Farmers Market, but he wanted his relationship with Paloma to grow and lying to her now would be the same as spraying weed killer on a beautiful rose bush just before any of the buds had opened. "Paloma, I wasn't a lawyer, or a doctor, or anyone important. In fact, I never walked on a college campus until I attended my daughter's graduation ceremony at UCLA. I was just a journeyman meat cutter. I worked most of my life behind a counter selling ground meat, pork chops, or steaks. Then I'd weigh, wrap, and while I smiled at the customer, I'd ring up the sale. The truth of the matter is that if it wasn't for owning my mortgage free home, and my wife's life insurance, I wouldn't have been able to pay the entrance fee at The Oaks. As it is, I'm concerned about how much the monthly rental fee could increase each year."

279

Paloma laughed. "Do you think a retired meat cutter and a lady who cleans apartments can afford to go out to dinner and a movie?"

Now it was Casper's turn to laugh. "I'm sure we'll make it. Between my pension and what you earn, I feel confident we've got the bases covered."

Paloma frowned., "Bases covered?"

"I apologize. That's an old baseball idiom. Sorry I was late picking you up tonight. One of the ladies who lives at The Oaks cornered me and I had to drive her to some drug stores so she could buy—"

Paloma turned toward Casper, at least as far left as her shoulder harness would allow her to turn. "It sounds to me like you're talking about Miss von Thurn?"

"One of the same. Do you know her?"

"Of course I know her. I clean her apartment every week."

Casper hesitated. "Paloma, I know you can't tell me what's in her apartment, but I have driven her on several drug store runs and today she confided in me that she was making packages for our soldiers fighting in the Korean War. The Korean War ended more than fifty years ago."

There was a moment of silence, then Paloma said, "You can never tell anyone I told you this or I'll lose my job. That poor old lady has three closets filled with packages, floor to ceiling, but until now, I didn't know who, or what, the packages were for."

"Don't worry. After today's drive, I think she trusts me. Tomorrow some of us who live at The

280

Oaks will knock on her apartment door and offer to help her distribute the packages. We have armed forces all over the world and I'm sure we'll find someone out there who will enjoy the efforts of Miss von Thurn."

Paloma snuggled a little closer to Casper, and said, "You are a good man, Casper Potts, but changing the subject, I hope we're getting close to the restaurant at The Farmers Market. All this talk has made me hungry."

While driving to the movie theater, Casper said, "What did you think of dinner at Du-par's?"

Paloma, not wanting to dent Casper's ego, tempered her review. "The food was well prepared, just not as spicy as I am used to."

After the Fellini movie, the two were seated in a booth at Ghirardelli's in Hollywood. Paloma, after spooning up a dollop of whipped cream off the hot fudge, said, "So what was your take on the movie?"

Casper sat back. He hesitated because he didn't want to hurt Paloma's feelings, but between hearing the rapidly spoken Italian words and trying to read the subtitles, he had missed so much of what was going on that he truly didn't understand the story line. "I'm sorry, but I'm afraid I didn't comprehend what was happening most of the time. And the scenes jumped around so much that I couldn't get my arms around the plot. Tomorrow I'm going to call my daughter and ask her if she can tell me what I missed."

Paloma was disappointed that Casper had so much trouble reading the subtitles that he missed the reason she wanted him to see *La Dolce Vita*, the similarity of his life-style with the casserole ladies and the untrustworthy Marcello, the character who continued to have multiple affairs despite being engaged. She now realized that her attempted subtle approach wasn't going to work and she would have to eventually tell Casper that she couldn't bring herself to trust men. Once that was in the open, she feared her budding relationship with this man could be in jeopardy.

Chapter Thirty-two

Date—Numero Tres

Toward the end of their third date, after dinner at El Cholo's, and while driving from Hollywood to Boyle Heights, Casper noticed that Paloma had not spoken a word. Just after midnight, when he double parked his car next to her vehicle, he turned toward her and waited for what he had hoped to be an actual lip to lip goodnight kiss, and perhaps something more.

Paloma leaned forward, brushed his forehead with her warm lips, and said, "Thank you for the date."

Casper was both disappointed and puzzled at Paloma's sisterly peck on his forehead and the joy of his after-date-high vanished. Tentatively, he said, "I thought tonight was great. I hope you had as much fun on our third date as I did."

"The dinner was good. I food at *El Cholo's* was spicer than *Du-pars*, but the movie was not my style."

Casper chuckled, "I agree my movie pick was not the best, but at least I understood the language."

Paloma laughed, "I agree."

Then Casper said, "It's funny, after my taco lunch at Guisados, I never realized how tame the food was at *El Cholo's*."

Paloma responded, "It did lack some heat, but then I'm Mexican and I'm used to real Mexican food."

Casper laughed. "So except for the blah Mexican food, and the bad shoot 'em up movie, how was the rest of your date?"

Paloma said, "The hot fudge sundae was perfect, and so was the company."

"I guess one out of three isn't bad." Then Casper looked directly into her beautiful brown eyes. "Paloma, are we on for next week?"

Paloma hesitated. That would be their fourth date. After their second date, she had sat down with her Tia Consuelo and they had talked, and talked, and eventually, Paloma felt comfortable asking for advice from her elder.

Tia said, "*Pequeña*, I love talking with you, but you have to be more direct. What exactly do you want to know?"

"Tia, you are much wiser than me when it comes to the ways of the world. You tried to warn me about my first marriage. Now I've gone on a few dates with the man I met at Guisados. Do you recall him? The day you went with me?"

284

"Ah, the gringo. What can I do?"

"Do you remember how you tried to tell me that marrying Ramon was a mistake?"

"*El Bastardo?*" Tia pretended to spit on the ground. "*Gue se pudra en el infierno!*

Paloma said, "Don't worry. I'm sure he will rot in hell, but he's not the reason I'm asking for your advice."

"So what can I do to help my favorite niece?"

"A couple of weeks ago I started to date the gringo you met at Guisados."

"And?"

"Tia, I want to kiss him. I want to run my hands through his hair. I want to . . . I . . ."

Tia said, "You want to go to bed with him?"

Paloma nodded. "Exactly! How will I know if I'm doing the right thing?"

"*Pequeña*, one thing I have learned by living this long is that you must love your life. If this gringo is the man you want to live with the rest of your days, and he wants you, and if he is a gentleman, then follow your heart. You alone will know if, or when, the time is right."

"Thank you, Tia."

That was the moment when Paloma decided to wait until the fourth date. If she still felt the way she did now, and Casper remained a gentleman, then she would invite him to her apartment after the movie.

285

But her casual decision to wait until the conclusion of the fourth date nearly cost the eventual happiness of two lonely souls.

Casper's voice cut through her thoughts. "Earth to Paloma. I asked you if we are on for next week?"

"I'm not sure." Paloma hesitated. It was now or never! She looked into his eyes and said, "I told you that I had been married before."

"Yes, and that you gave birth to a daughter who will soon become a Registered Nurse. But what does that have to do with our next date?"

"Casper, after I became pregnant, the man I married abandoned me and never returned."

Casper jerked back as if he had just seen a snake. "Oh my God, you're not still married to him?"

"No, but I had to hire a lawyer and wait many years until the court would allow my divorce to become official."

Casper glanced around. He was double parked, but the street remained deserted so he asked, "Paloma, why was telling me about your ex-husband so important that—"

It was as if Paloma's dam of angst burst. "Because after Ramon left me I stopped trusting all men."

Casper said, "But that was your ex-husband. One man. Not all men!"

Tears streamed from Paloma's dark brown eyes. "I know that, but I hear from the other cleaning women all sorts of stories about those women who come to your apartment. And there's that board on your apartment door! Casper, I'm not sure I trust you."

"Paloma, what have I've done that would make you doubt me?"

"It's not what we have done during our dates, but my lack of trust is why I haven't kissed you. Or let you kiss me. Don't you understand? I will never allow another man to hurt me. "

For a moment, silence settled over the front seat of the car as Casper wasn't sure what to say next. To the best of his knowledge, he had never done anything to Paloma that would cause her to distrust him. "Paloma, I can't say I understand how you feel because I don't. Before we met, I trusted both my mother and my wife, the only two women in my life. They always did the right thing and they never let me down."

Paloma brushed away a tear before it tumbled off her cheek. "Then you are a very lucky man who has lived a very lucky life."

Casper sat up and gently placed his hands around Paloma's face. "I have an idea. Next Friday, we'll go on one more date. We'll go to a movie, and then get some hot fudge after. While we eat our ice cream, we'll play a little game where you can tell me all the bad things I've done to you."

Paloma frowned. "But you've never done any bad things to me."

He smiled. "Exactly. But just in case I have, we will eat our ice cream with hot fudge and you can try to find the Mr. Hyde lurking inside of me."

"Mr. Hyde?"

"I'm sorry. That's an old horror story about a good man named Doctor Jekyll who drank a potion he had concocted in his lab. The potion turned Doctor Jekyll into Mr. Hyde, a man who murdered innocent people."

Paloma shivered. "Casper, I know you would never do that."

Casper's heart jumped with joy. "Then it's settled. One week from today we'll go on our fourth date. I'll pick you up right here, outside of Guisados at six."

"No! I still have to settle things in my head. I'll clean your apartment next Wednesday. Just like I did before, I'll leave you a note on your kitchen table with my decision. And you have to promise me that if I say no to our fourth date, you will have to agree that I am a woman who will never be able to recover from my first mistake with Ramon."

"But Paloma, I . . . "

"No buts. Casper Potts, you have to accept the fact that it's possible that I will never regain my trust of men and that lack of trust will include all males."

The color drained from Casper's tan face. "I understand. But, be sure to put on the note where we will meet."

Paloma shook her head and opened her door. "See, you still don't understand. My note could say that our relationship is over."

For a long moment there was only the sound of the two breathing inside of Casper's car. Now a tear slipped down Casper's cheek. He opened his door, walked around the car, opened the passenger's door and offered Paloma his hand. "Paloma, regardless of your decision, I trust you will make the right one. Good night."

Fighting to slow her tears, Paloma said, "Thank you. Good night, Casper."

Chapter Thirty-three

Casper Seeks Advice

When Casper woke Saturday morning, he realized that the next four and a half days were going to pass by at an agonizingly slow pace.

It might seem even slower than the time he was five, some three days before Christmas, when Casper noticed his name on many of the packages his mother had carefully placed under the Christmas tree. As he started to pull the boxes out, his mother had admonished him that he must wait until Christmas morning to open them up.

Those days before Christmas had been the slowest three days of his young life, until this Saturday morning, more than fifty-years later.

As Casper stood in the hot shower, and as he considered all of the casserole ladies who had supped with him, he realized just how important Paloma had become to him.

While Casper shaved, he looked into the mirror and considered a possible new strategy with his potential paramour. The next time they met, he could look her in the eye and say, "Paloma, I want to spend the rest of my life with you."

As he finished the right side of his face, a second approach popped into his head. "Paloma, there are over four million people living in Los Angeles, and I don't how, or why, but against all the odds, we've found each other."

As Casper finished scraping off the whiskers from his upper lip, he came up with a third tactic. "Paloma, I'm not now, nor will I ever be, another Ramon. Just give me a chance."

Showered, shaved, and as ready as he will be to face the day, Casper headed downstairs to the dining room where, still lost in thought, his morning greeting to Julio was barely more that a perfunctory, "Morning,"

Julio glanced around to be sure Mr. Bradford wasn't lurking about, and then said, "Sound a little grouchy this morning, Casper. Have a bad night?"

Casper considered Julio's question. What had happened last night with Paloma was private, not something he would share with a stranger. But Julio was not a stranger. In fact, without him, Casper would have never even talked to Paloma.

"Julio. I'm going to confide in you a very personal situation, but you have to agree to keep our conversation confidential."

"Dude, after we hustled Mr. Stevenson's dead body into Bradford's office, I don't see why you'd think that anything you do, or say wouldn't be just between us. But if I spot Mr. Bradford, you'll understand why I'll have to split for a while."

"Split?"

"Sorry. Sometimes when I talk to you I forget I'm not shooting the bull with some of the other waitstaff. Split means I might have to leave, okay? Now go ahead. What's the scoop?"

"My relationship with Paloma has reached a critical point and I don't know what to do next."

Julio wanted to hear everything Casper had to say, but just then Mr. Bradford entered the dining room, glanced around the large, nearly empty space, and snapped his fingers. "Boy! Over here! A coffee refill is required at Mr. Furchak's table."

Julio raced across the room and filled Mr. Furchak's cup to the brim.

Mr. Bradford walked over to Casper's table and forced a superficial smile. "Ah, Mr. Potts, are you enjoying your breakfast today?"

"I was about to order when you took my waiter away."

The manager glanced at Mr. Furchak's table. "That boy?"

"Mr. Bradford, his name is Julio, and I believe I provided you with that information before."

"Ah yes! Julio! Mr. Potts, I'm sure you understand that with the large staff I have working under me here at The Oaks, there are just too many names to remember."

"But I'm sure you also understand that the morning waitstaff consists of only two men, Julio and Manuel. I'd like to think that you could remember the names of two employees, a simple task, not too large a challenge for a manager of your caliber." As the words tumbled out of his mouth, Casper was surprised at the uncharitable, off-putting comment he had just made to the General Manager. Not that Mr. Bradford didn't deserve his reprimand. It was just that, after living for a year at The Oaks, Casper had to admit that Mr. Bradford's unpleasant demeanor had finally gotten under his skin.

Mr. Bradford paused, as if considering a response to Casper, then he said, "Mr. Potts, I am available in my office should you need my assistance concerning any of the luxurious facilities available here at The Oaks." He spun around on his heels and walked out of the dining room.

Julio scurried back to Casper's table. "I don't know what you said, but you got rid of him. Now, what can I do to help?"

"As I said, my relationship with Paloma has reached a critical point and I don't know what to do next."

"What's the problem?"

"She doesn't trust me."

"Trust you? Casper, I don't know many dudes your age, but you're the most trustworthy one I know."

"Let me try to explain. Paloma was married many years ago and her husband deserted her and her baby daughter. Since then, it has been difficult for her to trust men, and seeing that I am a male, her lack of trust includes me."

Julio pulled out a chair, sat down, and poured himself a cup of coffee into an unused cup that graced Casper's table. "You know, I thought that once a dude reached your age, you know, a guy like you who's been around the block more than a couple of times, you would know how to handle a relationship problem like that."

Casper picked up Julio's coffee carafe and poured himself a second cup of coffee. "I guess you could say that my block was a pretty short one. The only woman I ever dated was my wife. Then we got married and we were together until she died."

"But what about all those casserole ladies?"

Casper was now faced with a true dilemma. Did he dare risk telling his friend why he invited the casserole ladies into his apartment? After a pause, Casper said, "Julio, what I am about to tell you must be placed into your mental safety deposit box, right next to how we moved Clint Stevenson's body after he died here in the dining room."

Julio's Hawaiian tan faded a couple of shades. "Jeez . . . okay, shoot!"

Casper sat up and moved closer to Julio. "Those ladies come to my apartment to share their casseroles. Nothing more than that."

"But you can get all the food you want. Three meals a day in this dining room."

"The reason I don't eat lunch or dinner in the dining room, and I share a large casserole with the women five times a week at The Oaks, is because of a bet I have with Mr. Bradford."

Julio started to say something then stopped, as the puzzled look in his eyes indicated to Casper that he had not been given enough information to ask an informed question.

"Julio, the first week I lived at The Oaks, I discovered that Mr. Bradford tracked and recorded all the food consumed each day, by everyone who eats in this dining room. He then took that information and determined just how much he should increase the monthly facility fee for each resident."

Julio jumped up, as if suddenly startled by a live rattlesnake. "And if you don't eat lunch or dinner in the dining room, he would reduce your monthly facility fee?"

"You've got it!"

Julio sat back and shook his head. "So your whole casserole scheme was a clever scheme to get free food?"

"Bingo again."

"Wow! You've got a giant pair of cojones! Okay, now I understand the casserole ladies. But I haven't lived long enough to tell you how to make Paloma trust you."

Casper's face flushed with a touch of frustration. He stood and pushed his coffee cup away. "Julio, could you talk to Paloma and convince her to go on a forth date with me?"

"Like I told you, Casper, I don't have enough experience to help you with Paloma. Now, sit back down and let me do my job. What do you want me to bring you for breakfast?"

Casper sighed. "Bring the usual."

He wasn't really mad at Julio, just disappointed to realize that he was no closer to solving his problem with Paloma than he was when he went to bed last night.

Chapter Thirty-four

Casper Seeks More Advice

After completing his usual gargantuan breakfast, Casper decided to get into his car and drive to the beach. During the long days following his wife's demise, he had used the bracing ocean air to help make up his mind concerning his life as a widower. He took the stairway to the underground garage and just as he reached his car, he noticed, for the first time a door at the far end of the large parking area with a sign over the entrance that proclaimed, MAINTENANCE, in large, bright white letters.

On the chance that his maintenance friend might be there, Casper knocked on the door.

It popped open and Mr. June stuck out his head.

"Potts! Do you have a maintenance problem in your apartment?"

"No maintenance trouble this time, Mr. June. I'm seeking some advice concerning a personal problem. May I come in?"

Mr. June snorted, "Hell yes. Come on in and take a load off."

As Casper entered the small room, Mr. June continued, "You've got a personal problem? That sounds a lot tougher than clearing a stopped up toilet, but I promise I'll listen carefully and do what I can."

"Thank you for your hospitality."

Mr. June said, "Are you up for a brew?"

"I'm afraid it's a little too early in the day for me to consider drinking a beer."

"Hey, down here in the maintenance room, beer's the breakfast of champions. Did you know that the Germans call beer liquid bread?"

"Again, no thank you. Do you have any coffee or tea?"

"Hell, we emptied the coffee pot hours ago. The only time a guy needs hot coffee is when he's sucking down a couple of those big, fat jelly doughnuts. The kind where you've got to bite down just right or some of that sticky red jelly will squirt out onto your shirt."

While Casper tried to picture a glob of colorful jelly shooting out of a doughnut and landing on his shirt, Mr. June continued. "But me and the guys finished off all the jelly doughnuts more than an hour ago. And Potts, not wanting to cast aspersions or anything, but me and the men that work on the

298

maintenance crew are real men, not a bunch of tea sucking wimps, so it's a beer or nothing."

As Mr. June concluded his attack on the integrity of the world's tea drinkers, Casper noticed a large white board with names, dates, and room numbers, mounted on the far wall.

"Mr. June, is that the scheduling board you previously told me about?"

Mr. June glanced over his shoulder and nodded. "Yup, that's it. Now, Potts, we need to get something straight about the fact that we occasionally drink beer down here. I know I offered you a beer, but the scoop that some members of the maintenance crew might suck down an occasional brewski during our working hours must never get back upstairs to Mr. Bradford, if you get my drift."

Not exactly sure what Mr. June's drift had to do with anything, or in fact, what Mr. June's drift was, Casper nodded, and said, "I understand, I think."

Mr. June walked over to a small refrigerator, opened it, reached behind a wall of brown paper bag lunches, and pulled out a can of Coors. He popped the tab, took a long swig, and said, "You sure you don't want one?"

Casper shook his head.

"Okay, Potts, time's a wasting. What's the personal problem?"

Casper explained to Mr. June how his suggestion to ask one of the Mexican waiters to set up a meeting with Paloma had led to their first meeting for lunch. Then, how that first meeting was followed by an actual date. Then, a second and third rendezvous. Mr. June listened intently as Casper described how his relationship with Paloma had reached the point where, at the end of their third date, she had told him about her failed marriage and her lack of trust in men.

"Potts, that's a great story, but I'm still not sure what you want from me."

"Mr. June, based on your vast life experiences, is there anything you can think of that would help me gain Paloma's trust?"

Mr. June drained his beer, opened the refrigerator door and extracted a second Coors. He popped the tab, took another long swig, wiped his mouth on his shirtsleeve, and said, "Potts, there isn't anything that goes wrong in this joint that I can't fix, and that means the heating, air-conditioning, plumbing, carpentry, painting, anything, but when it comes to dealing with the broads, I'm all thumbs. I'm sorry, Potts, but you've asked the wrong guy for advice about your love life. Hell, I've been married a bunch of times. Not one of them worked and I don't know why. In fact, now that I think about it, the last one used 'lack of trust' as one of her reasons for our divorce and to this day, I don't have a clue what the hell I did, or didn't do, to make her feel that way." As if totally exhausted by his personal confession, Mr. June dropped into a chair and momentarily concentrated on his beverage of choice.

Casper, sorry to see that he had caused his maintenance friend obvious distress, said, "Thank you, Mr. June. I'm leaving now for a drive to the beach."

"Need a brew to drown your sorrows while you sit on the sand?"

"No thank you. Goodbye."

"Hold on, Potts. I just got an idea. Have you talked with a broad about how to fix this lack of trust crap? In my experience, it's the babes that know all about that stuff."

Casper stopped with his hand on the doorknob. Of course! That was the ticket, but who should he ask? And how to form the question? Ask Izzy. She'll know what I should do. "Mr. June, you provided me with food for thought. Thank you again for giving me some of your valuable time."

"No problem." Mr. June paused to let a loud belch rumble past his lips. "Hey, that's what us maintenance guys are here for."

Chapter Thirty-five

Casper Keeps Looking For The Right Answer

Casper sprinted back upstairs, burst into his apartment, grabbed his phone, and punched in Izzy's number.

"Hello?"

"Izzy, could you come over to my apartment? I want to—"

"Lover boy, it's about time. I knew that sooner or later you'd get around to me. Just give me time to freshen up, I'll be there in five minutes."

"Slow down, Izzy, it's not like that. I just want to ask you a personal question."

"So it's still a no-go between us?"

"Izzy, I'm looking for a female perspective on a relationship problem I have."

"Oh!"

Casper listened to his phone. Until this exact moment in time, it had never dawned on him that a man should never ask a woman's view concerning a relationship problem with another female. As he realized his massive mistake, he listened for a click to indicate that Izzy had hung up. Puzzled, he asked, "Izzy? Are you still there?"

Silence ensued for a few seconds before he heard Izzy sigh.

"I could meet you in the computer room in five minutes. It's a public place and usually empty."

Four minutes later, Casper was sitting in a chair that faced one of the six computer terminals when Izzy entered the room. She had been right. Except for the two of them, the room was empty.

Izzy sat down, turned her chair to face him, and said, "Let's get one thing straight before we discuss anything. Did I upset you in anyway, or do anything wrong?"

"Izzy, I'm confused. Why would you think you did something wrong?"

"Casper, when I heard your voice on the phone, I was hoping you'd finally come around. You finally figured out that you wanted to develop a relationship with me. Then you asked me for a female perspective on a relationship problem. That meant you had another woman. Frankly, for a moment, I considered telling you to go to hell. But then I remembered just how unworldly you are. You're like the twelve year old boy who has never kissed a girl. I decided you just don't comprehend that a man should never pose a question like that to another woman."

"Izzy, I didn't—"

"That's what I just said. You didn't know. I got over my anger and here we are. So what's the question?"

Casper pondered if he should continue. It was now obvious, even to him, that he had hurt his friend in a way that he didn't understand.

"Come on, I'm tougher than I look. What's your problem?"

Casper explained his first meeting with Paloma, then their date, followed by two more dates.

Izzy interrupted, "It sounds to me like you've got a good thing going. We all should have your kind of problem."

"Izzy, here's my dilemma. Twenty years ago, Paloma was married and her husband abandoned her and their child. In a few words, for what he did to her, she doesn't trust men. All men! And that includes me! Is there anything you can think of that could help me gain her trust?"

Izzy sat back and tears came to her eyes. "I'm sorry, but I was married for thirty years to the most trustworthy man on the earth and your question reminded me just how much I miss him."

"I apologize for—"

"Hey, don't apologize for reminding me how much my husband made me happy. But therein lies the rub. I can't help you because I never had to rebuild the trust in our marriage because I trusted Timor, and he trusted me."

Casper stood, beckoned to Izzy to stand up. She did. Casper reached out. She moved between his arms and he gently hugged her. "Izzy, thank you for being my only female friend here at The Oaks."

She gave Casper a playful punch in his ribs. "You're welcome. And if this thing between you and Paloma ever hits a snag, just give me a call. I still think you could do with a second shot at my world famous Chicken Paprikash with Dumplings!"

Chapter Thirty-six

A Catastrophe Befalls Casper

During the days following his meeting with Izzy, Casper began to realize how few true friendships he'd made during the year he had lived at The Oaks.

There was Julio, the young man who served his breakfast each morning and had helped him transport Clint Sullivan's body to Mr. Bradford's office.

There was Mr. June, the maintenance man who had built the two scheduling boards for his front door, and had offered Casper a beer.

There was Izzy, the woman who had served him his first casserole and who had stuck by him through thick and thin.

There was Clint Sullivan, the man who had invited him to his weekly Texas Hold 'em game.

Then Casper considered for a moment each of the women who had shared with him her life story along with her favorite casserole and he was ashamed to admit, that except for the seductive Delilah Madison, after the second month of casseroles, all of the women's faces, and their carefully prepared dishes, had coalesced into an indistinguishable mass of femininity and food.

Then there were those persons that he learned to avoid as he wandered the expansive facility at The Oaks.

There was Miss von Thurn, the crazy woman who would force Casper to drive her to drug stores.

There was James Stately, the man he had to remind himself not to ask how he felt.

And finally, there was Mr. Bradford, the manager who lurked around The Oaks as if he was sure the people who lived there had just been paroled from prison and required constant monitoring.

To put it simply, with the exception of his chance encounter with Paloma, Casper was beginning to question his resolve to move to The Oaks.

A few days later, the day of decision had arrived. Casper, nervous to the point of feeling ill, decided to skip breakfast and made himself a cup of tea.

After his second cup of tea, he ingested two slightly stale fig newton cookies he discovered next to the container of tea bags, and Casper's unsettled stomach improved. It was not as good as normal, but strong enough that he decided to attend the

Senior Strength Class to pass the remaining hours until Paloma left her note.

However, Casper's concentration was so intent on his future life with Paloma, he didn't spot James Stately who was seated in Clint Sullivan's old chair. Unwilling to endure the endless invectives James Stately would hurl against The Oaks, the city of Los Angeles, the state of California, the United States of America, and the world in general, Casper spun around and walked up the stairs to his apartment. As each step brought him closer to his front door, his mind and heart raced as he considered the possibilities in Paloma's note.

What would he do if her note declared their relationship was over?

What would he do if she said they would go on a fourth date?

Once Casper reached his apartment door, he stopped and took a deep breath. Paloma's message had the power to provide him with an extraordinary life, or to turn his remaining years into an unmitigated disaster. He slipped his key into the lock, hesitated for a moment, and opened the door.

He tentatively stepped inside, expecting to pick up the fragrance of Paloma's perfume lingering in the air.

But his olfactory senses detected nothing.

He called her name. "Paloma?"

No answer.

An uneasy feeling settled over him as he saw there was no note on his kitchen counter.

He ran out of his apartment into the hall and took a sniff.

Again no hint of Paloma's perfume.

He moved to the apartment next to his and carefully placed his ear on the door where he heard the whine of a vacuum cleaner.

She's here! He smiled as he decided that Paloma must have forgotten to leave the note.

Casper knocked loudly, knowing that the vacuum cleaner noise could overwhelm his rapping.

The door opened and a woman he had never seen before said, "Yes?"

The woman was wearing a blue uniform with a large, bright orange Spotless Cleaners logo near her breast pocket.

Casper said, "Excuse me, I was looking for Paloma."

"Sorry, Bud. Can't help you there. Don't know anyone named Paloma."

"But each Wednesday she cleans my apartment."

"Gotcha now. I guess nobody told you what's going on, so here's the skinny. This week The Oaks signed a contract with my company, Spotless Cleaners." She pointed at the bright orange S/C logo on her chest. "And we all started work today. Check your calendar. It's the first day of the month, right? Did your friend work directly for The Oaks, or did she work for an outside company like I do?"

A tiny portion of Casper's brain was trying to come up with a coherent response to the woman's question, while the major section was bordering on panic! He just remembered that he did not have Paloma's address, nor her telephone number. Without meeting her at The Oaks, or outside Quisados, he had no way of contacting her. It took all his will power to answer, "Yes, Paloma worked directly for The Oaks and she cleaned my apartment each week. Sorry to bother you."

Casper turned and raced down the stairs to Mr. Bradford's office.

By the time he reached the manager's door, he was gasping for air.

He took a moment to catch his breath, then he gave the door a cursory knock and burst in.

A man Casper did not recognize was seated behind Mr. Bradford's desk. The man looked up from a stack of printouts, frowned, and said, "Sir, I'm not used to people bursting into my office unannounced. May I help you?"

"Where's Mr. Bradford? And why are you sitting in his office at his desk?"

The man occupying Mr. Bradford's chair snapped, "Sir, I will respond to your questions after you introduce yourself."

Casper stared into the cold, blue eyes of the unknown male sitting in the office of his old adversary. The man's chiseled features looked as if they had been copied off a Marine recruitment poster. He had dark short hair with just a few wisps of gray in his sideburns.

Casper closed his mouth long enough to generate a sufficient amount of saliva to loosen his tongue that was stuck to the roof of his mouth. "Please excuse my ungentlemanly abruptness. My name is Casper Potts. I've been a resident at The Oaks for more than a year. Now, where's Mr. Bradford?"

"Mr. Potts, my name is Charles Mendenhall, and I am the new General Manager at The Oaks."

"Mr. Bradford is gone? But I just talked with him a few days ago and he didn't mention anything about being replaced by a new General Manager."

"One could say the change in General Managers was rather abrupt." Mr. Mendenhall frowned. "What did you say your name was?"

"Potts. Casper Potts. But my name has nothing to do with my need to talk with Mr. Bradford."

"Mr. Potts, as you are a resident here, and I'm the General Manager, any complaints or questions you needed to discuss with Mr. Bradford should now be directed to me."

"Okay, here it goes. Mr. Mendenhall, what the hell did you just do with my cleaning lady?"

"Just do? Mr. Potts, I don't have any idea what you are talking about."

"Did you fire all the in-house cleaning staff and replace them with an outside cleaning service?"

"Ah, now I understand. Yes, I laid off the in-house cleaning staff. The Spotless Cleaners Company will save the corporation more than a hundred thousand dollars to the bottom line over the next five years. Do you have any idea how much we paid the in-house cleaning staff in benefits alone?"

Before Casper could respond, Mr. Mendenhall continued. "Mr. Potts, I'm curious. Why is it so important to you who cleans your apartment?"

Casper, still stunned by the unexpected turn of events, said, "Um . . . after a year, and without any notice to the residents here at The Oaks, the change seemed very abrupt. Who cleans my room is not really important . . . I guess."

"You guess?" Then, as if a light suddenly switched on, Mr. Mendenhall leaned forward, "Is it possible that you had developed some sort of a relationship with your cleaning lady? Don't worry, that sort of thing happens more often than you'd think. At the last facility I was assigned me to turn around that problem was rampant. But I nipped that situation in the bud by bringing in outside people. I find it good policy to mix things up on a regular basis. Don't you agree?"

Casper forced a smile through his panic. "Mr. Mendenhall, I'd like to assume that we can act like two gentlemen."

The man behind the desk nodded. "I agree."

"Then provide me with the address and phone number for a former employee of The Oaks, Paloma Franco!"

"Mr. Potts, I'm afraid I cannot do that. To give you that sort of information is against corporate policy. Now, your name Potts rings a bell." He quickly shuffled through a stack of papers on the desk. "Ah, here it is."

As Mr. Mendenhall's eyes scanned the paper, Casper took the moment to size up his new adversary. He was well dressed in a suit and tie. His age landed somewhere between forty-five and fifty-five with short cropped hair, and a strong, square jaw. Based on appearance alone, Mr. Mendenhall looked to be a much more formidable opponent than Mr. Bradford.

Mr. Mendenhall set down the paper he had been reading. "Oh my God! Potts, you're the guy with that weird schedule board on his door. Bradford called you the casserole guy. Don't tell me that, with all the women who brought food to you each day, you had the proclivity, the time and the energy, to develop a separate relationship with your cleaning lady?"

"Mr. Mendenhall, what I do during my personal time has nothing to do with you, or your corporation. Now, if you'll excuse me, I have to take care of a few items—"

"Mr. Potts, before you leave, I have one more piece of news to pass on. During a quick audit of the books, I noted a mistake had been made concerning your monthly facility fee. You see, effective today, the corporation increased everyone's monthly facility fee by fifteen percent. In your case, there must have been some sort of computer error because your present monthly facility fee of $3,750 was decreased by fifteen percent. You'll be happy to note, however, that I caught the error and your monthly fee will now be $4,312.50 instead of the erroneous number of $3,187.50 you previously received.

"Mr. Mendenhall, from one gentleman to another, I will happily pay your exorbitant facility fee once you provide me with the address and phone number of Paloma Franco."

Mendenhall and Potts locked eyes, and to Casper's surprise, Mendenhall blinked first.

"Mr. Potts, I will take your request for information under consideration and I will personally contact you if and when I receive the go-ahead from corporate headquarters. Now, if we have nothing else to discuss, I have many papers to go through."

"I understand, Mr. Mendenhall. Until next time."

Chapter Thirty-seven

Will Casper's Life At The Oaks Ever Be The Same?

The following morning, Casper walked into the dining room for his breakfast. He sat down in his usual chair, at his usual table, and, as usual, Julio appeared with a pot filled with . . . oh my God! . . . the man filling his cup with coffee was not Julio!

Casper jumped up and cried, "Where's Julio?"

The man said, "I'm sorry. I don't know anyone named Julio. My name is Frank and I'm your waiter. What can I bring you for breakfast?"

"Frank, it's nothing personal, but my waiter for the past twelve months has been a young man named Julio. I demand to know where he is."

"I'm sorry, Mr. . . . what is your name?"

"Casper Potts."

Frank pulled out a note pad from his back pocket, scanned a page, then a second. "Ah, here you are, Mr. Potts. First I had to check to be sure you are a guest of The Oaks. I would be happy to take your breakfast order."

"Not until you tell me what happened to my favorite waiter, Julio!"

"I don't know, Mr. Potts. I can get the manager, Mr. Mendenhall. I'm sure he'll be able to answer your question. Would you care to order now?"

"No thank you, Frank." Casper sat back down. "You go offer Mr. Furchak more coffee."

"Good idea. I'll be right back to take your order."

While Casper watched the new waiter pour some hot coffee into Mr. Furchak's cup, he considered how much he would miss his young Hawaiian friend. He was still thinking when Mr. Mendenhall entered the dining room. He glanced around and walked over to Casper's table.

"Mr. Potts."

"Mr. Mendenhall."

"Mr. Potts, is the dining room always this empty at this time of morning?"

"Empty? I'm here and so is Mr. Furchak. " Casper shrugged. "Why is the population of the dining room suddenly important?"

"Because I can't afford to have my wait staff standing around empty tables."

Growing madder and bolder by the second, Casper said, "And what would be your solution to this monumental problem?"

"Open the dining room doors for breakfast at 7:30, or perhaps as late as 8:00."

Casper, who normally didn't express a contentious comment, was warming to the task. He stood and faced his adversary. "And what about Mr.

316

Furchak, and myself? Obviously, we both like to eat our breakfast early."

"Mr. Potts, I have to—"

"Mr. Mendenhall, when I moved into The Oaks a little more than a year ago, it was my understanding that the staff at The Oaks was here to serve the guests, not the other way around."

"Mr. Potts, I've only been here a few days, and I —"

"Mr. Mendenhall, I don't care how long you've been here! Now, what have you done with my favorite waiter, Julio?"

The manager took a step back from Casper and his lips took on an evil twist. "My goodness, Mr. Potts. First you have a favorite cleaning lady, and now a favorite waiter. Do you have any other favorites here at The Oaks?"

"Now that you mention it, yes. Miss Zeiss, the lady that runs the Senior Strength Class."

Mr. Mendenhall frowned. "I'm sorry to inform you, Mr Potts, but I have suspended the Senior Strength Class until further notice. We offer a wonderful gym room with state-of-the-art equipment that I'm sure will more than take the place of that silly little exercise session."

"Mr. Mendenhall, those 'silly little exercise sessions', as you called them, are important to many of us here at The Oaks. A large group of seniors of various physical abilities were brought together and Miss Zeiss knew how to get the most out of each of her participants. Now, why have you stopped the thrice weekly Senior Strength Class?"

"It should be obvious by now. It's the cost. We had to pay Miss Zeiss a monthly stipend, and as I previously stated, The Oaks has provided state-of-the-art exercise equipment in the gym for your use, without further cost. You don't seem to understand . . ." As Casper listened to Mr. Mendenhall drone on, his anger mounted and the memory of Casper's initial meeting with Mr. Bradford filled his thoughts.

"Mr. Mendenhall!" Casper interrupted as he moved so close that the two men's belt buckles were dangerously close to striking.

"Mr. Potts, I was attempting to explain to you why—"

"Mr. Mendenhall, I'm not the least bit interested in your convoluted explanations as to why you are cutting staff." Casper turned and called out, "Frank, get Mr. Mendenhall a cup of coffee, but first, inform the kitchen that this morning I want a special order of loco moco, six strips of crisp bacon, two pieces of sourdough bread with a light toast, butter, and a large serving of the imported cherry preserves."

Mr. Mendenhall's mouth dropped open. "Mr. Potts, we have a breakfast menu at The Oaks that the kitchen must follow. You can't go about ordering what you want. Frank, what's on today's menu for Mr. Potts?"

Frank, beginning to feel like a tennis ball during the fifth set of a long match, pulled out his note pad, flipped a page, and read, "Today is Thursday. Mr. Potts, you can order a soft boiled egg, or two eggs, fried sunny side up, or oatmeal with brown sugar, or your choice of dry cereal."

Casper said, "Frank, I gave you my order. Now go into the kitchen and tell them what I want for breakfast."

Frank hesitated for a moment, glanced at both men, and then said, "I'll do that right now, Mr. Potts." He turned and rushed out of the dining room.

Mr. Mendenhall shook his head. "I hope you're proud of yourself, Mr. Potts, you have caused that young man to lose his job."

For a brief moment, Casper considered his response, his usual polite, gentlemanly reply that would fit the moment. But then, a sudden, unexpected, and uncontrollable surge of testosterone raced through him as he realized that his opponent was incapable of acting like a gentleman, nor was he a decent human being. Casper now understood that he and Mr. Mendenhall were about to engage in an old fashioned verbal jousting match with Mendenhall wearing the villain's menacing dark armor while Casper, the hero, would be encased in shining bright protective metal. Through the slits in his face mask he would see his prize, the lovely Paloma waving an embroidered handkerchief in his direction as a token of her love.

As Casper realized that this moment was why he had been born a little more than sixty years ago in Anaheim, he faced his adversary, about to engage in a battle to the death for the hand of his beloved.

He squared his shoulders and looked Mr. Mendenhall directly in the eye. From that moment on, Casper was in a struggle to the end and he vowed he would give no quarter. With a level of conviction he had never felt before, Casper said, "While Frank is in the kitchen placing my order of loco moco with the chef, we will have a few moments alone. I believe just enough time to have a little talk."

Frank walked back into the dining room, stopped, looked at the two combatants about to do battle, turned and scampered away.

Casper stared directly into the steely-blue eyes of his opponent. "Mr. Mendenhall, your decision to lay off the core of The Oaks' employees, the very people who made this place endurable, has forced my hand. A year ago, I discovered, unknown to the other guests who live here, that the Oaks management was secretly monitoring the food intake of each guest. And that the cost of the food consumed by each guest, in excess of management's arbitrary baseline, was added to their annual rent increase."

Mr. Mendenhall's eyes widened to the point that they nearly popped out of their sockets. His whole body shuddered. "Potts, how did you access my office computer?"

Casper cut him off. "For once in your life, sit down, shut up, and listen!"

Like air escaping slowly from a balloon, the new General Manager dropped onto a dining room chair while his right eyebrow began to spasmodically twitch.

Casper stared down at his seated foe. "Mr. Mendenhall, last year I told Mr. Bradford that I would expose your secret food monitoring scheme to a local television investigative reporter." Casper paused to allow the magnitude of his threat time to sink in. "I'm talking about the local TV station with that investigative reporter who will broadcast the facts, night after night, until all the shocking details are made public."

Mr. Mendenhall's lower lip began to quiver.

"I see you are aware of the investigative reporter I am talking about."

"Look, Potts, I—"

"I have not finished!" snapped Casper. "I have four demands and they all must be met within forty-eight hours or I will contact the local television station. Do you want to hear my demands, or watch the eleven o'clock nightly news cast destroy The Oaks' reputation?"

Mr. Mendenhall's shoulders slumped, indicating to Casper he was on the right track. "Go ahead, Potts. What are your demands?"

"I recommend you write them down. You wouldn't want this thing to blow up in your face just because you forgot one of the four."

Mr. Mendenhall pulled out a note pad and pen from his inside jacket pocket. "I'm ready."

"Number one. I demand the address and phone number of Paloma Franco."

"Giving you her address concerns me. How do I know you are not a stalker? I will only provide you with her phone number. What's next, Potts?"

"Number two. As I will be leaving The Oaks, under less than desirable conditions, The Oaks must return one hundred percent of my entrance fee."

"But you know the rules. I can't—"

"Au contraire, Mr. Mendenhall, I have the feeling you can do whatever you need to do as long as the occupancy rate remains above the corporate target. So to assist you with that problem, I will continue to reside at The Oaks until you are able to find someone to occupy my apartment.

"Number three. You will hire back all of the former cleaning and wait staff with a five percent increase in their salary and a reinstatement of all benefits to full time employees."

Mr. Mendenhall closed his notepad and pushed his chair away from the table. "Mr. Potts, I'm afraid you've gone—"

"Remain seated! Number four. You must immediately reinstate the Senior Strength Class under the guidance of Miss Zeiss."

The skin on Mr. Mendenhall's cheeks started to glow red and his right eyebrow began to twitch faster. He thought it was obvious to everyone at The Oaks, including this casserole character, that the corporate Vice President had sent him to The Oaks to take over the helm of a truly troubled ship about to crash against the rocky shore. Now he finds himself in a battle for his career.

But with years of managerial experience had told him when to hold them and when to fold them. The general manager stood and backed away from Casper. "Mr. Potts, as I stated earlier, I will give you the phone number before you finish your breakfast. As to your other demands, I'm afraid that —"

Casper moved closer and again the two men were standing inches apart, mano a mano. "Mr. Mendenhall, face reality. I have left you no alternative but to capitulate."

"Never! I'm not that weak sister you had previously dealt with. This time you have a real fight on—"

The door from the kitchen burst open and the verbal combat stopped. Frank entered the dining room with a tray full of Casper's precise order—loco moco, six strips of crisp bacon, two pieces of sourdough toast, and a large serving of imported cherry preserves.

After he served Casper's breakfast, Frank said, "Would you care for more coffee, Mr. Mendenhall?"

His nose flaring with each breath, he cried, "No, damn it!"

Casper's heart was pounding so hard that he thought he might break a rib, but his expression remained stoically calm and collected. "Now, Mr. Mendenhall, there's no reason to take out your frustration on Frank."

"Damn it, Potts. I . . ." Mendenhall glanced at Frank who stood a few feet away with carafe in hand.

Casper said, "Thank you, Frank, I'd love more hot coffee, but I fear that Mr. Mendenhall will be too busy completing his new morning assignments to partake in a second cup." Casper returned to his seat at the table, placed his fresh linen napkin on his lap and nodded at Frank to pour his coffee.

Before Frank could pour some coffee into Casper's cup, Mr. Mendenhall, his right eyebrow now furiously quivering, growled, "Potts, if you'll excuse me, I have some pressing business."

Mendenhall slipped his note pad into his jacket pocket, and obviously struggling hard to control his anger, said, "As I previously stated, I'll have that phone number you requested before you finish breakfast. Concerning the other items, I will keep you informed as to their progress."

"Thank you, Mr. Mendenhall. I never had a doubt that we would come to an amicable agreement. I look forward to the results of your efforts on my behalf. Frank, after Mr. Mendenhall leaves and you have made sure that Mr Furchak's coffee cup is full, come back and sit down next to me. I want to learn more about you. Are you a student?"

Mr. Mendenhall having been summarily dismissed, turned and stormed from the dining room. Once he had disappeared into the hallway, Frank sat down and said, "No. Last year I graduated from UCLA's School of Theater, Film, and Television."

"My boy, that sounds very exciting. Are you an actor?"

"Yes, I am. I took this job because my afternoons will be free so I can audition for TV shows."

Casper was pretty sure he'd never see Julio again, but his old friend had been replaced with a bright, young man, eager to learn and just starting his life. "Frank, this afternoon you might want to head over to the offices of Potts and Panns Production. Tell the lady at the front desk that Casper sent you. My daughter is—"

Frank's eyes widened. "Oh my God, your daughter is the Potts of Potts and Panns. He thrust his hand in Casper's direction. "Thank you. This just might be the break I'm looking for."

"No problem. And Frank, please give the chef my compliments on the loco moco. As usual, my breakfast looks outstanding!"

Chapter Thirty-eight

The Fourth Date

As Casper waited for the promised phone number, he forced himself to remain calm and to do his best to enjoy breakfast. About the time he was buttering his sourdough toast, Frank walked into the dining room holding a piece paper in his hand.

He handed it to Casper and asked, "More coffee?"

Casper pushed his chair away from the table and started toward the entrance to the dining room. "No thank you, Frank, and I'm finished with my breakfast."

While Casper walked down the hall in the direction of the stairway, he heard Frank call, "Did you want your last piece of toast?"

Normally, the polite Casper would have responded to Frank's question, but he held his future happiness in his hand and that was all he could think about at that moment. He sprinted up the stairs, opened his apartment door and ran to his phone.

After keying in her number, he heard one ring, then two. Casper was about to burst when the ringing stopped and he heard Paloma's voice. "Hello?"

"Paloma, it's me, Casper. I just found out that you were fired and I didn't know how to find you."

"Obviously, you found my telephone number. How are you?"

"Not good. I walked into my apartment to read your note and there wasn't a note. Paloma, I nearly cried. Please, just tell me over the phone that we're still going on a date tomorrow. That news will make me the happiest man on earth."

Paloma hesitated for a moment to be sure she could talk through her tears. "Yes, Casper, if you still want to date an out of work cleaning lady, you can come to my apartment for dinner and if you want to see a movie later, that sounds good to me. Will that work for you?"

Casper's heart skipped a beat. She invited him to her apartment. That meant she finally trusts him! Overjoyed with Paloma's invitation to her home, he nearly yelled the words into his phone, "I'll be there at six and I'll bring a bottle of wine. Would you prefer red or white?"

"Make it a red. I'm going to fix you a real Mexican dinner, but don't worry, I'll give it the gringo touch. See you tomorrow evening."

"Wait! Don't hang up, I don't have your address."

After Paloma recited her address to Casper, he said, "I'll be counting the hours, and thank you."

The following evening, in Paloma's modest apartment located in Boyle Heights, Casper and his hostess sat down for dinner.

She started her sumptuous meal with a delicious Albondigas soup that contained beef stock, sautéed onions, garlic, cumin, tomatoes and meatballs made from ground beef with a hint of fresh oregano.

The first course was followed by Green Chile Chicken Casserole. As promised, Paloma had substituted Anaheim and poblano chilies in place of her usual roasted New Mexico Hatch peppers, an ingredient that could have had as much as four times the heat of Anaheim and poblano chilies—far too hot for her gringo date.

For dessert, Paloma served Casper a creamy flan with a drizzle of caramel sauce.

As the last bite of flan slipped down Casper's throat, he realized that Paloma, along with her Green Chili Chicken Casserole, had won his heart. He took a sip of wine to build up his courage, and said, "Paloma, I knew you were a wonderful person and a delightful date, but I never knew that you were a great cook."

She laughed, "My auntie told me that the way to a man's heart is through his stomach."

"She was right. Paloma, I know that my next question might catch you a little off-guard . . . will you marry me?"

Now it was Paloma's turn to take a sip of wine, but it was more like a gulp. She whispered, "Yes."

As tears streamed down her face, she jumped up, ran around the table, kissed Casper, and said, "In case you didn't hear my answer, YES! YES! YES! I want to become Paloma Potts."

Then Paloma took Casper's hand and led him down the hall toward her bedroom. "I hope you don't mind, but we can see a movie next week."

The next day, Paloma called her daughter and younger brother, Carlo. She told them the great news about her pending wedding and asked them if they would both be willing to 'give the bride away'. Of course, they said yes.

Paloma's Tia Consuelo agreed to help. The elderly woman, moving quicker than she had done during her last thirty years, checked various venues in the Boyle Heights neighborhood and discovered that the Community Center Annex was available and she immediately rushed to the annex with a deposit to lock in the wedding date.

That same day, back at The Oaks, Casper called his daughter, and gave her the news of his coming wedding. She was excited for him, his soon to be new bride, and offered to be her father's 'best man'.

On the Monday after Casper's proposal, and four days before the wedding, Mr. Mendenhall knocked on Casper's door, handed him a check for one hundred percent of Casper's entrance fee, and departed without a word.

An excited Casper called Paloma. "Mendenhall just handed me a check for my total entrance fee."

Paloma wanted to ask Casper how much the check was for but decided that he might consider her question inappropriate. She said, "Does that mean you can move out of The Oaks?"

"I could, but where would I stay?"

Paloma said, "I know my apartment is small, but until we find a bigger place, you could move in with me."

"I was hoping you'd say that," said Casper.

"One problem, if you move in with me now, what would happen to all that furniture I dusted so diligently for a year?"

Casper laughed. "My sweet, I was just handed a check for $750,000. We'll cross that bridge when we come to it."

The thought of three-quarters of a million dollars momentarily stunned Paloma. After a moment to collect herself, she said, "But Casper, that's your money!"

"Sweetheart, from the moment you said you would marry me, my money became our money."

"But—"

"No buts. You've made me the happiest man in the world. The kind of happiness that money can't buy."

Paloma hesitated, then said, "Okay, I give up, but first we have to find a place to live. Are you locked into a neighborhood?"

"Where you live, Boyle Heights, sounds great to me, but with one caveat. Please don't ask me to live in a place that only allows seniors. I want our home to be in a neighborhood mixed with seniors, working people, and families with children."

Paloma smiled. "I didn't know that you were so fond of children."

"Paloma, on Halloween night, I want to answer the front door and hand out candy to the little neighborhood kids in their costumes."

"Casper Potts, every day you surprise me."

"Thank you. Now get ready. If the traffic is light, I'll be knocking on your door in forty-five minutes and we can go look for a place to live."

The moment Paloma and Casper's call ended, she got on her phone and called a friend who was a real estate agent. The couple's search for a house or apartment in the Boyle Heights area had begun.

The first day most of the single family homes, and apartments they looked at were too big, or too old, or in need of too much renovation. The second day, and third day had the same results. Casper was growing a little frustrated at their lack of success but on the forth day, they got lucky. The agent took them to a brand new duplex a few blocks North of E. Cezar Chaves Avenue. After a quick inspection of the single story, two bedroom apartment, Casper smiled and turned toward Paloma, "I like it. Lots of room in the living area. Both bedrooms are good size. What do you think?"

She responded, "As you said, all the rooms are spacious. The kitchen has lots of cabinets, and I've never lived in an apartment with a kitchen island."

Casper said, "And how about those beautiful quartz counter tops!"

Paloma gave him a hug. "And I love the patio with our private garden. I can see a new grill sitting under the tree where we can cook steaks and vegetables in the summer. I want to move in tomorrow."

Casper said, "That's all I needed to hear."

On the quartz counter top Casper and Paloma signed a twelve month lease, and the agent handed each a set of keys.

An hour later Casper and Paloma returned to her apartment where Casper said, "We need to break out a bottle of champagne."

Paloma said, "Not before we have made an important decision."

"Decision about what?"

"In a few days, we're going to move into a very nice two bedroom apartment with two households of furniture."

Once the word furniture rolled past Paloma's lips, Casper said, "I think I understand what's bothering you needn't worry. All we have to do is walk through both of our apartments with a note pad and jot down which couch, chair, table, and lamp we want to keep. Or, we can splurge and buy all new furniture for our new life."

Paloma's heart skipped a beat. She was uncomfortable about spending that much money on furniture when she knew what they owned was serviceable. "Casper, I"m not sure if I'm ready to spend—"

"Sweetheart, we're starting a brand new life in a brand-new duplex with brand new neighbors."

Paloma said, "I know, but—"

Casper took her in his arms. "Paloma, we don't have to worry about money. We won't be rich, just very well off. We'll have my pension from the union. Next year I can apply for Social Security. And don't forget the $750,000 entrance fee I got back from The Oaks. If we invested that at—"

"At three and a half percent interest we would receive $26,250 a year."

Casper chuckled. "Ah ha! Besides falling in love with the best looking fiancé in Los Angeles, I'm marrying a money management maven."

"Don't make fun of me. As a single parent I had to learn how to live within my limited income!"

"I was only kidding. So have we solved our first kerfuffle?"

"Kerfuffle?"

"A kerfuffle is not really an argument. More like a conflict of views."

"Yes! No more kerfuffle. We're going to buy new furniture."

And the two spent the rest of their day shopping for new furniture.

That evening, Casper and Paloma called their daughters, explained they would be moving into their new apartment and offered them any furniture they would like to keep before the rest would be donated to the Salvation Army. They also asked them if the daughters would agree to meet with Salvation Army at the two pick-up locations while they were on their honeymoon in Hawaii. The daughters agreed and Casper and Paloma's first kerfuffle was resolved.

Two days later, after receiving permission from the local bishop, Casper and Paloma were married by a local priest at the Community Center annex. In addition to their families, their vows were witnessed by Izzy, Mr. June, and Miss Zeiss.

Soon after the couple returned from a week in Hawaii, Paloma discovered that Casper had no concept of how anything worked in the kitchen. She suggested the two take a series of cooking classes at the Boyle Heights Senior Center.

After a few months into the classes, and as Casper became more confident, he would select one of Paloma's recipes, drive to the local supermarket, buy all the ingredients, then go home to cook that night's dinner. Within a year, Casper's culinary talents had reached the point where he cooked most of the couple's breakfasts and an occasional dinner.

The couple continued their two times-a-week dinner out routine, but at Paloma's suggestion, they swapped restaurants for their Mexican night from El Cholo's to Quisados.

Paloma, out of her love for Casper, recommended they return to Du-pars every few months so her husband would be able to return to the Farmers Market for a bit of nostalgia. On the nights they skipped Du-pars, they sampled Thai, Lebanese, Peruvian, Sushi, and threw in an occasional hamburger as long as the hamburger was, to quote Casper, so juicy that the sandwich would be difficult to pick up.

So there it is. The tale of Casper Potts and how he struggled through a year's worth of casseroles, designing and building two scheduling boards, inept and overbearing managers, grouchy and looney members of the Oaks family, and Anglo and Latino angst, to find his true soulmate out of the giant melting pot of more than 4,000,000 people of all ages, colors, sizes and shapes who populate in the Los Angeles basin.

Casper and Paloma's declaration love for each other, and marriage goes to prove what Maya Angelou once wrote, 'Love recognizes no barriers. It jumps hurdles, leaps fences, penetrates walls to arrive at its destination full of hope.'

Epilogue

Read on and find out what happened to the rest of the characters that played a major influence on Casper's life during his thirteen month stay as a member of The Oaks family.

Mr. Bradford

Mr. Bradford, his managerial incompetence now obvious to everyone at corporate headquarters, was transferred to a small satellite office located in Sacramento, California, where he had little to do. The reason for his sudden move was because his boss in the corporation did not want to take the blame for promoting so poor a manager, so he used the corporate's 'water torture' method of continual movement to hopefully convince Mr. Bradford to resign.

Three months later, Mr. Bradford was relocated to a slightly smaller corporate office in downtown Detroit, Michigan, where he discovered that he had almost nothing to do.

Two months later, he was transferred to a single room office in Austin, Texas, where he had absolutely nothing to do.

After his fourth move in six months, this time to a refurbished massage parlor located in a decaying strip mall in Camden, New Jersey, Mr. Bradford finally took the hint. He quit his corporate management position and moved to Atlantic City where today, he successfully sells life insurance to the unwary.

Mr. Mendenhall

As soon as Casper moved out of The Oaks, Mr. Mendenhall reneged on two of his promises—he did not reinstate the in-house cleaning staff, nor did he bring back the Senior Strength Class under the guidance of Miss Zeiss. Those decisions, added to his other drastic cost cutting measures, caused many of the once-happy active senior family members to follow in Casper's footsteps and move out of The Oaks. Within three months, the occupancy rate at The Oaks had dropped far below the corporate target. After two more months of falling occupancy rates, Mr. Mendenhall discovered that meeting, or exceeding the corporate target was mandatory, not just a suggestion to aim for, and he was fired.

Mendenhall's replacement, Mr. Callahan, had the presence of mind to listen to the remaining residents complaints and immediately reinstated the in-house cleaning staff, and the college student wait crew. Within six months, the occupancy rate inched back above the corporate target and Mr. Callahan was given a raise.

Izzy

Izzy Timor never remarried, but she continued to have flirtatious flings during her long, and enjoyable tenure at The Oaks. She died at eighty-nine, not long after she had turned over the reins of The Ladies' Casserole Club to a new, sixty-year-old blonde bombshell who promised Izzy that she would try to do as good a job as Izzy had done during her leadership role of the unsanctioned activity.

Delilah

Delilah Madison moved to a downtown condo where she lived for three months, but as she had feared, she never felt comfortable leaving the building due to the undesirables that lived nearby. Her next move was to another active senior living facility in Medford, Oregon. There she met a man with better lineage than Casper Potts who was willing to sign Delilah's prenuptial agreement. Together they shared a tolerably happy life. But to this day, no part of Delilah's long life ever reached the height she achieved at her coming out debutant ball in Savannah, Georgia.

Mr. June

Mr. June continued in his maintenance position at The Oaks until the day Mr. Mendenhall discovered the six-pack of beer tucked behind the wall of sack lunches in the refrigerator. In one of those unusual twists of fate, however, his dismissal turned out to be a blessing for the maintenance man. After a few days of unemployment to think things over, Mr. June put an ad in the local paper extolling his virtues as a handyman and lucrative fix-it jobs started to pour in. In fact, so many jobs that he had to hire an office manager to schedule the work. The woman he hired was rather attractive in Mr. June's opinion and soon became his trusted workmate. They soon married and worked out a perfect balance between the business and marital bliss.

The Ladies' Casserole Club

When Mr. Callahan was installed as The Oaks new manager, more than two hundred and fifty single women resided there. Had he followed the corporate guidelines to the letter concerning approved senior activities, he would have been required to close down the unapproved Ladies' Casserole Club.

Mr. Mendenhall replacement, Mr. Callahan, however, was quick to realize that something was needed to allow the more than two hundred females the opportunity to blow off a little steam. In in his opinion, without The Ladies' Casserole Club, The Oaks would face a rebellion along the lines of the French Revolution.

And that is why The Ladies' Casserole Club at The Oaks, while it remains an unsanctioned activity, the club continues to this very day.

Julio

Julio Santana graduated from UCLA with a BA in International Business, possibly the world's fastest growing career opportunity. He took a position at the American headquarters of a Chinese conglomerate located in in a high-rise building along Century Boulevard just outside the Los Angeles Airport. Although the beaches of Playa Del Ray were within a few miles of his office, he found it impossible to escape his responsibilities and surf daily like he used to on the island where he grew up.

After six of the longest years of his short life, fed up with the traffic, polluted air, and the lack of surfing, Julio resigned his high pressure position with a six figure salary and returned to Nawiliwili Bay on the garden island of Kaua'i.

Once back on his island paradise, Julio realized that he wasn't cut out for the mainland lifestyle. He got a job as a guide escorting tourists on a walking tour at an old sugar plantation. The short trek took the haole's through a rain forest, pineapple fields, and orchards full of fruit and coconut trees, all that remained of the old sugar estate. As Julio reverted to the island lifestyle he had once abandoned, he discovered another job as a fire dancer at a major hotel on Poipu Beach. Between his fire dancing and tour guide gigs, he made more money than he needed. When he added in all the free bananas and mangos he could eat along with surfing in Nawiliwili Bay, three hours a day, seven days a week, fifty-two weeks a year, Julio knew he had returned to paradise.

Miss Zeiss

Miss Zeiss, a retired ballet dance teacher, was mentally and financially devastated when Mr. Mendenhall shut down her Senior Exercise class. Lucky for her, she had not burned her bridges with her exercise class members, and once Mr. Mendenhall left The Oaks, they besieged Mr. Callahan to reinstate the program. Mr. Callahan called Miss Zeiss and requested her return. She told him she would, but only with a mutually agreed upon letter of understanding.

The letter stipulated her salary would include an annual ten percent increase. The class would be offered, Monday, Wednesday, and Friday, and the hours of the class, would be one-thirty to two-fifteen with no input from the General Manager. Two weeks after Mr. Callahan signed the letter of agreement, Miss Zeiss, to the appreciation of the family members of The Oaks, The Senior Strength Class was back in business.

Miss von Thurn von Taxis

Miss von Thurn passed away in her sleep a few weeks after Casper and Paloma were married, but she lived long enough to see all her packages shipped to various Army, Navy, and Air Force bases around the world. How did all that happen? Izzy and her merry band of Casserole Ladies' completed the project as a wedding present to Casper and Paloma.

Mr. James Stately

Mr. James Stately was the man that everyone at The Oaks attempted to avoid because no matter what you asked him, he would come back with a negative response.

If you asked the question, "How did you sleep last night, Jim?"

Without fail his response would be: "Terrible. I haven't had a good nights' sleep since I moved into this dump. And my name is James, not Jim."

Or, "The weather looks great today. Are you going outside and sit by the pool?"

"In all that smog? Are you crazy? Breathing five minutes of that crud is guaranteed to give you a case of terminal lung cancer."

Or, "Hi, Jim. There's an empty seat at our table. How about joining the rest of us while you eat your lunch?"

"I've told you more than once my name is James, damn it, not Jim. And no to the empty chair. I can't listen to all of your inane babble and read my book at the same time."

So Mr. James Stately spent the rest of his days alone, sowing his seeds of discontent. He soon found himself ostracized by everyone who lived at The Oaks with the exception of Miss von Thurn, possibly because she was also rebuffed by all.

James Stately, still unhappy with everything. died three months after Casper and Paloma were married and his death brought more of a feeling of relief than sorrow to the other family members that remained at The Oaks.

Author's Notes

I must confess that along with a teenage Casper Potts, I was fascinated with the Farmers Market where my mother began her lifelong career in the world of restaurants. As a pre-teen, I spent many happy days wandering up and down the aisles of the Farmers Market marveling at the perfectly displayed fruits and vegetables and spending time at a souvenir shop delighted by a myna bird who would talk back.

While I researched this novel, I was amazed to discover that the Farmers Market was once the largest oil field in the Los Angeles basin. Today, the dirty old oil derricks and pump jacks are long gone from public view, but based on photos of the 1920's, at the corner of Third and Fairfax, you would not have see perfectly displayed fruits and vegetables, only tall, wooden oil rigs, and black dirt that had been saturated with the oil residue from the producing wells.

During my last visit to the Farmers Market, I bought a cup of coffee, a sticky bun, and sat down in the warm sun of Southern California where I watched the shoppers and the tourists while I relived the surroundings of my childhood.

Speaking of food, you may be curious why *Casper and the Ladies' Casserole Club* has such a focus on food, such as Casper's breakfasts, the endless casseroles, and the restaurants that were important to Casper, Margaret, and his first 'date' with Paloma.

The reason is simple, Casper, and this author, are both foodies.

My mother was in the restaurant business, and when I was in my freshman year at high school, I would drive the two of us to her restaurant located in downtown Los Angeles. After we arrived, my mom would whip up a batch of fresh cinnamon rolls while I would make the coffee. By the time I left for school, the alluring aromas of fresh baked cinnamon rolls and coffee filled the lobby of the Union Oil building on Olympic and South Flower Street in downtown Los Angeles.

There are three outstanding Los Angeles restaurants highlighted in the book: Guisados, Dupars, and El Cholo, all Casper's favorites. Those restaurants exist today and still serve outstanding food!

Guisados is the newest of the three and is based on the single, but mouthwatering item, the humble taco!

After an unpretentious beginning, Guisados now has seven restaurants located throughout the Los Angeles basin with their flagship still located in Boyle Heights. The restaurant has thrived on a limited, but delicious menu of homestyle braises that cover handmade corn tortillas. All the tacos featured in the book can be ordered, but if you are a gringo, watch out for the Chiles Toreados, the taco with habañero, serraño, jalapeño, and thai chiles blistered together over high heat. But don't worry, you can always ask for a dollop of sour cream to calm down the heat.

Du-pars, Casper's first favorite restaurant, opened at The Farmers Market in 1938 and continues to serve breakfast, lunch, and dinner to this day. Famous for their pancake breakfasts and Chicken Pot Pies for dinner, Du-pars has branched out with three additional locations in Studio City, Pasadena, and West Las Vegas.

El Cholo's, another of Casper's favorite Mexican restaurant in the Los Angeles area, opened its doors in 1927 in a storefront at 11th and Western Ave. with eight stools, three booths, and a hot top stove where the cooks warmed the tortillas. Today's menu includes my favorite, Albondigas Soup, Margaret's favorite, Green Corn Tamales, along with other delicious Mexican dishes such as their historic Sonora Style enchilada and the more modern Blue Corn enchilada. El Cholo's now has six locations but the original, my favorite, is still located at 11th and Western Ave. near downtown Los Angeles.

Concerning Casper's prodigious breakfasts, the plot of the novel required that he pack away a good amount of food each morning. But this writer has to admit, as one who only eats two meals a day, breakfast and dinner, I also eat a substantial morning meal. Quite often an omelet with two to three strips of bacon, wholewheat sourdough toast, imported black cherry preserves, and two cups of coffee, ground fresh each morning. Some years ago, I started to experiment with blending coffee beans and have perfected my personal combination, known around our house as Ken's blend. It consists of two pounds of Columbian beans, one pound of mocha java beans, one half pound of French roast beans, and one half pound of vanilla flavored beans.

Trust me, once you find your own perfect blend of coffee beans, you will never be happy with anything less.

And now for a few casserole recipes that tempted Casper Potts. These are tried and true dishes that you may want to prepare at your home. But which casseroles of the hundreds Casper consumed during the story did I chose? First, I will start with Paloma's favorite, the casserole that captured Casper's heart.

I have attempted to make sure that each recipe appears on one or two pages so you can open your book to the recipe page and make a copy. And you have my permission to make a copy of all the recipes. But please, only the recipes, not the whole book as I enjoy buying good wine.

The first recipe is Paloma's Hatch Green Chili Chicken Casserole, and it is printed on the next page.

Paloma's casserole is followed by Izzy Timor's Chicken Paprikash with Dumplings.

Finally, there is Delilah Madison's Shrimp & Grits with Fried Egg.

Let me know how the three casseroles worked in your kitchen. If you have a favorite casserole recipe, email it to: ken@kendalton.com

Who knows, your favorite casserole might end up in Casper's next adventure.

BON APPÉTIT!

Hatch Green Chili Chicken Casserole

Ingredients

One baked or roasted chicken.
One pound of whole Hatch green chiles (you can substitute Anaheim chilies).
Two cups chicken broth.
One pound of Mexican Cheese.
One medium onion.
Two cloves garlic.
Twelve yellow corn tortillas.
One can of cream of mushroom soup.

Chili/Chicken Sauce

Strip the meat from the cooled chicken and chop into medium sized pieces.

Chop the onion into small pieces and sauté over medium heat.
Add minced garlic.
Sauté together but do not allow the garlic to brown.
Add in chopped Hatch, or less hot Anaheim chilies, cream of mushroom soup and the chicken stock.
Season with salt.
Add in the chopped chicken.
Cook at a medium temperature, about 15 minutes, until the mixture comes to a boil.
Remove from heat and allow time to cool.

Assemble the Casserole

Spray a large casserole dish with nonstick cooking spray.
After the chili/chicken sauce has cooled, place a layer of tortillas on the bottom of the casserole dish and cover with one third of the chili/chicken sauce.
Sprinkle about one third of the cheese and repeat until you have assembled three layers.
Sprinkle the top layer with the remaining cheese.
Bake at 350 degrees F. for about 25-30 minutes until hot and edges are bubbling.
Serve immediately with side dishes of sour cream, chopped cilantro and diced tomatoes.

Chicken Paprikash with Dumplings

Ingredients

Two and a half pounds chicken legs and thighs with the skin.
Three tablespoons unsalted butter.
Two pounds yellow onions sliced lengthwise.
Two tablespoons sweet Hungarian paprika.
One tablespoon hot Hungarian paprika (adjusted to taste).
One cup chicken broth.
One half cup sour cream.

Salt the chicken pieces well and let them sit out while you slice the onions.

Melt the butter in a large Dutch oven over medium high heat. When the butter is hot, pat the chicken pieces dry with a paper towel and place them skin side down in the pan. Brown the chicken on all sides. Once browned, remove and set aside.
Add the onions to the pan and cook them until lightly browned.
Add the paprika and black pepper to the onions and stir to combine.
Add the chicken broth and deglaze the bottom of the pan.
Add the chicken pieces back into the pan on top of the onions.
Cover and cook on a low simmer for about 25 minutes or until the chicken is cooked through.
Once the chicken is cooked to your liking, remove the chicken once again from the pan.
Allow the pan to cool for a few minutes and slowly stir in the sour cream. Add salt to taste.
Put the chicken back into the pan and coat with the sauce.

Dumpling Ingredients

One half teaspoon salt.

Three quarters cup of water.
Two eggs.
Two cups all-purpose flour.

Place a large pot of water with salt added on the stove and bring to a boil.
While the water is heating, combine eggs, salt and water, mix well with a whisk.
Add flour, a little at a time enough to make a soft, sticky dough.
Let dough rest for 10 minutes.
Drop small pieces of the dough mixture using a teaspoon into hot water.
When dumplings rise to the top, they are done.
Remove with a slotted spoon and rinse under cold water.
Cover with the chicken paprikash and serve.

Shrimp & Grits with Fried Egg

Ingredients

Four cups water.
Salt and pepper.
One cup stone-ground grits.
Three tablespoons butter.
Three oz. of Monterey Jack cheese.
One pound shrimp, peeled and deveined.
Six slices bacon.
Four teaspoons lemon juice.
One cup thinly sliced scallions.
One large clove garlic, minced.
Four eggs.

Bring water to a boil.
Add salt and pepper.
Add grits and cook until water is absorbed, about 20 to 25 minutes.
Remove from heat and stir in butter and cheese.
Rinse shrimp and pat dry.
Cook the shrimp in boiling water until they turn pink. Remove from water.
Fry the bacon in a large skillet until browned.
Remove the bacon from the skillet, pat dry, and chop.
In the hot bacon grease, add shrimp.
Add lemon juice, chopped bacon, scallions, garlic and sauté for 3 minutes.
In a separate pan, fry four eggs sunny side up.
Once the eggs are ready, spoon grits into a serving bowl.
Top with the shrimp mixture.
Top with a fried egg, sunny-side-up.
Serve immediately.

Made in the USA
Columbia, SC
31 July 2020